REDEMPTION

A LORDS OF SIN NOVEL

ANGEL PAYNE

REDEMPTION

A LORDS OF SIN NOVEL

ANGEL PAYNE

WATERHOUSE PRESS

CHAPTER ONE

Marcus found her. At last, after a bloody hour of pacing the catwalks and searching the chaos of sets, costumes, curtains, animals, and humanity below, he found her.

Now that he had, he did not veer his sights from her. She joined the mayhem by way of the green room door, strolling with two other actresses who shared her confident look of a successful preliminary rehearsal. Marcus never blinked as he watched their bustled and flounced forms trek across Drury Lane's stage.

He never blinked, and he never breathed.

He felt the heat surge through his senses, centering behind his temples—as he expected it would, as he hoped it would not. Slow yet intense, the fire momentarily scorched away his vision, heralding the need and pain wracking him. As if he needed a reminder.

The resulting glow in his eyes would give him away like a lightning flare if she tilted her gaze an inch toward him, but Marcus didn't care. He stood there, paralyzed as he'd been last night and the two months of nights before that, and watched her. And watched her.

And he remembered why he had given up on this insanity called feeling two hundred eighty years ago.

Loneliness was hell.

★ ★ ★ ★

People weren't supposed to feel lonely with a hundred other people around. Gabriela Rozina ordered herself to accept that as she stopped at the center of the Drury Lane Theatre's stage, in the midst of preparations for the show's first full dress rehearsal.

Yet as the scenery whizzed by, the stagehands shouted, the ballet girls giggled, and Act Two's flock of lambs bleated on their way to their cue, an irrational emptiness surrounded her...an aloneness so complete, she might as well have stood on that wooden expanse in solitary blackness.

Circling to face the theatre's empty seats didn't ease her ache. And that, Gaby ruminated, tied her thoughts in their most confusing knot. For the last two months, this sight hadn't given her even a quiver of joy, where once a glimpse of Drury's magnificence gave her flurries of anticipation.

Two months...they'd dragged miserably by, since that afternoon she'd gone to Buckingham Palace and stood in the rain with a throng of other actors and actresses, sharing their silent pleas for the arrival of the notices signed by Victoria's own hand. And the queen had answered their supplications. At four o'clock that day, the word became official: the Prince's Grand Theatre Troupe would be transformed from ambition to reality within a year. The finest works of English theatre would be rehearsed, then taken to every corner of the globe welcoming them, performed by the best of the best. A meticulously-selected company would be comprised from the finest stages throughout Britain.

Gabriela had gasped in amazement along with the hopeful faces around her. A royally sanctioned company, cheered by throngs in houses across the globe…

It wasn't just the opportunity of a lifetime.

It was the chance to call the whole world *family.*

Affirmation. Approval. Acceptance.

At last.

In short, it was the fulfillment of all her dreams. And more.

Her heartbeat doubled with just the thought about the Prince's Troupe again. But Gabriela ordered herself back under control. She couldn't fall into the trap of deluding herself. Shattered expectations were no longer her specialty. And she'd never aimed her hopes at such a spectacular goal before. Dear God, could she earn the rank as one of Her Majesty's "meticulously-selected" few? She didn't have all the experience. She didn't have all the credits.

But she had all the passion. And she carried every ounce of the precious dream in her soul. That had to matter, didn't it?

Somehow, Augustus Harris had seen that. Yes, *the* Augustus Harris, London's most innovative producer, and he'd decided she deserved a chance because of it. It was far from a pumpkin-coach-and-glass-slipper chance, but it had landed her here, beneath the gaslights of London's most famous theatre, rehearsing the first part "Augustus Druriolanus" himself cast her to.

Gaby still thanked Providence every night for the blessing. As Augustus's new prodigy, she'd catapulted from "nothing" to "promising" inside of three months. *She* still felt the same, but a few daring journalists even began their raves in this week's papers, extolling Augustus's "fresh flower in the dying London theatre garden."

So why did she still feel like a sapped daisy, ready to be pressed and forgotten in a book? Why did this loneliness return each night to claw at her, shredding even the crumbs of confidence in her soul?

Even at the age of seven, when only a chipped chapel bench had been her stage and a dozen other orphans her audience, the anticipation of performing had stirred her blood. Each "show" had surged her heart with fulfillment, her soul with completion. There wasn't any sweeter ecstasy on earth, any greater way to quell the emptiness that had yawned inside since the day, a week after her fifth birthday, when she'd dropped tear-soaked daisies atop both her mother and father's graves...

Just like the emptiness clinging to her heart now.

She tried to concentrate on warming up. While humming a series of vocal exercises, Gabriela read through her script again, taking note of her underlined dialogue prompts. In truth, it was just a way to pass the time. She'd memorized the scenes weeks ago. Augustus had, of course, reserved the female leads of the next three productions for the French diva gracing Drury with an extended visit, but the parts he assigned Gabriela were still a far cry from chorus girl. From the first rehearsal on, Gaby vowed to prove herself worthy of the honor.

Now she prayed she could satisfy that commitment.

"Ready for first cue?" a throaty voice asked at her shoulder.

Gabriela turned to meet the confident smile curling Donna's lush lips. Her roommate's name stood proxy for the actress's full stage title—"Donna, as in *Prima* Donna," she always reminded the tabloid writers—and Gabriela didn't think she knew a person who filled the requirements of the persona more.

"Depends on how we're defining *ready*." Gaby's nerves raced faster as Act One's backdrop, an ornate ballroom scene, unfurled from the flys over the stage.

"Oh, dove," her friend drawled, "none of us is ever *ready* ready."

Donna looked ready to expound on that theory when her tapered eyebrows leapt by an inch. "But Lord," she amended on a sultry undertone, "at least you've got *that* on your side."

A bevy of squeals from the ballet coincided with Donna's appreciation of the top-hatted, leather-gloved blade striding down the center aisle on patent leather boots. But Gabriela's tension only climbed with every step those boots took. The sight of Alfonso Renard transformed her empty stomach into a churn of dread.

Why, she lamented, tonight? Why did the man have to appear at a rehearsal he had nothing to do with? Why did he have to dissolve what poise she *had* gathered by forcing her to battle his octopus hands? For being, in his own words, one of the city's "most up-and-coming producers," the letch had an astounding amount of free time to take advantage of Augustus's hospitality—and actresses.

"Oh, he's good," Donna crooned, eyeing Renard's "bashful" wave at the dancers. "Modest, but manly. Rather like...Lancelot crossed with a bit of naughty Black Irish."

Gabriela rolled her eyes. "Black?" she finally snorted. "Now *there's* an apt description."

She underlined that by jerking her script open and burying her face so far between the pages, the text blurred. If the dancers wanted the viper's attention, let them have it.

Her heart sagged when she heard Renard stride right by the giggling girls. Her spirit plummeted to her toes when the rustle of his coat ceased at the edge of the stage; directly in front of her.

"Miss Rozina?" came that slick-as-oil voice. "Don't tell me you weren't even going to say hello."

Was it her imagination, or did the man's line evoke stage-wide silence faster than Augustus's throatiest bellow? Balancing her breath against the ballet's gossipy whispers, Gabriela slowly lowered her script, forcing herself to meet the dauntless stare waiting at the stage's edge. "Good evening, Mr. Renard," she leveled with queenly calm.

A mock scowl fell across Renard's aristocratic forehead. "Come, come. It's just Alfonso, remember?"

She gripped her script—and locked her teeth—tighter. "Alfonso."

His satisfied grin replaced the frown. The ballet loosed another collective sigh. Gabriela struggled to take a decent breath of air. It wasn't easy, especially when he reached beneath his overcoat to produce an eye-popping bouquet of red tulips and roses.

At that, even the blasted lambs fell into silence.

"I've brought you a gift," her visitor murmured into the expectant pause.

Gabriela turned her gaze into a glower. The man's smirk didn't falter.

"Mr. Renard—"

"Alfonso."

"Stop it!" He hadn't crossed the line of her patience; he'd demolished it. Gaby stomped down the stage's temporary steps and hissed, "I have made it perfectly clear that I will not accept your gifts!"

Renard shrugged. Loomed closer toward her. "Gaby...oh, little Gaby. I apologized for the pearls, did I not?"

"After I threw them in your face."

Now the man had the grace to color. "That's water in another tide now, isn't it? Now please; think nothing of these blooms but what they mean—"

"Another lure into your bed?"

"You're witty today, dear. They are but a tiny reminder of my admiration. A fleeting token of my wishes—"

"I don't want them."

"For your good luck."

Gabriela's sharp breath was drowned by the collection of everyone else's. *Devil take him.* He'd done it now, and his cocky grin showed it. To wish a performer "good luck" anywhere near the theatre, let alone three steps from the stage, boded certain failure to the performance.

To undo the damage, for the entire cast's sake, she'd have to take his wretched flowers. And the knowing kiss he trailed on the back of her hand when she reached for them. And the possessive, almost brutal rake of his eyes over her body as she turned the blooms over to a stage boy.

"There, now." He leaned and whispered it into her ear as the final dagger in the ordeal. "That wasn't so bad, was it?"

Gabriela forced herself to breathe, though it meant suffering Renard's opulent cologne. At least it gave her the strength to reply, in a voice dripping with acid-laced honey: "If you must know, sir, it was as pleasant as letting a maggot kiss me. And if you dare such an underhanded stunt on me again, I promise I'll dispense of your roses, and their thorns, in an area much further below your pretty face."

She only made one mistake with the proclamation: firing the words so near him. Alfonso coiled a hand around her elbow before Gaby could step away. But she willed her gaze to remain steady, her posture proud.

"You used to welcome my face," he growled.

"And you used to be a kind and considerate friend."

"Friend?" His glare drilled into her, black with the force of his acrimony. "You little fool, Gabriela. I have no need for *friends*. I'm not a milksop who wastes my money or manners on enterprises that won't pay me well in the end. That's why I'm going to be bigger than your precious Augustus someday. I'll produce the biggest plays London has known, with the biggest ticket take, as well."

"That's splendid." Though her throat quivered with the effort, the retort flowed with cool disdain even Victoria would applaud. "I do, however, apologize that I won't be in London to see this conquest."

Gaby expected his answering tremor of fury. And the bruise he twisted tighter into her arm. She maintained her composure despite both.

She did *not* foresee the laugh that snorted out of him, low and mocking. "The lady won't be here," he repeated. "I see. So we're still entertaining our pipe dream of stardom with the Prince's Grand Theatre Troupe?"

The slur slid in, twisting beneath her armor. It was the one barb capable of deflating her back into a mass of raw vulnerability. "What do you know of dreams?" Gaby gritted back at him. "What do you know of beliefs or hope?"

Renard laughed again. The sound ripped Gabriela deeper than any audition dismissal she'd ever been dealt.

"I only know that most dreams don't come true," he sneered. "So why you pine away to join that company, royally sanctioned or not, is beyond me."

Gaby tilted her head at him, sad and curious about his skepticism, even at the same time that her mind's eye filled with the vision...her dream. Yes, it *was* a vision, wasn't it? The images she'd seen so many times, she often wondered if she'd been born with them.

"Don't you see?" she said, not bothering to struggle against him anymore. "Don't you realize the feat they plan to accomplish? Only the finest English works will be showcased, from Shakespeare and Marlowe to opera and musicals. And the entire world will be waiting. The entire *world* will remember the performers who take these works to them. It's a chance to inspire thousands, perhaps millions, across the globe."

"But you can be an inspiration right where you are." Renard's soft protest blew into her ear again. "You inspire *me*," he continued in a coarse murmur. "Can't you think of it, dear Gaby? My brilliant scripts and staging, complementing your hot-blooded Italian delivery..."

"Wh-What?" she blurted. "What does my blood have to do with—"

"You little vixen," Renard returned, "as if you didn't know. Gabriela, you'll seduce all of England on my stage. All that Italian passion, inspired by the private lessons you'll receive in my arms...we'll be unstoppable together. Just think of it!"

But Gabriela could think of nothing but the bile roaring up her throat. And the need to push back the outrage and hate she'd jammed into a sole cubicle of memory...

Aye, that's right; her seventh birthday tomorrow, Parson Reeves. That will make two years she's been here at the orphanage with us. Such a delightful child. What's that? Oh aye, you be right again, that does makes it harder to discourage her dreams. And she always dresses so pretty when the families come, looking to adopt. But it's that tainted blood of hers, Parson. That thick Italian hair. Those eerie Italian eyes. The girl can see straight to my soul with those eyes, I'm certain of it. It's too bad. Just too bad.

She got away from Renard's talons with a desperate shove. Then Gabriela ran. She ran from the loneliness and the fear, and she didn't stop.

★ ★ ★ ★

Marcus had known something was wrong. He'd suspected it from the instant Gabriela had stopped on the stage, looking for all the world like nothing more than a wax figurine for expression. Usually, it was as if Christmas morning occurred for her beneath those lights, the gold flecks in her almond eyes as luminous as the gas glow surrounding her. He knew that expression well. He'd memorized the sight.

But the popinjay with the flowers didn't see anything. Even now, when she bolted from the man as if he had sprouted leprosy, he just lifted a calm brow at the ballet chits who still swooned at him. Finally, the clod strolled after her as if retrieving a recalcitrant puppy, not an angel he was blessed to have on loan from heaven. Marcus decided the man was daft, dangerous or as dead as—

He fought to cut the thought short. No use.

As dead as me.

He spun and raced back along the catwalk, as if the words were wasps giving chase. For an instant, he wished they were. He would verily welcome the stinging onslaught, if he could feel it. He would invite the pain, if it replaced the sensations she'd forced upon him in the last two months. All this wanting and dreaming, this confusion and frustration—

What the hell was wrong with him? He had never

encountered trouble distancing himself from any mortal, physically or mentally, since he had made the mistake of trusting a doe-eyed Hungarian farm girl in the early seventeenth century, and found himself stalked by the whole of her crucifix-bearing village.

After that, it had been no grand feat to discern the obvious: losing control would mean losing his life.

Losing control made him into this beast to begin with.

The reminder came at the right moment. Reaching the end of the catwalk, Marcus faced the choice of taking the secret walkway over the dressing rooms, to his right, or the ledge over the now-empty green room, to his left. Just a few strides would take him atop the dressing room Gabriela Rozina had assuredly locked herself into at this very moment.

Marcus turned toward the green room.

He dropped onto the dark ledge with a weary sigh. He usually visited the green room later in the evening, as the cast filtered in to relax after rehearsals or performances. He greedily eavesdropped on their rowdy regalements, for the simple assurance that he could still laugh at a joke or feel compassion at a tragedy.

Then Gabriela had come, and shown him he could feel far more than that. Before she had even entered the room on that fateful night—was it only a day over eight weeks ago?—his supernatural psyche whirled into chaos, rejoicing in the kinship he immediately sensed in her lonely soul. But then there had been more. So much more. The life she provoked him to feel again...the hope she dared him to believe in. Oh, God...the hope. He had not needed it or wanted it in such a long time...

"No!" he gritted, shoving the memory away.

God's damned teeth. Coming here had been a bad idea, after all. He shoved from the ledge, preparing to head back along the catwalks, toward home.

His legs buckled on his first step. His heart slammed in his chest.

He was in trouble this time. Just like that first night, but a hundredfold more intense, he felt her. She was approaching, and fast. He smelled her: warm, smoky stage scents blended with pearl powder and female essence, the way he had breathed her in so many times, when he allowed his mind to wander in fantasy. Only now she wasn't fantasy...

She dashed into the green room, but didn't turn up the dimmed lamp. She whipped an angry circle around the faded couch, marking each step with a huff. She stopped and clawed errant tendrils of thick, dark hair from her flushed face. A vein beat wildly in her neck.

Marcus barely contained his agonized growl.

He wanted her. Sweet Jesu, he wanted her. Her body, perfectly formed for his. Her spirit, searching for the answers his could give. Her life, her dreams, such lights in the darkness of his.

And her blood...

He opened his mouth, struggling for the right words, for once wishing that a mortal—*this* mortal—was under his unearthly power and he could just close his eyes, willing her to his side.

I shall not. I cannot. Damn you, Gabriela!

"Gabriela!"

The command, striking out from the same direction she'd come, was loud enough to jolt the lamp's glass chimney. And her.

"Gabriela…" Marcus repeated, his voice a primal whisper, yearning to shield her from the waves of trepidation that possessed her in deepening waves. He felt all of it in her, saw it in her urgent tugs at her skirt.

She dropped her hand an instant before the dandy appeared in the doorway. In that moment, comprehension slammed Marcus. She was not nervous. She was afraid. The scent of her fear reached him between her sweet talc and the intruder's cologned stench.

"We aren't finished yet," the intruder growled.

"The devil we aren't." She took a breath and amended, "Alfonso, please. Just leave me alone. We're two different people, with different ideas—"

"No. Not different." The clod stepped forward, arms coiled across his chest. "Gabriela, don't you see? We're so much alike, it's frightening. Why don't you just admit it? Why don't you just give in to what you want?"

She stopped tugging at her skirt. Her hands curled into tight white fists. "You don't know a thing about what I want."

Renard cocked a knowing smirk. "Oh, really?"

"Stop it! Can't you just stop it? I know I *don't* want you, your plays, or your version of stardom. Not at your disgusting price."

Silence. Then the bastard's mocking retort. "Then what do you want, girl?"

She turned and looked away, looked *up*, as if pleading to a higher power. She nearly found Marcus instead, still fallen to the catwalk beyond his ledge. But he easily remembered the instinct for dissolving into mist, and slid back into the shadows with less noise than a puff of fog.

She looked back down. And answered the clod with three words that echoed in Marcus's soul with the terrifying ring of memory, from when he had uttered them himself a hundred lifetimes ago:

"I want more."

Another heartbeat of silence thumped by.

Before the popinjay exploded in laughter.

Marcus tried to emulate her incredible show of will. He tried to clench back the lust to swoop down on the sadistic boor and rip his head from his body. But like a fool struggling in quicksand, the more he fought, the more he fed the ugly force. He was lost. And he was thirsty, so damn thirsty.

"Gabriela," he grated as he spun and stumbled away. "I am sorry." *So sorry.*

Too far gone with the madness to take the catwalks, he groped his way to the stairs, instead. It seemed an eternity until he reached the bottom of them, then clawed his way to the end of the dank subterranean passage. Did his own breathing rage in his ears like the panting of a beast? Were those his hands before his eyes, fumbling to turn the copper key in the huge iron door, slipping because they dripped with his saliva?

Was this the hell his existence had come to?

He burst past the door with a groan. Folded to the stone floor in a mass of heated gasps and icy sweat. For long minutes, he remained that way, attempting to soak in the calming effect of the black air in the deep, buried chamber.

The calmness never came. But a measure of strength returned. With it, Marcus pushed to his feet and staggered to the small rise of packed dirt in the center of the room.

Room?

His lips curled up at that, but the sound he let out wasn't a laugh. Oh, when had he started to glorify this place by calling it a *room*?

It was a crypt. Nothing could alter that God-forsaken truth.

And the earth at its center was where he now tumbled, his looming fatigue in a battle against savage despair.

"Gabriela," he whispered once more, pulling a thick satin blanket around his shaking, hungry body. His mind, even in its exhaustion, called out to her, too. But she'd no more hear or respond to his thoughts than she would a wisp of wind.

Only one feat could make that possible. And he'd never subject her to that debasement...that repulsive confirmation of the sick creature he was. *Never.*

The injustice of it all reignited him in fury. Marcus clawed out at it with a snarl. Only desperate echoes answered from the black world beneath London. Inviolable dark surrounded him once more.

"Damn you," he whispered. "Damn you, Gabriela! I will not let you do this to me. I *cannot.*"

Gabriela...I shall not let you turn me into a monster!

CHAPTER TWO

"I won't let him do it to me again."

Gabriela underlined her declaration with a jab of carmine to her chin. But upon surveying her work in the dressing room mirror, she tossed the color pot aside. The stage paint worked no miracle on her pale and glowering face.

Donna didn't lift her mood by sliding into the other chair before the glass, already the picture of glamorous serenity an hour before the rise of opening night's curtain.

"Dove," her friend cooed, toying with a copper curl, "I don't understand your frostbite toward the man at all. Renard doesn't pick his teeth or his nose, dresses better than Prince Eddie, then showers *you* with gifts befitting a princess—"

"With his personal price tag attached to each," Gaby shot back.

Donna threw her head back on a husky laugh. "So?"

"So, despite what the better portion of London thinks about the women of our 'trade,' I am *not* on the market."

She emphasized the retort with such a stab of frustration, a miniature snow storm of pearl powder flew off her camel hair face brush. Donna's chuckle sprinkled the air along with the tiny specks. "One laughs at farce, Donna," she scolded, "not tragedy. Well, not *this* tragedy." She stood, tightening her dressing robe sash. "I'm just...tired of it. We aren't interchangeable commodities, to be written into any producer's portfolio at whim—"

"The hell we aren't."

Gabriela's gaze shot up. Her friend's heavy-lashed observation met hers in the mirror. A faint smile loosened the red bow of Donna's lips.

"Gaby," she queried softly, "what do you think you're doing here?"

A tenuous pause fell. "I'm doing my job," Gaby finally said, jerking her chin higher. "I'm improving my craft, in the best way I can."

"Fine. Call it that. You can even call it art, or magic...but under any title, it's all still an illusion." She looped a finger back at the mirror. "That illusion is what London pays to see. And it's what the producers will pay *us* well to see. Dearest, how do you think we got a nearly free lease on a two-bedroom Mayfair flat? Where do you think my fur parka came from? My ruby earrings?"

"Stop." Gabriela raised a flat hand. "I don't want to hear any more."

A soft *tsk*ing began behind her. "Oh, dove. Tell me you cannot be that fresh a berry?"

"I'm not." Gaby turned to where her opening scene costume hung, tried to busy herself straightening the fringe of forest-green beads along the sleeves. The turn of the conversation unnerved her. Despite Donna's affectionate nickname, Gabriela was not a mindless dove. She knew what happened when a man and a woman kissed in a certain way... then touched in certain places...

Those caresses led to feeling certain things. Sometimes, when heaven smiled upon the destined lovers, magical things. But those feelings also led to actions—and consequences of those actions. Consequences like a baby. A baby who grew into a child; a child who could be beautiful and bright, cared for and cherished—

Or orphaned. Or abandoned. Despite the best intentions of all, sentenced to an existence marked by days of loneliness and nights of tears...

"Look." She laughed in an effort to banish the dark memories. "I know about your amusements, Donna, and I don't mind them. But that's your life, not mine." A sigh escaped her, and betrayed her by quavering. "It—it won't ever be mine."

One of Donna's perfect brows arched. "You don't ever want steady work, beautiful clothes, and exciting companionship?"

"Oh, I *will* succeed." The statement didn't wobble this time. "But I want a success different than yours." She gazed back into the mirror, the reflection going hazy to her eyes, taking her into a faraway vision. "I...dream different dreams."

"Ahhh, yes," Donna replied. "How could I forget? The Prince's Grand Theatre Troupe. Your 'opportunity of a lifetime', yes?"

Gabriela waited a long, telling moment before slowly turning back to her friend.

"I will obtain an audition with the company, Donna." She leveled each word the same way she meted out her gaze— with the conviction of her dreams. "And I'll astound them... somehow. I have to. I don't care what stories Renard is telling the rest of the cast; I don't care if they all think me the next candidate for the freak show. I will do it—no matter what it takes—but I'm going to do it with my soul intact."

★ ★ ★ ★

"I refuse to put up with any more of this nonsense, Gabriela."

The popinjay's ultimatum echoed effortlessly through Drury's empty house. Aye, even up to the fifth tier box to which Marcus confined himself in hopes of rendering himself deaf to the now-nightly confrontations—and the fury these episodes summoned in him. The anger that brought the burning appetite to every corner of his aching mouth—a thirst he thought he'd quelled two and a half centuries back.

But no. As he rose and leapt from the box down to the passage over the dressing rooms, he actually had to concentrate on controlling his ire. He had to think about his steps along the way, steps that used to be gracefully silent. He forced the acid in his throat to erupt a hiss, not a snarl.

Amazing. Three months ago, he could not remember how to growl, let alone snarl.

His body tensed as he stopped over the dressing room Gabriela shared with that Donna creature. He found himself shaking with the desire to bury his claws into the shoulders of the hulk who loomed over her now, instead.

"You aren't being asked to put up with anything," Gabriela told the bastard. Marcus's muscles constricted harder. The strain in her voice stood out as clearly as the fatigue lines around her mouth. "As a matter of fact, I should have had you barred from backstage long ago," she continued, "but out of deference to your friendship with Augustus, I have been more than tolerant. My tolerance, however, has reached its limit, *sir*. So good night."

She started for the door, but in a savage sweep, the hulk yanked her elbow and flattened her against the wall.

"It's not going to be that easy," he commanded. "Not tonight."

Marcus lurched forward, but stopped when Gabriela

fought back with twists worthy of the most vicious snake in India. "Let me go."

"Not until I get some answers. Not until you tell me how much longer these after-hours stunts will continue."

"*Rehearsals.* For the last bloody time, I've been staying after performances to *rehearse.*"

"For three weeks straight?"

"Yes!"

Renard released a weighted huff. "Gabriela, you've gone over the line."

"And you, Mr. Renard, don't draw my lines."

"Damn it, your cast mates agree with me!"

Reflexively, her eyes widened. The bastard seized on her surprise. He leaned harder against her, savoring his moment of control. "Why does that surprise you, darling? Nobody sees you anymore. You hardly wave your hand past the green room every night. They don't just call you the cast eccentric any more. You're now the cast lunatic."

Marcus yearned to roar a *bravo* at the glare she raised in response, a copper and gold sensation of defiance. "Because I'm bettering myself and my craft? Because I'm pursuing my dreams? They're rehearsals for my audition piece, not séances. You know rehearsals, Alfonso? Practicing until one gets the thing perfect? It's a concept you might want to try sometime."

Renard's grip visibly tightened on her. "And you might want to try looking at this Prince's Grand Troupe as the garbage it is, and resign yourself to the role you were meant to play."

"In your bed?"

"For a start."

"I'll be dead first."

"Be careful what you wish for, darling."

Marcus started forward again. It was not the whoreson's threat as much as the undercurrent of tone—the malevolence so strong, it slashed through his senses, ripping a violent, protective instinct through him. His vision clouded red. He shook his head just enough to clear his sights, so he could aim his attack on the bastard correctly—

But his gaze refocused in time to watch Gabriela beat him to the task. Without lowering her gaze, she jabbed her knee up between the man's legs. Renard's moan filled the dressing room. Gabriela stepped out of the lout's way as he crumpled to the floor, snapping her skirts out of his path.

"Well," she said, "I'm very happy we cleared that up. But ah, yes—" She flicked a three-inch swath of skirt back at him. "One further item. Please be notified that if you refer to my work as 'garbage' again, you'd better pray you've bedded half of London, because you won't be able to again."

Without looking back, she reached for a script on the dressing table, a lace shawl hanging over the dressing screen. "I pray you have a good evening, Mr. Renard," she commented with so much respect, the Shah of Persia might have sat clutching his groin at her feet. "I am now very late for my *rehearsal*. Good night."

Marcus raced her to the main stage via the catwalks, wondering when the overhead paths had become so complicated. A faint remembrance came of that night, seemingly so long ago, when he condemned her and himself and sworn off the sight of her forever. But he was like an opium addict who knew bloody well what he did, yet could not control his self-destruction. The need to see her, to watch her in all her furious life, had become an unthinking obsession.

He likened the feeling to distant memories of mortal lust.

As he found a dim corner formed by Catwalk Five and the House Curtain, his heartbeat pounded a cannon rhythm; he clenched his thighs against the joyous arousal at their juncture.

But the sensation, as wondrous and exhilarating as it was, served as just the overture.

When Gabriela appeared, his senses burst beyond desire. His mind detonated beyond thought. His body detached from his awareness and soared beyond his control. An agonized groan escaped his throat, despite his effort at restraint.

This woman would burn him alive long 'ere he saw the sun again.

★ ★ ★ ★

"Someday," Gabriela spat as she stalked out onto the stage, "I'm going to burn Alfonso Renard alive."

The angered beat of her stomps reverberated in the wings—and her bloodstream. She forced herself to halt at the House Curtain line and take several breaths, hoping the action would cleanse the grime clogging her senses, and scrape her skin clean where Alfonso's touch lingered in its foul aftermath.

She froze when a low moan echoed around her.

For ten more seconds, she didn't breathe. Then she spun toward the open green room door and demanded, "Who's there?"

Only a shaft of yellow gas light spilled from the portal... just as it had last night *and* the night before, when this strange, "something's-out-there" sensation had also washed over her. She'd attempted to describe it to Donna, who'd shuddered in reaction—which had made Gabriela promptly go quiet about the whole thing. The truth was, it *didn't* frighten her—which did nothing to fade the ghost of Alfonso's "cast lunatic" insult—but how could she ever be afraid here, beneath the lights and standing on the floorboards that served, for all intents and purposes, as home?

No, this awareness stemmed from something else. It was tangible; so close; as if something was waiting just beyond her reach, filled with sights, sounds and perceptions she'd never experienced before...

Only tonight, the feeling possessed a voice. More jarring than that, a voice that groaned.

"The wind," she scolded herself. "Pull it together, Gaby, or you really will be three steps short of Bedlam."

She laughed at that, and the sound drifted into the blackness of the theatre. No groan echoed back this time. But invisible fingers seemed to reach out and pull at her, encircling her waist...and, for the first time in months, her empty core was filling with a strange but stirring warmth...

She heard herself laugh again. Her eyes slid shut. Her head rocked back. Her whole body reveled in the magnificent heat, flaring further inside her, reaching straight for her soul. Flowing flames. Fantastical fires. Liquid lightning.

What in the world is happening?

She slammed her eyes open and whirled back toward the green room. But her footing slipped, and a panicked shriek tore out of her. Common sense took over with relieving speed. She regained her posture and swung back toward the stage, irritation in place of fear.

"Bloody leaking roof." Gaby examined her twisted ankle. "Somebody's going to kill themselves on one of these puddles."

She regretted the remark instantly. With her words came the repetition of another observation, like a demon haunting her mind. *Be careful what you wish for, darling.*

"Stop it," she commanded her rampaging imagination. "Stop it and get to work. Phantom voices and misplaced rain puddles are no excuse for the sorry state of this audition piece."

She pulled the script from beneath her arm and smacked it open. Then she cleared her throat and read from the top of the page in a strong, sure voice. "*Hamlet, Act Three.* Denmark, here I come."

And, beginning to recite the three hundred year-old dialogue, she climbed into the heart and soul of a maid named Ophelia...sort of. Oh, blast it, she tried. But every line came clumsy as an elephant's minuet; every inflection she tried ended with a rant against either her childish pitch or her forced delivery.

Finally, eyes feeling like they contained half the Sahara, she declared the rehearsal another fruitless effort. With a frustrated sigh, she made the trek back to her dressing room.

Once there, she turned the lamp halfway up and sank into the corner chair. She wished Donna were here. But a glance at the table clock placed her friend deep beneath the covers of her satin-blanketed bed, or about to climb there with somebody else. The thought, which normally brought a squirming discomfort in Gaby's chest, caused a different, but even more intimidating reaction tonight.

The feeling that kept calling itself loneliness.

"*No.*"

She looked to the clock again. And was grateful she did. There on the table, in the shadow of the soft-ticking hands, she discovered the weapon to keep her solitude at bay. Her leather journal. She'd neglected her entries in the past week, as the news of Harris's "latest theatrical success" had spread across

London, turning her life into a frenzy. Now the book came as her ideal confidante in this silent hour.

But ten minutes later, the page still loomed white and blank. She tried to summon words—and words came—but the ink scrolling them across her mind came with cruel assurance, carving each syllable like the glide of a torture master's blade.

See it all for the garbage it is, Gabriela, and resign yourself to your true role.

He wants to make you a star, Gaby. Steady work and beautiful clothes.

Your true role, by my side.

Your true role, in my bed.

"No!" Her fist trembled around the pen.

Why was she the only one who knew where she belonged? Who believed it with all her heart?

And why, so suddenly, did it hurt so much to believe it alone?

She sucked in a breath, struggling to re-lock her emotions, but in that moment, it didn't matter. She didn't care. She didn't want to fight; she didn't want to believe anymore. She was tired and discouraged and lonely. *God, so lonely.*

The lock sprang open. The tears came. She let the pen and the journal slide to the floor, curling in on herself as the pain stormed her heart.

Gabriela had no idea how high she'd fortified the ramparts of herself, until she gave herself permission to let them down. Her sobs filled the room, but stopping the release was impossible as damming the Atlantic. It felt horrible. It felt wonderful. How perfect, she thought, would it be to just die.

"No. No, you do not want to die."

Her cries caught in her throat. "Who—" she stammered,

but gulped the rest down. The voice. *That* voice. The same ghostly, but silken tone behind the moan over the stage...she was certain of it!

Dear God. Alfonso was right. I'm insane. Raving starkers. The Prince's Grand Troupe will never want me now.

The thought made her cry harder.

"God and the angels," the ghost muttered. "I pray you to cease, sweeting. Or 'twill be but moments before you drown in your tears."

"So what if I do?" she choked.

The ghost, believe it or not, also had a laugh. His chuckle rumbled over her like a distant thunderstorm, powerful and musical. "I should have to haul you out of the puddle, you nit. And I am not partial to salt water."

"So let me drown."

"I could not do that."

"The devil you couldn't!"

"Do not shout. 'Tis not good for your voice."

"Stop it!" she shrieked. She balled fists at her temples, yearning to beat this insanity out of her head. "Just stop it! You're not real! I'm not insane! And it's not all garbage, it's my dream! I'm not...insane...I'm not!"

"Oh, sweeting."

Now the voice returned to its near-groan. Gabriela bunched tighter, trying to ward off the aching seduction of that voice, so rife with grief, as if experiencing this sorrow right along with her. He sounded so *real.*

"Gabriela," the dream called again, "do not cry. You are saner than the bloody lot of them. I shall kill them all if they say not."

"But you're not real. You're just—"

Raw shock sucked the rest of the outcry off her lips. Somewhere between one sob and the next, a hand brushed her tear-soaked hair off her neck. Then gentle fingers brushed up to her temple, soothing and caressing, back across her scalp. Strong and wonderful. And real.

Her heart stopped. Her head snapped up.

Lightning struck her world.

She'd yearned for him so many times. She'd invoked him in the realm of her fantasies, where the world at last understood her, and the world was nothing but him. Yet those daydreamed concoctions didn't do justice to the man filling her vision now. Thunder-black hair slashed against his strong forehead and his straight-cut jaw; the dark cascade rained to just inside the collar of his white shirt. And oh, that *shirt*—or more appropriately, the V of dark muscle the material folded back to reveal, down to where a rugged black vest took over, blending into rust-colored breaches and black laced-up boots that outlined his thighs and legs so well, Gaby blushed at the masculine glory of him.

But the power of the lightning came from his eyes. Dear God, the force of his stare...it almost *glowed* at her, in a color she could only label...silver. Every thought she'd ever had, every dream she'd yearned to fill, every desire she'd ever known...he held them there, in his eyes, in his soul.

"Oh, my God," Gabriela rasped. Her fingers flew to her trembling lips. "Oh...my God."

CHAPTER THREE

Words spun in Marcus's head. There were so many things he wanted to say, so many sensations begging for release. Nothing broke past his motionless lips.

Mayhap that was for the better. Mayhap he could disappear while she still sat in her shocked daze, restoring himself to the realm of simple hallucination in her mind's eye. Mayhap there was time to correct this disaster his stupidity created in the first place.

Bloody hell, how had this happened? Three weeks ago, he had vowed never to look at her again. And tonight, merely the sight of her unhinged his fatal groan over the stage. Just the sound of her weeping froze every nerve in his body like January icicles. So he had come to her; he had come as swiftly as every extra-human muscle in his body could manage...

To face the biggest terror he had ever known. The terror of staying with her. The terror of ever leaving again. The dread of shattering this moment in any way at all; this miracle of sitting here as the sole object of her shimmering stare, beholding him as if he were a god and not the sickening opposite.

Do not! The depths of his soul snarled it. *Do not look at me! I'm a monster. I want your blood as bad as I want your exquisite soul. Run from me. Run and end this ordeal before we are both annihilated.*

Gabriela did not move.

Damn her.

Ah God, damn her for the beautiful stare she unleashed upon him, those copper depths absorbing the unhuman silver beacon of his. Damn her for the joyous tears slipping down her cheeks. Damn her for her unknowing sensuality as she slid one trusting inch toward him.

He flinched from her outstretched finger. *Do not trust me. Do not touch me!*

"Who...are you?" she whispered.

I am...a freak. Get back. I shall love you. I shall kill you.

"Are you real? Or am I just dreaming again? Oh, please tell me I'm not dreaming."

Hell.

You are not going anywhere now, Stafford.

"Dreaming," Marcus echoed on a gruff, awkward laugh. "If it were only that simple."

Her lips parted on a tearful sigh. Marcus's fists clenched in fury and remorse. Apparently, no matter how violent his effort at control, her mind had fallen prey to the psychic influence of his. She could nay be experiencing this battle of exhilaration and terror on her own.

But then she reached out, and took his hand.

A wolf's snarl escaped him, pure instinct, before he could check the reaction. They both jerked back, breathing hard.

Marcus wrapped his hand around the knuckles her fingers had brushed. He wanted to hold the heat of her there forever. He wanted to push her energy through his skin and make it flow through his body, his heart. He wanted her life pulsing inside him.

He wanted to be inside her.

The thought slammed him back further. Strange. This sudden weakness in his every muscle and bone...it was almost *mortal.*

He stumbled from her, plowing into the door frame, letting out another humiliating growl.

"No!" she cried. "Please don't go. I won't do it again; I promise!"

Another laugh escaped him. Marcus braced a hand against the wall, clawing at the wood. Splinters embedded under his fingernails as he fought the self-loathing in his reply. "No," he concurred in a harsh breath. "We shall *not* do that again."

"All right. Fine."

Her comeback vibrated with the anger he'd hoped to incite. And a breathtaking sizzle of rebellion. They had dubbed him a rebel in his time, too, he recalled...all those Whitehall wenches hiding beneath their pious pearls and "virgin's" lace, dropping the suggestive words between weather remarks and whispers about Drake's latest adventure in the name of his sovereign.

All but Raquelle. Raquelle, all satin and skin and blatant, coyless sex, who had brought his end—and his beginning. The end of his life. The beginning of his hell.

But she is not Raquelle, a voice told him from deep within. It spoke the assertion entirely too easily. *She—is—not—Raquelle.*

"I have to go." He forced himself out into the hall. If one woman had seduced him into this existence, another had only one disaster left to lead him to.

"No. Please, I've only just found you!"

"Let me be, Gabriela." His voice sounded animalistic even to his own ears. Grating. And hungry.

"Why? And how do you even know my name?"

"'Tis not important. Let me go."

"The devil it's not important. How did you know I was

here? Where did you come from? What's going—"

"Damn you!" He spun back upon her. His lungs heaved with heat; his blood turned to flames. "Damn you, go away and leave me be!"

He appeared Satan's cousin. Her eyes told him so, reflecting his imposing height, bared teeth and burning stare. *Judas Iscariot.* Any self-respecting chit would be daintily unconscious on the carpet by now.

Gabriela Rozina barely flinched.

She stood there, mussed and gorgeous, her hands clenching and unclenching as if preparing to go to fisticuffs with him right there. Then there was her heartbeat, hammering blood to those straining fingers. Then came the whole chorus of her, the irresistible symphony of her entire body, daring to defy him like this. Daring to not only brave his wrath, but throw it right back at him.

"I have to go." He dragged his gaze over her once more, needing this last heaven of a moment to take into eternity with him. "Please," he rasped, "do not follow me."

She didn't move either way. Nor, for a tight silence, did she speak.

In a shaking murmur, her words finally came. "Bastard. You malicious bastard. You come to me like this, saying you understand, saying you care—" She shook her head. "Damn *you.* I don't even know your name."

"Gabriela—"

"Nor do I want to know it. Go, then. Go."

The word came out of him without a thought, let alone a chance at restraint. "Marc," he finally uttered.

"Marc?"

"My name. If you need anything—*anything*—just call for Marc."

"Marc." Unbelievably, a smile wobbled on her lips. "Marc. That's nice."

"Now..." He pretended to adjust the lamp in the wall sconce, instead disguising the moment it took to focus a mild hypnosis over her. Amazing, how swiftly the powers returned; how easily he could summon them for his own self-serving purpose. "Go home, Gabriela."

It's for her own good, he silently justified. *And yours.*

She blinked slowly at him. Then again. Then murmured with all the tender trust of a three-year-old, "All right."

He smiled, then, too. He imagined kissing her on her high, smooth forehead, running his mouth along her hairline. Then he willed the image to oblivion.

"Good night, Marc," she said.

"Goodbye, Gabriela."

For a long while after the door slammed behind her, he simply stood there. A thousand times, he commanded himself to outcast her warmth from his blood and his soul. Two thousand times, he ordered an exorcism of the life he had slowly allowed himself to revel in the last two months.

Hours passed. The lamp's oil burned down and died. Darkness, the starless gloom that permeated the world in the last hour before dawn, descended.

Gabriela's warmth still clung to every inch of him. Her life still filled his nostrils, his sights, his mind.

Let her go, a voice ordered, seemingly from thin air. His conscience did that when it said things he nay wanted to hear.

You could have only hurt her. And she could have hurt you. Irreversibly. Do you remember the last time you were so hard and hot and obsessed over a woman, you thought with all the control of a bonfire—

"Go to hell."

He stormed down the hall. For the first time in a long time, he felt pricks of the approaching sunrise—and welcomed the hot needles in his skin. He contemplated giving in. Of at last choosing the finality of eternal damnation over the torment of eternal loneliness.

But he would not. He was too much a goddamn coward even for that. For all the drinking and swordplay and bedded wenches he'd crammed into his depraved mortal existence, Marcus was, deep in his rotten gut, passionately afraid to die.

So he would descend to hell once more.

The exhausted weight of his body pulled him toward the locked door at the end of the hall. Curiosity about what lay beyond it had long ago waned among Drury's ever-changing tenants, their histrionic tales of the theatre's famed "ghost" replaced by the more stylish excuse of a never-used broom closet. In this sole matter, Marcus appreciated the intervention of style. He just wanted to get out of here.

But he had to take the steps past Gabriela's dressing room first.

With a determined curse, he approached the portal fast. He steeled his gaze straight ahead. *He would not look.*

But she had left the lamp turned up, just a little bit.

Like distant recollections of autumn sunsets, the view beckoned to him. All the elements of her world lay still but vibrant in the deep umber light. The gleam of her crystal hairbrush on the dressing table. The twinkling beads on her costume, hanging on the dressing screen. The frayed copy of *Hamlet* she'd been working from earlier.

And a dark leather book on the floor, its pages soughing the floor as his boot bumped it.

No, Marcus amended as he picked it up. Not a book.

"*Gabriela.*" He now gripped the journal with both hands,

drinking in her words as if they were written in water from the spring of life. Knowing he should hurl the damn thing away. Clinging to it harder with each passing moment.

"Gabriela," he grated, slumping against the door frame, "I do not know how I am going to survive you."

But how, his soul roared back, would he exist any other way again?

★ ★ ★ ★

Lightning.

A hundred times the next morning, Gabriela berated herself for the comparison—and for the irrational jolt in her nerves whenever the memory of *him* struck. She even indulged herself in some breakfast, and lingered over the latest issues of *Theatre* and *The Contemporary Review*. But the remembrances hit without timing or care; the visions of stormy black hair and a rain-smooth touch, coming and paralyzing her just like—

Lightning.

In the form of a gaze from a beautiful stranger named Marc.

Now, as she reentered her dressing room by the gray light of the rainy afternoon, that silvered sensation overtook her again. She didn't move to turn up the lamp. At this moment, the room appeared just as it should: draped in shadows, unreal; just as she remembered it from last night. Just as she recalled the magical scene which had transpired here.

It all *had* been real...hadn't it? And if it had, what strange being had it transformed her into? One minute, she'd burned with the most intense anger she'd known, matching Marc snarl for snarl. The next, she found herself trapped in a whirlpool of light, emanating from the splendor of his eyes, wanting only to please him. Like a puppet-headed maid transfixed by a wizard from a penny novel, she'd left the theatre in a mindless haze, leaving behind her cloak, her manuscript, her reticule, and her journal.

Oddly, the misplacement of the latter filled her with the most anxiety. She'd kept the journal updated with every thought, feeling, and experience she'd had this year...including some things so intimate, her cheeks colored just thinking about them. She had to retrieve the book—and the deep secrets the pages kept safe for her.

She stopped at the big chair she'd curled into last night. She'd been waging battle against a blank page in the journal before the tears had come, and *he* had appeared. But a search around the chair, the table, and soon the rest of the room turned up everything except the journal. Three face powder brushes, two boot-lacing hooks, and a handful of hair pins richer, Gaby slammed hands to hips and threw an exasperated scowl about the chamber.

She turned and strode down the hall, toward the main stage. "Louis!" she called on her way. "Louis, I need your help."

Just invoking the stage manager's name helped usher a calming flow into her heart. If anyone could help her locate the elusive journal, the grizzled but good-hearted hulk was the man for the job.

"Louis," she shouted again, pushing open the stage door, "are you able to help—"

A chaos of hammering drowned the rest of her sentence. She would have started again, but her mouth dropped open in astonishment.

The scene resembled the area she knew as the main

stage—vaguely. Only now, props and sets were ghosts draped in sheets, the stage floorboards flooded by a sea of muslin tarps. That sea sprouted several ladders and one island of carpenter's tools. At least ten dirty-bibbed workmen lumbered around her, whistling in time to their heavy strides.

She located Louis at last, practically pacing a hole into the tarps downstage right. "Good afternoon," she greeted, deliberately dry about the tone. "To what do we owe the pleasure of the chaos?"

The man's head, topped by a tumult of brown, ropy hair, jerked up. "What are you doing here, Gaby?" he snapped.

She stepped back instinctively. "I left my things here last night," she said softly. "But I can't find my journ—"

"Haven't seen it. Gaby, you're in the way here."

She hurried behind him as he stomped to the opposite wings. "In the way of what?"

"What the bloody hell does it look like is going on? We're fixing the damn roof."

"Today?"

"Today."

Gabriela barely checked her jaw from dropping. "But we've all been having trouble with those rain puddles for months."

"Yes; yes, I know. Listen, I have to have this done by tonight."

"But I told you about this repeatedly, and you—"

"Well, somebody decided to listen!"

His growl erupted with an extra dose of vehemence due to the approach of a workman bearing several bills to be signed. Louis swore at the figures, but signed the papers, anyway.

"By the devil's own mother," he muttered halfway through

the third invoice. "I've only met the lunatic once, but it's like he has eyes and ears everywhere."

"Who?" Gabriela asked, but only partly from curiosity. Mostly, she wanted to know who to thank for this miracle.

"Marcus I-want-it-done-by-tonight Stafford, that's who. Calls himself a silent owner of this place but causes more chaos than six of Augustus could. Thinks he can leave a note on my desk like a bloody royal decree, and the roof will patch itself overnight, good as new. I swear to you, Gaby, I'd leave this place, if..."

But Louis's stormings faded to a drizzle beneath the thunderstorm of his first sentence. Gabriela turned and clung to a ladder for support as the words resounded in her head. *Marcus Stafford.*

Marcus "Marc" *Stafford.*

Like regaining perspective after a triple pirouette, comprehension came between one blink and the next. Gabriela laughed; yet the sound held no mirth. "It can't be," she whispered.

Yet it could. It made so much—too much—sense. She recalled the moment her gaze had first locked with Marc's. She remembered the quicksilver sensation through her veins, and thinking he'd been watching her with that surreal intensity for hours. As if he was perfectly at home in this building, and she the strange new creature in *his* private forest.

Haunting thoughts loomed at her. How many times before *that* had he watched her like that? How long had he been studying her every move?

Long enough, Gabriela suspected. Enough to know the backstage rain puddles had caused her a number of precarious slips, then wield his power as silent theatre owner to order the problem rectified within a day.

Theatre owner.

Why hadn't he told her?

That was a silly question. There were a multitude of things Marcus Stafford had never told a soul about himself. She'd stake her own soul on the fact.

A barrage of *whacks* resounded through the theatre. The workers had started on the roof. Gaby's heartbeat thundered loudly enough to join the din. She searched the expanse of the theatre and each box on both five-tiered sides, wondering if he watched her even now. Wondering if he even took notes...

She pushed away from the ladder. Icy fear dueled with searing anger along her nerves. She marched through the green room, but didn't turn back to her dressing room. No, she angled the opposite direction, through the back door and into the street, welcoming the rush of April wind on her cheeks and through her hair. She hoped the cold blasted away the skirmish raging inside her, but admitted she might as well wish the Thames to stop flowing.

She didn't go back in to look for her journal again.

Because she knew exactly who had it.

Eight hours later, just after the last orchestra member shouted goodbye from the back door and the theatre fell into a silence, Gabriela stomped to the middle of the stage. She threw back her head to make her voice carry to the highest rafter, and shouted as loud as she could:

"Marcus! Marcus Stafford! I want to see you *right now!*"

CHAPTER FOUR

Silence.

Had she expected something else?

He's not there.

It was the same inner demon that delighted in tugging at her insecurities before auditions...and long ago, had heckled her each visitor's day at the orphanage.

A voice she fought now with shaking fists.

The heckler persisted.

He told you to go away once. He meant it. You didn't listen. He's not there.

"No."

She secured her stance tighter. Blast it, she knew what she felt, despite the dark theatre answering her desperate gaze. Freezing fingers of sensation claimed her skin more boldly than they'd dared this morning. Her heartbeat pounded like a triple timpani with each passing second into the night. Worst of all, she couldn't shed this breath-catching awareness...this super-real sensation that he still watched her, followed her, haunted her.

She moved to the edge of the stage. Stopped when her toes jutted out into the dark—and tried not to liken the view to the unreadable abyss of her senses.

"Coward!" she accused into the chasm. "Backing down from the challenge, now that I've figured out a little more than I should? Hiding in your precious shadows, Sir High and Mighty Theatre Owner? Enjoying the drama of the hopeless actress, going slowly insane?"

As she backed off the edge, she shook her head in slow-burning fury. "I hope you like tonight's repertoire, Marcus. It's the last you'll get. I don't play to ghosts." She pivoted toward the wings. "Or thieves."

As she marched across the stage, she refused to let the dry heat behind her eyes liquidate. She refused to let her shoulders sag or her step falter. She'd give in to her humiliation only after escaping those all-seeing silver eyes.

Wherever the bloody hell they were.

Two steps from the stage left wings, she gasped and skidded to a halt. Two black-clad, black-booted legs stepped into her path. Her journal and reticule hit the floorboards between those boots with a forceful thwack. They were tossed there from a long-fingered hand.

Gabriela's stare connected that hand to an arm, the arm to an endlessly broad shoulder, encased in billowy black silk. Her sights continued up the cords of a taut neck, to the spiritual intensity of Marcus's face.

If it were possible, the otherworldly force of him radiated even more potent impact tonight. He looked hewn of dark gold granite under the gas lights, his hair swept around his high forehead like onyx turned to velvet.

But most of all, he looked furious.

He glared at the purse and the journal, then back to her. "I am not a thief."

Gaby didn't pick up the items. Not yet. She nudged one foot forward, her reticule on one side, his boot on the other.

She raised her stare, issuing the same challenge to his eyes. "You took them without my permission. You stole them."

"I borrowed them."

"Borrowed?" She sliced out an incredulous laugh. "Oh, this is a new way to play the scene."

"Gabriela—"

"You mean to tell me you decided to *borrow* my reticule—"

"Aye."

"Planning a big evening out and didn't have one of your own?"

"Gabriela."

"And my journal. That's the worst of it, Marcus. Did you stop to think what you took from me—the record of my deepest thoughts and feelings? Did you consider *asking* before you violated my privacy, my life?"

For a long moment, he issued no reply. But with the slightest motion, he'd pressed his boot against her foot—beckoning her sights up to his again. She cursed the thousand butterflies in her belly that lifted wing along with her gaze.

"If I asked...where would your answer have lie?"

Gaby compressed her lips, letting silence stretch again.

"I rest my case." He dropped his gaze. But not before Gabriela glimpsed a flash of silver light beneath his dark lashes—his surrender to a moment of such intense pain, his eyes looked as if they really did glow...

She shook her head. This was no time for such hallucinations. Blast it, *he'd* wronged *her*, not the other way around. She snatched her pity back from him, recognizing it for the dangerous emotion it was. But she held on to the anger.

"Well?" She locked her arms across her chest.

Marcus didn't look up. "Well, what?"

She slid her foot away from his. Suddenly, her voice didn't come so strongly. "Well...did you read it?"

He considered her question for what felt like hours.

Finally, he looked up again. Slowly leaned toward her, appearing like a great beast used to watching every step for fear it would crush something.

"Aye."

Damn him.

Damn him for saying it with such meaning, for looking penitent yet proud as he did. Again, as if *he'd* experienced every fear and feeling, every triumph and sorrow she'd expressed on those pages.

"Bastard."

"That will not procure you an apology." He towered closer. So mesmerizing. A fine wine in human form, dominating her senses, whether she liked it or not. "I am not sorry I did it."

"Yes." She snorted. "I know."

"Your words are beautiful."

"Stop it."

"I memorized them."

"You think that's going to redeem you?"

"Sweeting, nothing can redeem me."

The night held its breath around them.

He meant it. Gabriela was forced to recognize the fact as she watched a shadow descend over the noble angles of his face, casting them into rigidity that he might as well be one of the prop statues. Her anger inverted to amazement turning full circle, firing her blood all over again.

"Why?" she rasped. "Why are you doing this to me?"

His taut silence told her everything. And nothing. Once more, their gazes locked. And once more, Gabriela stared into a silver storm roiling with every tear she'd cried, every laugh she'd freed, every emotion she'd known.

Dear God. This man moved her. And terrified her.

"This—this isn't just about the journal, is it? It's about what happened the other night, when we first saw each other."

Marcus raised his hand as if to touch her. His fingers curled into a ball, instead. "I never meant to frighten you."

"You didn't frighten me."

His gaze tightened. "What?"

"For a moment, I was startled. But then I looked into your eyes, and I felt only that I'd known you for a very long time. But now I realize it's because *you* knew *me*. You'd been watching me, every night—"

"*Nay.*" He slammed the fist to his thigh. "I mean—God's blood, Gabriela, I meant you no ill."

"Then I'm right." Her voice wavered. She didn't know it until now, but a part of her had held on to some strange hope, desperately wishing any other expression to his face but the confirming grimace on his lips. "Dear God. I'm right."

"Gabriela—"

"How long? How long has this been going on, Marcus? Do you follow me everywhere? To my dressing room? Do you follow me home?"

"Nay—"

"Stop lying to me. How else could you know everything about me? How else can you look at me and make me feel like you look *inside* me? How else can I feel this way every time I look back, losing myself in your eyes...losing myself in your—" She stopped, her throat constricting on a bizarre clutch of grief. "It's not fair."

Marcus's nostrils flared on an audible intake of breath. She tried to breathe, too. Tried to understand, no matter how the confusion and fear drained her strength.

Her hands fell to her sides, palms open and entreating.

"What the blast are you doing to me? Damn you, just tell me what you want from me. Tell me why you're doing this!"

She still held her breath. Marcus's face didn't change. Except...

Except for the haunted grimace that parted his lips, revealing his locked teeth beneath. They were straight and perfect but for the slightly extended tips on opposing sides of his front pair. Gabriela wasn't sure why her stare was drawn there...but she couldn't stop looking...hypnotized by the ferocious sensuality of his mouth...

"Because..." that mouth said then, the word a sibilance of raw need, "you are the most beautiful thing I've seen in my miserable existence."

★ ★ ★ ★

God's wounds.

He might as well have stripped naked then stood there before her. He would be eminently more comfortable, and equally as exposed.

Yet even with the tremors of the confession still rocking his body, his mind struggled to believe he had said it. From the look of Gabriela's wide stare, so did she.

So much for the pretty-worded stud who carnalized half of Whitehall behind Good Bess's back. Admit it, Stafford. You are old. Very old. And you are nay near worthy enough for an angel like Gabriela Rozina.

He let out a weary sigh and nothing else, not trusting his mutinous mouth to release safe words any more.

Slowly, he turned to plod heavy steps toward the door leading to safe, wretched darkness.

"Where the bloody hell do you think you're going now?" she called.

He stopped. Not voluntarily. Another oath escaped from beneath his breath. His boots grated against the floorboards as he faced her again.

Sweet God.

She had aroused him before, but always from the heights of the spiritual realm he would never achieve again or on the stage far below and far away—either way, a reaction he quelled with the understanding he would never find fulfillment.

Yet now she stood there visually sparring with him, just as confused as him. And close, so achingly close. Again, she squared off at him in that let's-cuff-it-out-right-now pose, bracing tapered fingers to a waist he could span with his hands— though a man could not gauge that sort of thing anymore, with the barbaric underpinnings they currently called "style." Still, the corset contraption thrust other things into perfect view. The swell of her creamy breasts. The soft lines of her hips.

Hell.

Somehow, he managed to bite out a retort. "I shall go where I bloody well please, if it concerns you, which it does not. But suffice it to say I will not tamper with your precious sanity again. Goodnight, sweeting."

"No!"

He gritted back an obscenity he had not heard for at least a century. And swung his gaze back toward her.

She still stood proud as an empress though had shifted her hands to intertwine in front of her, forming a V that centered his sights straight to the crux of her—

Hell.

Again.

He forced his stare back to her face. Then almost laughed. Gabriela's glower had faltered into an uncertain scowl. The woman did *not* enjoy ambivalence.

"Believe it or not, Mr. Stafford, my sanity was in trouble long before you came along." Then, in a swift mumble, "And I do, in fact, care where you go."

"Well, do *not*," Marcus countered.

"Why not?"

"Just...do not, Gabriela. Do not begin to care. I—you—we are two worlds crossing at the wrong time. God's wounds, that should not have crossed at all."

"I don't happen to agree."

"You are hardly qualified to render such a verdict."

For exactly two heartbeats, she said nothing. But during that silence, Marcus felt every moment of her two hard breaths, every muscle coiling tighter in her two white fists.

They were the calm before the storm.

"How dare you." The third heartbeat exploded with her tempest. "How *dare* you. *You're* not the one whose thoughts and dreams were last night's bedtime reading, sir. You're not the one most exposed here, most vulnerable!"

As she tightened the distance between them, finally stopping a step away, Marcus swung his gaze down. *Oh, sweeting, if you only knew.*

"I think," she seethed, "that if anyone has the license to care here, it is I." She attempted to smooth the creases she had imparted to her dress. "And—and what I really need to care about here is this bloody script," she rushed on. "But you already know that, don't you?"

He dared one careful word. "Aye." After a pause as comfortable as disrobing for a first-time lover, he could not repress the rest of his thought. "Your rehearsals..." he ventured. "You wrote many times of them in your journal. And of your vexation with them."

Gabriela chose a moment of circumspect silence. But when she turned back, the stamp of pain on her face was a mallet of confirmation on his heart. He fought the yearning to hold her, to command away that mortal frustration from her senses.

But another force bested him to the job. Her features changed. Wildly. Some instantaneous power ignited her. She beamed a glorious smile.

"Marcus!" His name was a miracle of joy on her lips. As he stood numb from the wonder of it, she grabbed his hands with the mischief of a lass contemplating her first May Day kiss. "Marcus, *you* can help me. You're just what I need. A partner to help me run lines!"

He went even more numb, despite managing to jerk his hands free from her. "Nay. I am humbled and honored but I am also contrite. Nay, sweeting. I cannot."

"Of course you can. Of course you *will*. Come on, grump. Stay and make yourself useful for once."

"I am not a grump." Whatever the blast that was.

"Marcus, I need help with these lines. I need...you."

Her last words tumbled out so swift and so soft, they would be inaudible to a mortal man. But Marcus heard. Oh aye, he stood there and soaked in every word. And then the nervous breath she drew in after...and the pound of her heart as she awaited his decision. So swift and urgent a heartbeat, the tempo could claim only one dance master.

Fear.

Panic took over his actions. In one sweep, he whirled back

to her. Before she could fight, he curled a finger under her chin, commanding her sights to his. Despite the surprise of his move, Marcus did not expect her to meet his challenge so directly, enabling him to secure an instant link with her psyche. And her soul.

And for once, without hesitation, he delved his mind into the deepest core of hers.

Oh, aye. She *was* afraid.

But not that he would stay.

She was terrified he would leave.

He swallowed as the glimmer of a tear swelled in her right eye. She tried to fight it but lost; the heavy drop defied her with a slow descent across her smooth cheek.

Ah, God.

He knew tears like that. He had battled back tens of thousands like them. Tears of rejection. Anger. Frustration. And loneliness.

In short, all the pain he had known himself over the last two hundred eighty years.

And now, terror gripped him, too.

What the hell have you started, Stafford?

"Gabriela." Though he whispered it, raw torment permeated his voice. He slid his finger from her chin to her cheek, retracing the path left by her tear. He tried, without succeeding, not to meet her gaze again—and was hopelessly lost in the dark copper beauty of her gaze.

"Oh, Gabriela." The more hard-edged mutter helped him regain a measure of control. But not enough to hold him back from saying, "You...were working on *Hamlet*, were you not?"

CHAPTER FIVE

She broke into a watery grin. She couldn't help herself. She also had a devastating urge to hug him but squelched the temptation with the memory of his reaction when she'd touched his hand last night.

Not that he made it at all easy. Her body clenched, battling the need to sway closer to him as his features changed again. His eyelids lowered. His fingers raised to roam her cheek. His firm lips parted, as if the picture in her mind became the fantasy in his, too.

Dear God. A woman could lose herself in that look.

All of herself.

As in hopes, dreams and goals, too.

Again as if he read her soul more clearly than the acts in a program, Marcus yanked himself back. Yet as he did, her heart slammed to another stop. In the deepest fathoms of her mind, Gaby swore she heard, in the most fervent whisper: *I cannot touch you. Sweet God, Gabriela, I could never hurt you.*

But before she could work her jaw around a reaction, Marcus found her script atop a prop boulder and started to thumb the worn pages. So blithely, as if he'd heard—or said—nothing.

"So." He braced his bent knee to the boulder and the script to his knee. "My mate Augustus is staging the great *Hamlet,* hmm?"

It took a few moments for Gaby to realize he lent a *voice*

to the words this time. "What? Oh, yes. We begin rehearsals in three weeks but I want to prepare more thoroughly. This production is particularly important to me."

He turned another page, noting her marked lines and cues there. "Ophelia is that tightly entwined to your soul?"

She frowned. "I beg your pardon?"

"'Tis a play close to your affections. You just said so. And you stay so late, laboring on your lines. Surely it is because you liken yourself to the poor Ophelia."

"Great saints," she sputtered. "Whatever gave you that—this is just the role Augustus assigned to me! I'm going to learn it and perform it as best as I can, but—well—" She threw him a perturbed glance. "Ophelia was a lovesick sagmop who drove herself insane because of a *man*."

He lowered the script and slanted a vast stare back at her, unfaltering as polished pewter. "And you have never wanted to go insane because of love?"

Gaby fired back another snort.

And that maddening man on the boulder continued his unnerving scrutiny. By the stars, didn't he ever blink?

Marcus returned the script to the boulder and paced toward her. "Are you telling me your heart has never been broken, Gabriela Rozina? That you have not lost so much or grieved so deeply that you wanted to die, too?"

She didn't answer him in words. But her soul returned the question loud enough. *More times than you'll ever know. More times than you* want *to know.*

But his eyes told her he already knew that.

His eyes told her he wanted to know more.

A *more* she'd never give anyone.

Gabriela dropped her head. Jerked up her skirts, attempting to sidestep the approaching scoundrel, but Marcus moved three steps ahead, slicing each escape route short. How did he *always* move three steps ahead?

"Look," she gritted as they squared off for the fourth time, "I said the production was important to me, not the role. And I never said it was 'close to my affections'."

"Ahhh." He nodded with too much confidence for her comfort. "Yes, how could I have forgotten? You have that honor reserved for the Prince's Grand Theatre Troupe."

She didn't question how he knew that. Between the teasing she weathered from everyone and the reminders she railed at herself during her extra rehearsals, the man didn't need Pasteur's genius to deduce where her aspirations lie.

She dared another gaze up at him. But this time, she met his examination with pride, perhaps a little defiance. All right; a lot of defiance. "All right. Yes. Making the troupe is my ultimate dream. There's nothing wrong with that."

"Nothing at all."

His lips remained a solemn line, but now his eyes smiled. The combination befuddled her. Gaby didn't know whether to embrace him for his understanding or slap him for his insolence.

"You're serious, aren't you?" she said in lieu of either choice. "You truly think I can do this?"

She didn't know how he'd respond to that. She only knew her imagination didn't include Marcus sweeping her beyond clueless and into speechless. He did it by first sliding his hands into hers, and lifting them to his lips as gingerly as crystal roses. His kiss to her knuckles was the barest brush of a touch. She didn't even feel his breath on her skin...

She didn't feel *her* breath any more, either.

She'd never fainted before, but certainly this sensation

counted as the prelude to such. A tingled fuzz replaced her brain. Languid warmth flowed through her cells instead of blood.

Marcus's murmur, low and musical, only spun the spell thicker. "I think," he told her, "that you can do anything, dream anything, and become anything you want."

She squeezed his hands to test if this moment was real. When she knew it was, she couldn't hold back her joy from bursting on a misty laugh. Even the odd drop of his left eyebrow added to her delight.

"This is—I mean, you are—" she tried to explain to his puzzled expression. "It's just that you're the first to ever believe in me."

"Nay," Marcus countered. "*You* were the first."

"But I'm not important."

"Is that what Alfonso told you?"

She jerked her hands down. Just that word from his mouth made it physically necessary to move.

Blast. She should have known! He knew everything else about her life, didn't he? That didn't make it less frustrating that he'd brought up the one thorn that could ruin this sweet bouquet of a conversation.

"Alfonso is—" she stammered, "it's a complicated—" An irritated huff. She took several more steps. "I will thank you to simply leave the subject of him alone."

"He is a clod. You know that, do you not?"

She snapped back around. His voice loomed directly behind her—and so did he, suddenly standing so close, she shook from the tremor her spine composed in answer.

How had he gotten there so fast?

Dear Lord. The man's ability to sneak his large body

around, silent as death...it was wholly disconcerting.

Gaby funneled her agitation into a caustic comeback. "Thank you for the insight, but I've discovered Mr. Renard's filthy fortitude on my own. And I'll dispatch the wretch just as simply."

To her surprise, a chuckle underlined his response. "Oh, I do not doubt that."

"What's that supposed to mean?"

He spread open hands again. "That is, most verily, rather obvious. 'Tis no secret you hot-blooded Italian misses have a talent for dispatching wretches with—"

She cut him short with a cracking slap—but the sound was caused by her wrist slamming into his steeled grip, not the stinging ring she craved, of her hand against his face. She struggled against his hold. Marcus held on with amazing yet effortless power.

"Let. Go."

"Hmmm. Nay." He drawled the words with infuriating calm, practically caressing her with the tone. Gabriela glared up at him. His gaze answered with nothing but with smooth silver serenity.

A shocked gasp escaped. "Did you—bait me with that on purpose?"

"Aye."

"Why?" She gulped hard, forcing tears back. *Not now. Don't let him in. Don't let him see the pain.* "I thought you cared about me," she rasped.

"Sweet Gabriela." To her deeper astonishment, his voice shook in tandem to hers. He lifted his other hand, bracketing it to her face. "I do care. Do *you* not fathom it is why I long to know your shame of what you are? Of why you fear your true self?"

Stillness stretched, uncomfortable and thick. Finally with a strength she didn't know she had, she wrested free of him. Her mind and senses reeled. Dear God. He'd hit the target of her soul with fatal accuracy, and she didn't know whether to cry or die.

"Gabriela?"

"Because it's not good enough!" The pain burned beyond tears now. Her sobs came dry and fast. "Don't you see? *I* will never be good enough!"

"So you pretend to be someone else."

"If I have to." Her fingertips lost blood as she curled them around her sleeve ends and pulled. "Now...let us close the subject. Permanently."

"We have not discussed Renard yet," he objected.

"Yes, we have."

"Gabriela—"

"The matter is closed!"

"Damn it, now why do *you* not see? The man is dangerous! You are in mortal jeopardy!"

He raised his arms, hands shaking, muscles straining. Gaby swallowed back a shameful urge to laugh. "Mortal jeopardy? Oh, Marcus. Where did you grow up? In the Age of Chivalry?"

He dropped his arms but not his glower. "You said you trust me."

She sobered enough to give that a moment of sobering thought. "Yes," she murmured. "I did."

"Do you still mean it?"

"Yes."

"I only want to prove myself worthy of that gift, Gabriela."

"I know that. I *do*. So stop brooding. Your intention is not a sin."

The relief she expected to grant him never manifested. Instead, she watched her words render the same effect as a knife through his middle. Something between a sob and a grimace marred his handsome face.

"Not a sin." He emitted a harsh laugh. "Oh, dear nymph, in thy orisons be all my sins remembered."

He looked to the blackness of the theatre as he said the beautiful line, imbuing it with intimacy, as if truly speaking to someone out there in the dark. Watching him, Gaby knew she'd treasure this instant as one of *her* most precious memories. With his dark hair falling over his high forehead, his stance proud and strong, his jaw a searching uplift of an angle beneath the noble slant of his lips, he appeared to see beyond even the building's paltry walls, windows and confines.

He looked like he gazed along the very depths of time.

He took her breath away.

Several moments passed before she comprehended he'd turned expectantly back toward her. It cost him an impatient snort to get her attention.

"Wh-What?" she stammered.

"Act Three, Scene One," he leveled with sudden, not to mention strange, efficiency. "'Nymph, in thy orisons be all my sins remembered.' 'Tis your cue, young lady. You told me you stayed to rehearse, didn't you?"

"Uhhh…yes." He was right. The line *was* her cue. And he *was* Drury's silent owner, signifying his devotion to the arts beyond mere lip service—

But none of it dimmed this latest addition to the surprise that continued to be Marcus Stafford. Actually, this was the biggest eye-opener so far. Gaby hadn't considered this factor when she blurted her plea for him to stay. She'd only watched him trudge toward the wings with the certainty that he carried a piece of her soul with him—and had scrambled for the swiftest excuse to bring him back. The entreaty for his help with her lines came logically.

It never occurred to her that he'd be good at the job.

She revised that assessment over the next two hours. "Magnificent" fit the bill better. Breathtaking. Beautiful. He countered her Ophelia with a Hamlet so real, she wondered if the Danes had lost a prince sometime in the last thirty or so years. His deliveries bettered even the Lyceum's Breezy Bill Terrace, fluent to the point of poetic, speaking each word as if the ghost of Shakespeare possessed him. He entranced her so completely, Gabriela fell into continual lapses of awed silence, her own lines forgotten to the conviction in his face, the desperation in his tone, the eloquence of his body.

She gaped her way through at least the fiftieth of those pauses, staring at his wide-legged pose just downstage of the prop boulder. His posture held the tension of "Hamlet's" last line, from his broad, coiled shoulders down to the defined angles of the calf muscles straining at his boots. Not that she cared about *any* of his muscles...

"Gabriela?"

She jerked her sights back up. The scowl had transformed to his expectant stare.

"I'm...so sorry," she stumbled. "Was that my cue again?"

As she expected, he folded his arms—as if making her stare at the perfect muscles between his wrists and elbows was going to assist his cause. If tendencies of the evening continued, a lengthy sigh would ensue, succeeded by the what-am-I-going-to-do-with-you shake of his head that, Gaby rapidly discovered, shot the strangest arrow of heat between her breasts before inching its way downward...

To her surprise—and odd disappointment—he smiled, instead. "Perhaps 'tis a good juncture to stop."

"*No.*"

She hated herself for the plea but couldn't dam the fear his action flooded through her. On that same surge of alarm, she rushed toward him.

"Sweeting, it's late." Marcus untwisted his arms and reached his hands for her elbows.

"No. No, it's not." But a traitorous yawn selected that moment to surface. She ignored his corresponding chuckle. "Please," she persisted. "We still have so much to work on."

To her further disconcertment, his touch remained light, almost fearful, around her elbows. It wasn't enough. Not nearly enough...

Hold me. Please, Marcus. I need your strength and your insight and your insane beauty around me.

"You—are progressing well with the material now, sweeting. Just remember to keep your head lifted at the end of the monologue—"

"No."

His right eyebrow hiked, a precursor to his sharp scowl. "What?"

"I said no. I'm sorry, but I don't remember a thing of what I learned tonight." It wasn't too far from the truth. "I really need much more rehearsal—with a master. Someone who knows this play like the back of his hand."

I need you.

"Gabriela." His hold clamped around her hard. Then released her swiftly. "Nay." He turned and stepped away but whipped around when she tried to follow, sweeping his hand between them. His fingers, long and fluid and commanding, issued a directive as powerful as a shout. Despite every protest of her mind, her body obeyed.

She retaliated with her most vehement scowl. No effect. His beautiful eyes continued their steady torment, holding her in place like the hangman's noose. Tighter, tighter—until it was too late. Her brain recognized the assault of the same lethargic fog which had descended before she'd stumbled home last night. It took over her will, controlled her actions. She struggled to banish the murk. In vain.

"Don't!" She gasped it as that invisible force pushed her further from him.

"Don't?" It sounded as if he stood in China, not four steps across the stage.

"Don't—do this to me." Her voice sounded like she'd just practiced drinking, not drama. "*You're* doing this, Marcus. I—I don't know how—but *stop.*"

A long pause preceded his reply. In it, strange and horrible emotions assaulted her, almost as if another person stepped into her body then leapt back out. Confusion. Despair. Sadness. Longing. *Lust?* Then confusion again...

"Go home, Gabriela."

"No."

"*Aye.*"

"Say you'll come back tomorrow night."

"*Gabriela.*"

"Say it."

He sighed. At least she thought he did. The sound echoed in her head more than her ears, a breath full of weight and longing. As if he were an old man waiting to die, not a vibrant, magnificent dream come to life.

"I will think about it," he finally murmured. "Damn you, I will think about it."

★ ★ ★ ★

He had only said the words to make her leave. God's blood, what else could he have done? The woman gave persistence a new meaning, standing there swaying like a feather under his hypnosis but blurting her impossible commands as if she held Queen Bess's own scepter.

The muck of the whole thing was, he really did think about her pleas.

No, he corrected himself over the next fourteen nights, he thought nothing through at all.

No other excuse justified why he returned to meet Gabriela every one of those nights, drawn like a star to the moon...or an opium addict to his pipe. He cursed himself with each step up the secret stairway, only to renege on the doubt when he moved close enough to feel her presence again. Her excitement, her dreams, her drive—

Her smile.

That unabashed, unpretentious smile showered him with warmth each evening when she met him in the golden glow of the stage lights. She saved it for his eyes only. He did not have to delve an inch into her psyche to determine *that*. The magic of their deepening connection shined in every inch of that smile. It glimmered in every bronze fleck of her gaze, resonated in every step she moved at his directions, manifested in every nod she rewarded to his suggestions—and aye; demands, as well— to better her performance.

Oh, she certainly snapped back a few demands of her own—

but between their rows and their discrepancies, her obstinacy and his pomposity, Gabriela began to grasp the essence of a woman named Ophelia. It came first in tentative dialogue changes here and there, then in growing breakthroughs of emotion and spirit...and the result was going to be an absurd success on this stage. Marcus knew it.

But most importantly, he saw that Gabriela knew it.

Especially when each of her triumphant smiles thanked him for it.

At the current moment, however...

Marcus tried not to gawk too hard at her bustled little bottom as she indulged in a spirited huff while attempting to pull one of the prop trees to center stage.

For a long moment, despite himself, he enjoyed the view. Then he halted her foolery by moving up and gripping the limb over her shoulder. "May I take the presumption of asking what the hell this is for?"

She straightened and turned.

God's bloody wounds.

He'd planned his positioning with the intelligence of a baboon. With her pinned between his body and the tree, she was too damn close and tempting. He would only had to press a step closer, and—

His cock hardened. Instantly and painfully. And damn it, he had worn only a pair of his old loose knit hose tonight. If she moved even a few inches, she'd feel every pulsing inch of his desire. She'd finally know how much he wanted her.

For a moment, however, she looked as if she already knew. And for another perilous moment, Marcus thought she might feel the same torturous ache—unless he'd slept through some decade and a woman's high flush, moistened lips and shallow breath now stood for a contrary meaning.

"I—" she finally got out. "The tree—it's for—I've got to die tonight."

So much for arousal.

A storm of freezing sensations saw to that—most of them terror.

What the bloody hell provoked her to say that? Had she found out about him somehow? Gotten curious during the day, during the hours of his deepest sleep, and broken into the vault? Nay. He would have noticed the damage to the door locks.

Then what?

Perhaps that whirling mind of hers merely suspected his truth. It would not come as a surprise. The cursed newspapers screamed with that *Varney the Vampire* serial, enough to give her a few suspicions about a teacher who only came to her in the dead of night, complexion fading or glowing depending on his feeding schedule, always refusing bites of the fruit or bread she brought...

"What are you talking about?" He managed it with convincing incredulity. If he maintained a guileless charade, she would toss off her suspicions as imagination and everything would return to normal. Or as normal as things could be.

But her intent expression didn't falter. He braced himself for another comment hinting at subjects like wooden stakes and silver crucifixes. Or mayhap a take-no-prisoners accusation, more true to Gabriela's form.

He did not expect her to duck beneath his arm and begin a casual saunter downstage. "Stop teasing. You do remember our friend Ophelia? The one who falls out of a tree, into the stream, and dies? I want to start work on the scene tonight. Come on."

He let out a long breath of relief. Thankfully, his breath contained no substance and therefore, no betraying sound. "Ah, well...of course I remember." He yanked the tree forward with a cheerful spurt of unnatural strength. Thankfully, Gabriela busied herself at a side table, slicing an apple and some cheese. "But the scene does not get played on stage," he added. "Gertrude laments the matter in retrospect."

"Not in Augustus Harris's version." She sucked stray apple juice off her thumb with a laughing smack. "This is modern theatre, remember? Nothing sells tickets faster than characters loving, lying, fighting, riding, or dying on stage. Augustus has guaranteed his *Hamlet* contains generous portions of all—so he attracts 'good society' by presenting a classic but collects from the masses with the violent spectacle." She stopped with the knife halfway through the cheese. "Why am I telling you all this? You not only know it but stand to make a shiny shilling from it. Surely *you're* happy about the revision."

Marcus couldn't quell a sardonic grunt. "Be careful what you assume."

She frowned. "What do you mean?"

He leaned against the tree and regarded her steadily. For once, he knew exactly of what he spoke. "I did not invest in Drury Lane to make a 'shiny shilling,' Gabriela. Shine will one day fade. But truth and integrity are constant beauty. I am concerned that the theatre stays true to that beauty, and the artists who made it that way. It seems that nobody will listen to me unless I own a piece of their weekly salary."

"That's likely the truth. But Augustus *has* stayed true to Shakespeare's text. He's only given it extra imagery."

The comment filled him with an unexpected rise of indignation. Before he could tamp the anger, Marcus shoved from the tree. "Do you think if Shakespeare wanted to show Ophelia's death, he would have written in the blasted scene?" he growled. "Perhaps the man had a reason, a bloody good one, for leaving the *imagery* out."

Gabriela only answered by popping a cube of apple into her mouth. She watched him as she managed to chew and grin at the same time, a look Marcus usually found adorable—but tonight, he turned from her. Her opinion was clear, and tonight it stung. She thought him eccentric, just like the rest of these "modern" geniuses who butchered beauty for the sake of next week's ticket box take.

But Gabriela was not like the rest. Marcus wanted her to know, needed her to understand.

"Perhaps," she ventured, "When Shakespeare wrote the play, he didn't dream this kind of production would be possible."

"Oh, he knew." He lifted his sights along with the assertion. His gaze took in the backdrops rolled there, a collection of a dozen new worlds waiting to be unfurled to an audience's imagination. The setting sent his own vision traveling back, lost for a precious moment to those days of laughter and music, of daring new dreams. "He imagined all this, and more. God, how people laughed at him for those ideas. But he never gave a care. I do not think Will Shakespeare knew the meaning of fear. One day, he even marched right into Whitehall, and—"

"*Will* Shakespeare?"

Her question crashed his thoughts back to the present. And froze his heartbeat in his chest.

He jerked his sights around to her—another moment he should have thought about in advance.

An instant that became a disastrous mistake.

Her face had maintained that half-amused mien, until the truth came flying from every corner of his shocked stare.

Her smile dropped. Her face paled.

Just before her hand, still holding the knife, sliced through her apple and into her palm.

"Oh, my God," she cried. "I'm such an idiot!"

At the sight of her grimace, Marcus rushed forward. With his senses so stupidly uncloaked the moment before, he felt every jolt of the knife's slide into her skin. He knew only her pain, and only that he longed to stop it.

That changed when he smelled her blood.

He slid to a stop three feet from her. A hungering moan went barely controlled in his throat. Sweet God, she smelled so sweet and heady. Her life force consumed his nostrils. Flung open his senses. Aroused every cell in his body. His cock ached more, thrumming in time to the primal beat in his own blood. It ordered him to join that rhythm with hers, to take her...*now.*

Sweet Christ, help me.

"Marcus, would you help me? The cut's not deep but I'm clumsy with only one hand."

Unbelievably, his feet carried him forward. The journey felt like a hike over the Alps. Upon reaching her, he forced himself to find his sanity again, and cling to it. He commanded his sights down to avoid her scrutiny—God's teeth, what his gaze must look like when the rest of him quivered like this— but the action only aligned his view with her injured hand. Her beautiful hand. And her blood, such a perfect ribbon across her silken white skin.

Her life force. *His* life force.

Take her!

"Thank goodness I wrapped the cheese in this cloth."

Her murmur tickled his ear, intimate with awkward humor, innocent of the battle he raged within. "Bet the poor thing didn't know it would be doing double duty as a tourniquet."

She laughed and held out the cloth. Marcus inhaled excruciating breaths. And kept staring at her hand.

"Marcus?" came her faint prompt. "You need to wrap the cloth around my hand. Like this—oh!"

She cried out as he lunged like a panther, bringing her hand to a breath away from his lips.

"Yes." It escaped him on a whisper, closing his eyes, savoring her scent. His mouth watered. So close. Her essence teased him, so intoxicating.

"Marcus?" There was no mistaking the lilt of fear in her voice.

He released her, nauseated with his self-hatred—

Until her psyche burst over his with the power of a lightning flash.

Sweet Jesu. He read her completely, realizing she wasn't afraid *of* him.

She was afraid *for* him.

Gabriela. You darling, trusting fool.

"Marcus." Again as if through a fog, he heard her nervous laugh. "Come now. It's just a little blood. An accident like this can't effect you so deeply."

Try me. God, don't *try me.*

But she would not let him escape. Her presence beamed brighter into his darkness, seeking even the blackest corners of his despair. She repeated his name, dragging him farther out of his night each time, finally compelling his gaze up and into the copper sun of her own.

But that euphoric dawn lasted only a moment. As he

dreaded—expected—the moment Gabriela took in his features, a horrified gasp eclipsed her smile.

"Marcus. Wh-What's wrong? Your—your eyes. And you're shaking..."

"I know. *I know*. Please Gabriela, just—"

Just go. Leave me to my hell.

"No," she insisted. "Just tell me what's wrong."

He had no fathoming how he lifted his head back up. But when he did, amazement pummeled the air from his gut. The gas lights reflected in a lone, salty droplet on her cheek. He clenched his teeth with the torment of it.

Her tears. Her blood. Her body. It was more than he could bear. Marcus felt a growl form deep in his throat, and the will fled him to swallow the sound. No more strength. No more sanity. He shook harder, fighting his need, battling his lust.

He growled while turning his head, capturing the inside of her wrist against his lips. He gently grazed her soft skin as he nuzzled aside her lace cuff with his nose. Her gasp joined his moan as he suckled toward to her elbow.

Sweet Jesu. She smelled so good. She would taste even better.

"Marcus," she rasped. There were more tears, forcing him to blink his way back to reality on a damn-near impossible breath.

"I know," he replied, gently rolling her clothes into place. "I know, sweeting. I am sorry. So sorry."

"I'm not."

Her protest narrated a moment of magic...as she replaced her wrist with her lips.

God save him. She moved so shyly, so honestly, and that brave innocence proved his undoing. Her warmth flowed into him, tasting of apples and woman and life. Her trusting arms wrapped around him, full of hope and passion.

It was the first time he'd been kissed in over two hundred years. But Gabriela, his bold, beloved Gabriela, was worth every second of the wait.

Nevertheless, he swiftly set about making up for lost time.

CHAPTER SIX

Gabriela had never been more terrified in her life—not even on the day Lord and Lady Rothschild had come to the orphanage for a second interview with her, and she'd taken the kitchen bleach to her hair. Surely, she'd thought, if she *looked* the part of a good little English ten-year-old, they could teach her the rest...

But this need burned far deeper than chlorine. Her heart's hunger for acceptance had gone so much longer without nourishment. And these new aches through her body...she whimpered against Marcus's mouth with a yearning she'd never dreamed she'd know, never *wanted* to know, until now. Until this man.

She kissed him, desperately showing what she couldn't say in words. She embraced him, despite the stiff, almost angry response of his limbs. His hands tightened into fists and the thighs she pressed against were stone pillars, but she delved on, wanting him, needing him.

She knew the precise moment he got the message. Marcus's surrendering groan vibrated through every inch of her. His hands flattened, releasing their coiled energy into restless grasps at her back, pulling her closer with commanding intensity. He seized control of their kiss in a dominating sweep, teaching her the ages-old colloquy of man and woman, soft and hard, desire and surrender.

When he prodded her lips apart with his own, she yielded.

When his tongue sought hers, she responded. And when she heard his voice in her head this time, she set her senses free, reaching out to him in answer.

Yes. I want you, too. Take me. Complete me.

On an explosion of breath, he tore back from her.

His wide stare raked over her like she'd just turned into a ghost—but Gabriela knew the truth in the brief instant his eyes strayed to hers.

"You heard me," she gasped. "You really heard me, didn't you?"

He twisted away. "Gabriela—"

"Answer me! Marcus, who are you? How did you—what did we just—"

His shoulders shuddered. "It was wrong."

"No, it was beautiful."

He froze again, fingers curling once more with wordless fury. Gabriela rushed to hold him, to make him wrap her in his strength and passion again—

But she blinked on the way. And he was gone.

★ ★ ★ ★

You're a fool.

Marcus stopped counting how many times his mind bellowed the condemnation, especially after he ignored it enough to order his private box made ready for the next evening's performance. Now the phrase showed no mercy. The dooming words thundered louder in his ears than the standing ovation of the audience below.

And he sat in the darkness of the box, its sole occupant, agreeing with every echoing syllable. *You're a fool. You're a fool.*

The agony grew unbearable when Gabriela reappeared to take her bows.

His heart strained against his ribs as the footlights captured her from beneath, still dressed in that forest nymph costume from the last act of the play. Its flowing layers celebrated her siren's body, her angel's beauty. He moaned, aching with need, but his grief went engulfed by the crowd's roaring approval. As she moved forward, the crescendo rose. A chorus of "bravissimis" embellished the din.

Marcus gripped the handles of his chair, weathering an agonizing swell of pride. London loved her already.

Gabriela barely noticed.

Oh, she smiled and waved as she accepted a bouquet of flowers. She even bowed again, blowing a demure kiss to the source of the loudest "bravissimi," somewhere in the second tier. To this crowd, she exemplified grace, beauty and happiness.

To Marcus, she might as well have been a wooden cut-out for a child's toy theatre. He felt the locking of her teeth beneath her pleasant smile. He felt the tension of her hands as they curled around the flowers.

He felt her heart aching as she looked up to his box.

Damn it. She somehow knew he was here. She wielded her stare relentlessly, telling him how deep her pain went. Assuring him she was far from ready to let him forget it.

Surely enough, the moment the last house lamp was turned down and the last stagehand slammed out the back door, her determined footfalls clattered across the stage. She shook even the catwalk beneath Marcus's feet, where he stood listening to her, over the stage right wings. He dared not actually watch her. The chance ran too great that she would sense him doing so. But he could not move, either. She effectively cut off his only route home as long as she stood there, fists on hips, waiting for the slightest abnormal noise or motion in the building she knew so well.

"Marcus."

She did not yell it this time. Despite his effort to resemble the wall in his stillness, she spoke as if he stood next to her.

All before subjecting him to her most painful tactic of all.

Purposely reaching her mind out to him. Ruthlessly, doggedly seeking him.

His legs nearly buckled in the battle to keep her out. By Jesu's bloody wounds, how was this connection of theirs possible?

It was not. He knew the rules. Fate had given him two hundred eighty years to memorize them. Before anything like this became remotely possible, a vampire had to initiate a mortal: take in their blood once, sometimes twice, then reach inside their mind, literally touch their soul.

But what if...

What if Gabriela had already given him her soul?

He did *not* want to know the answer to that.

"Marcus." Her voice rose in an uneven pitch now. Her hands fell to her sides, began coiling into her skirt. "Damn you, I know you're here. Answer me!"

I cannot.

"Please don't do this to me." Her shoulders sagged. "You *can't* do this to me."

His heart broke along with her voice. *I never meant to hurt you.*

"Is that it, then?" she sobbed. "You won't even talk to me anymore? You won't even let me explain?"

But it's not your fault!

"No."

He started at that. She issued the word as a suddenly hard—and determined—ultimatum. Her head jerked up as she latched her fists to her hips.

"No. I refuse to believe it. You don't get my white flag, Mr. Stafford."

If she startled him before, she utterly baffled him now. She offered no further explanation but the view of her back as she pivoted toward the opposite wings, then marched on as if taking the field at Waterloo.

Before disappearing.

Marcus opened his senses as wide as he dared, straining to discern what the bloody hell she was up to—

Before he realized what she was *up* to.

He barely checked a maddened growl. She was coming close again—this time, taking a vertical path. A moment later, he spied her scrambling up the same rickety wall ladder the stagehands used to get to the catwalks, with one critical difference. Gabriela could barely grip the rungs, she was so tightly bound in that moronic corset. Her feet fared no better, wrestling past underlayers surpassing ridiculous.

The devil only knew how she guessed to look for him up here. No matter, really, because the chit would kill herself doing it.

As she pushed off the ladder and onto the catwalk, Marcus could not decide whether to let either relief or rage guide him. He debated the issue as Gabriela pulled herself upright—but tossed both options out as he observed her first shaky step on the narrow wood plank. Her gait was an unsure totter at best. Her face drained three shades of color as she peered down to the stage.

"Blast you, Stafford, Heights have never been at the top of my talent bill."

Now she told him.

"You impossible, beautiful fool," he whispered.

Just keep walking. Keep walking, and for God's sake, don't look down again.

She kept walking. While she looked down again.

And in a dizzy stumble, blundered into a stray scenery rope in her path.

All too clearly, Marcus watched the line snap around her ankle. Then the confused thud of her other foot, trying to compensate. Then every second of her scrabbling struggle, her hands flailing for purchase against the thirty-foot fall to the stage.

He did not remember the two hand rails and three prop clouds he demolished while charging to make sure she fell into him, instead.

For a moment of raw horror, he nay knew if his effort yielded success. He gulped down relief when he looked to her ashen face against the crook of his arm, her eyes blinking dazedly. She waved a hand about, trying to balance herself. When her fingers collided against his face, he turned and kissed them fervently, angrily.

"It—*is* you," she murmured. "Wh-What happened?"

"You almost killed yourself." His growl emanated from the deepest part of his gut. "God's blasted teeth, Gabriela. That was the most ludicrous, damfool stunt I have ev—"

"Wait a minute." As she dropped her hand to his shoulder, it became a fist. Indignant fire flashed in her eyes. "Don't try to hang this on me. You're the oaf responsible for my 'damfool stunt.' Just put me down and let me go. I don't know why I even bothered. You're clearly happy being a cowardly bastard.

I should have remembered that."

"What the devil's eye is that supposed to mean?"

"You ran from me in the beginning. You tried to run that second night. You only stayed after I begged for your help with my work. Your *gaze* runs when I look at you." She punctuated that with a bitter laugh. "Need I go further? You're happy when you're running, so put me down and I'll let you do just that."

He should have called her game. He should have dropped her on her well-bustled little bottom, given her his retreating back, and let her toss slurs at him until she turned blue—but an undeniable instinct said she wasn't playing games. That same impulse flooded him with the vehement need to prove her wrong.

With a growl, Marcus flattened her to him as he spun around. He ignored her stunned cry as he stalked toward Drury's pitch black wings, a singular destination in mind.

★ ★ ★ ★

Darkness. More darkness.

The description didn't apply just to the labyrinth of halls and stairwells Marcus carried her along. She felt him attempting to throw that black fog over her senses again, though his anger turned the cloud into more of a thunderhead. Ridiculous as the notion sounded, she concentrated her conscious on fighting back—and she sensed him letting her win. No. That wasn't it. His thoughts were focused elsewhere, as if his mind fled from thinking of—

What?

At last, after stomping up an endless stairway, he stopped and kicked a door open. The chamber he carried her into didn't provide much more light than the corridor.

Until he set her down on a velvet couch and swung aside two wide window shutters.

Gabriela broke the silence with an awed gasp.

She was facing toward the back of the theatre. Lamps glowed through the midnight mist far below on Drury Lane, but she preferred the more breathtaking landmarks across London's nightscape as markers. Far out and straight ahead lay the distinct oval of Finsbury Circus. Inward, her sights took in the soaring dome of St. Paul's. To the right was the ribbon of the Thames and crossing the river, London Bridge's stately lights. Everywhere else, street lamps comprised a maze of mystical night glow. Stars seemed to stretch below them as well as above.

"Oh, my God." She smiled. "It's...like heaven."

Marcus's responding grin was a crescent of white in the spectral dimness. "'Tis the general idea."

He released another set of shutters, adding enough light to help her see the luxury of the apartment's interior. Two wide Renaissance chairs matched the dark indigo shade of the couch where she sat. A massive oak dining table filled the wall between the two windows, buttressed by a pair of chairs with intricately-embroidered cushions. Tasseled tapestries draped the far wall, replacing the mirror that should have backed the oak sideboard. Atop that, a large Italian washing set and a well-stocked wine rack kept each other company.

Elegance. Majesty. Beauty for the sake of being beautiful. Magic.

"Beautiful," she at last breathed.

She looked up. As much as she resisted noticing, Marcus was beautiful, too. A small smile flickered his lips at her praise; his dark lashes dropped to hide an undeniable spark of pleasure.

"Many thanks," he murmured before lighting one more candle then crossing to the wine rack. His free hand closed around what looked like a very old vintage, the liquid echoing the candle's light with a shimmering amber glow.

"I didn't know this apartment was up here."

She issued the comment to rid herself of nerves as much as curiosity. Marcus moved and acted differently in this heavenly hideaway, a recognition she didn't know what to do with yet. Despite his simple white shirt and unassuming brown breeches, he walked with an owner's bold stride. He uncorked the wine with deft confidence.

"*Nobody* knows this is up here," he qualified to her statement. "You are the first I have ever brought."

He followed that with one of his long, unblinking stares. Gold candlelight and silver soul light combined there, burning their way across the room at her. Still angry with her—but adoring her. The recognition relieved her, but didn't give the jolt of confidence it normally did.

She laughed nervously. "Well, I'm certain Augustus will be happy to hear that."

"Not unless you wish him to think you even more a loon."

She shot an amazed stare. "Not even Augustus knows about this?"

"*Especially* not Augustus." He answered as if stating that one and one obviously made two. "I claimed the top and bottom of the theatre as mine. I gave Augustus a liberal hand over the rest. And of course, I did all the interior design and construction of the apartment myself."

"Oh, of course." Gaby rolled her eyes before circling

another glance around. But yes, she indeed saw Marcus everywhere in the apartment. She admired scrolled friezes carved with a mastered masculine touch, intricate paintings along the mantel depicting a romantic hunting tale, fabrics selected for comfort as much as appeal.

And an element she hadn't caught in her initial discovery. A half-draped doorway to her right, opening to a room with the biggest bed she'd ever seen.

"My God." She couldn't help herself. She vaulted off the couch and tugged the drape aside. "Who did you get that from? Queen Elizabeth?"

His breath caught sharply. She was tempted to ask why but her head decided to try its luck at another dervish dance. She stumbled to the bed's nearest post, latching onto it with a weak moan.

Almost immediately, Marcus pressed behind her again. His broad torso anchored her; his hands circled her upper arms, slowing the dance. He eased her down to the bed's wide counterpane, made of cloud-soft white down.

"Got up too quickly, aye?" he rebuked in a rough murmur. "Little fool." He pressed a silver goblet of wine into her fingers. "Drink this. It will smooth your nerves."

Though she gained a secure hold on the chalice, Marcus didn't let go, assisting her with several long sips of the rich, earthy vintage. Gabriela didn't resist, simply for the pleasure of feeling his fingers over hers.

"Thank you," she finally murmured.

"Better?"

He deposited the half-downed glass on a dark wood night stand. His other hand raised to skim some stray curls from her cheek. Gaby leaned her cheek into his broad, hard hand.

"That's...feels good," she whispered.

It was more than the truth. While the wine mellowed her tattered nerves, Marcus's touch swirled magic through her blood. Silken warmth enveloped her. A slow, aching need rose inside her, like nothing she'd ever felt before. A need to hold him, touch him...

"Gabriela." He began the word a protest but ended in a guttural grate. He tried to lower his hand. She wouldn't let him. She took his hand in both of hers, urging him closer toward her.

"*You* feel good."

Good? It was only the beginning, wasn't it? God had made this man with such infinite care...even his hands were so carved, so magnificent. Gabriela ran her marveling touch over his knuckles and palm, through the valley created by his thumb and forefinger, over his wide wrist, up his broad forearm.

"And I trow you are feeling much better." Marcus extricated himself, his movements suddenly tense as his voice. After rising from the bed, he turned and held out a hand to assist her up, too. Gabriela didn't accept. She stared up, only to watch him throw his gaze back out to the apartment's main area. He breathed as if he'd just swum the Channel to France and back. "Come. I'll escort you back now."

She gave his hand a cursory glance. "I don't think so."

That prompted his eyes back over. "Damn it, Gabriela. If I must be rude—"

"Go right ahead." She rearranged her skirts with dainty tugs. "I'm staying right here until we discuss a few things, Mr. Stafford—namely, why you feel you can appear and disappear from my life on your whims."

His lips twisted. "I owe you no explanations."

"You owe me quite a number of explanations. But tonight,

I'm only interested in a few."

"I want you to leave."

"And I said no."

"Then I *order* you to leave."

"No."

In a fierce sweep, he hauled her up by the waist. Though she half expected it, Gabriela's breath exploded in a whoosh. Despite *that*, as he snapped her head within inches of his, she swore she heard a snarl resonate from his throat. *Not* a frustrated male snarl. Something more akin to a...hounds of hell snarl.

Marcus didn't give her time to wonder about the occurrence. "You. Are. Leaving." His grip clamped harder. His eyes roiled with dark gray thunder.

But despite all the ways he tried, he didn't frighten her. The old hurt that throbbed anew in her heart—*that* frightened her. "No," she rasped from the depths of that pain. But she wouldn't cry. He would *not* make her cry.

"Damn it to hell," Marcus spat. "Why are you being so difficult about this?"

Too late. Her cheeks burned with wet heat. Furious with embarrassment, she fired a glare up at him. "Why did my kiss repulse you so much?"

His left brow plummeted. "What?"

"You—you heard me."

"Aye," he answered, slower and softer. "But what the bloody—why do you think—"

"Answer me, damn you." She wrenched free from him, taking a shaky back step. Marcus matched her, closing the space and reaching for her hands. Gabriela slapped at him. If he was going to reject her, then the lout had better get it over with, damn it.

Instead, the man trapped her against the bedpost, looming powerfully, undeniably close.

What the hell?

"What makes you think your kiss repulsed me?"

Each word hung between them, drenching her senses like moonlit snowflakes melting into crystalline rain. Beyond her control, Gabriela's soul sucked up those precious drops. Like the idiot she was, she accepted them even in all their feigned tenderness. She closed her eyes and cursed herself for this unrequited weakness; hated herself for the fresh rush of tears down her cheeks.

She finally twisted her head away. "Don't," she implored. "Please don't keep making me believe you care. Just tell me the truth this time, Marcus. I want to hear it from your own lips, then I'll be gone."

"God's blood." He followed the oath with a grunt of dark laughter. "How you arrive at these conclusions, woman, pales my comprehension."

"Damn it!" Gaby pushed a fist into his chest. "Stop it! I've been dismissed enough times in my life that I know how to accept it, all right? But I will not be lied to about *why*. Not by you, Marcus!"

"Gabriela." He caught her fist and held on, enveloping it with his hand. "By all that is in me, I am not dismissing you."

"Liar!"

"I do not lie. But there are things I cannot tell you—things you nay want to know—"

"Tell me."

His jaw locked. "I cannot."

"Tell me!"

She didn't dare imagine the expletive he bit back. It was

prelude to his animalistic bellow. "Why?" Marcus grabbed her other wrist and hauled her against his heaving chest. "*Why* do you push me like this?"

The answer erupted out of her before thought or reason or fear could throw themselves in the way.

"Because," she sobbed, pressing her hand against the side of his storm-dark face, "I'm falling in love with you."

CHAPTER SEVEN

The breath snagged in Marcus's throat.

Gabriela's stopped at the same time.

She stared at Marcus through aching tears, enduring the inevitable barrage on her brain. *Oh, Gabriela Angelica. What have you done now? What have you said now? Nothing you've thought about, that's for certain. You're still dizzy from the catwalks. Or fuzzy from the wine. Or hopelessly furious with this man.*

Or hopelessly in love with this man.

No inner argument retaliated to that—which only squeezed more painful tears from her heart.

But he'd made things clear from the beginning. Had all but commanded her not to need him, declaring his world—and his heart—forbidden ground to her. But she hadn't listened. Once more, she'd gambled her soul on the conviction that if she believed hard enough, wanted strong enough and worked diligently enough, somebody would open the gates of their trust and love her in return.

And God, how she'd wanted Marcus to be that someone. She just had to be an extra good person this time. And she had been good, hadn't she? Surely God would see that and give her the miracle she'd prayed so long for...

But his face, taut and strained, told her differently. He dragged in harsh breaths through his nose. His eyes, searching over her, were more intense than a limelight...

His face said all she needed to know.

She'd gone and blurted the completely wrong thing.

"I'm sorry." She pushed away, aiming the words at herself as well as him. "I'm so sorry."

But then he reached out. Stopped her with a hand that completely encircled her forearm.

Gaby gasped. Leapt her gaze up to his.

A luminous sheen had drenched the heat in his eyes. The new silver glint was a piercing brand on her senses. He continued to breathe hard, in and out, the rhythm corresponding to the rhythm of his lips over his teeth.

As if he were very hungry. For her.

He jerked her close. Then even closer to him. He was now all she could see...and feel. His towering body pressed against every inch of her. The beautiful angles of his face were just inches away.

"Say it again." His voice was bare and guttural.

"Say wh-what again?"

"You know what." His hold tightened—if that was possible. His chest expanded and dropped against hers, as if forcing himself to maintain their proximity. But then he repeated, nearly implored, "Say it to me again, Gabriela."

"You want to hear me say I'm sorry *again*?"

To her shock, the hint of a laugh skipped across his lips. "Nay. The other." Then, in a whisper along her cheek and her neck, "The *other*."

"Oh." Realization, warm and incredible, surged her. The sensations hit at the same time his lips captured the bottom of her ear. "Oh..." She reached, instinct leading the way, to twine her fingers through his hair. "Marcus."

"Say it."

"I love you."

"Again."

"I love you."

"Yes..."

He trailed the word down her nape then into her hair, swiftly searching for her coifing pins and tugging them loose. When her waist-length tresses tumbled free, Marcus caught them in his shaking fists then plunged his lips over hers with bold, conquering strokes. He was clearly through with being distant or even terrified, parting her mouth with his in masculine possession. His kiss assaulted and savored. His touch cherished her, excited her.

And wanted her.

Somewhere in Gabriela's conscience, an answering voice of need shouted to him—a voice she never imagined herself capable of. She'd thought this part of her heart incinerated, using her childhood as kindling. But it had never been destroyed...merely waiting.

Waiting for the silver destiny in the eyes of Marcus Stafford.

Thank you, God. She conveyed it with the tears in her eyes and the love in her heart. *Thank you for this, at last.*

But as her words flew heavenward, Marcus broke off their kiss. Even before his startled gaze speared her, Gabriela knew *he'd* heard her prayer, too. It only made her smile.

Yes, she told him with that same inner voice, kissing him softly. *Yes, I was thanking God for you.*

No silent answer echoed in her mind. But his deep moan proclaimed what a thousand love-sonneted words couldn't. The sound reverberated through Gabriela, awakening her spirit. The matching spark to his ember. The aria sung to his polyphony. The woman fitted to his man.

They kissed again. Tenderly, then deeply. Mouths fusing. Hands claiming. Hearts twining. Marcus stroked her everywhere, as if memorizing her form. Gabriela rejoiced in his assault, arching and sighing against him. Her own hands raced along his shoulders, down his chest and back again, reveling in this new, hard discovery called male.

They finally dragged apart. Their breaths mingled at the same rhythm, heavy and fast, excited and expectant. She opened her eyes, yearning to see her new emotions made into something even more magic by their reflection in Marcus's gaze.

But that captivating silver world didn't await her. Instead, she traced fingers over facial angles which had, strangely, tightened—and over eyes that trembled in his effort to remain closed to her.

As if his bloody obstinacy would deter her. Without hesitation, Gaby followed her fingers' paths with her lips. She nipped his strong chin and straight jaw, suckled the end of his nose, finally adored each set of his black eyelashes with soft, deep kisses.

His breath caught again. Hard.

She trembled. All over.

Her lips tingled as if she'd just kissed two burning stars. Considering the man those eyes belonged to, Gaby didn't cast away that theory as impossible.

She wanted more.

She lifted her mouth again, lingering in the creases between his eyelids and brows. The mesmeric warmth flowed from him again, filling her mouth, too. Gabriela smiled.

Marcus moaned. "Gabriela," he grated, "Sweeting—I pray you—"

"Ssshh." She drew him into her arms, burying her fingers into the thick waves of his hair. "Marcus, whatever it was," she murmured, "whatever you did…"

"Nay—"

"Thank you."

"Gabriela—"

"You're beautiful."

He moaned into the crook of her neck. "Nay! Gabriela, you must—"

"Love you. That's all I must do. I love you."

"Dear God."

His lips croaked the surrender as they raked from her throat to her mouth. He plundered as if he couldn't get enough of her; a drowning man sucking his last moments of life. New tears spilled from Gabriela as she joyously gave him what he needed, opening her senses to his hunger and her heart to his passion.

She gasped when his hands became desperate claws at her back, grazing the row of tiny buttons along her spine. His arms trembled. His thighs clenched. The massive ridge at their juncture made her achingly aware of the pooling wetness between her own.

She didn't need to see his eyes to know what he wanted now.

Because she wanted it, too.

And for the first time in her life, she knew why Ophelia flung herself from that blasted tree for Hamlet.

She tore away from their kiss, her lips seeking his ear. "Love me back," she implored when she found it. "All of me, Marcus."

His body clenched tighter. His throat vibrated, battling

to hold back a growl and sob enjoined, but he did so in vain. Primal instincts surged up in Gabriela. They guided her hand to slip past Marcus's waist, embracing the solid swell between his thighs.

"Gabrielll—!"

She stole the rest of it from him in a bold, open kiss. As she did, her other hand yanked on the back of his head. She never dreamed of kissing a man like this, caressing a man like this, or whispering the very intimacy she'd hushed from Donna a month ago.

But she'd never imagined Marcus.

She never thought she'd want him so badly. Yes, all of him, around her, inside her. And if that meant taking the seed of his babe, too, she'd thank heaven again. Things would be different. She'd *make* them different. Marcus's child would never know a day of heartache or loneliness in their life. Not with all the love she'd shower on the beautiful being. Not with the way she adored their extraordinary father.

She clasped his arousal tighter. His new tremor bespoke the effect she rendered. Her lips curled in a pleased smile as she pressed herself to the heavy bulge of him. Marcus answered in action, sliding his hands to her bottom, teaching her hips the same undulating rhythm set by their thrusting tongues.

The fire consumed them. Up and down. In and out. Sparking and flaring—and scorching away the rest of the world. They breathed desire. They drank of need. Past the point of any control. Past the point of no return.

Marcus fumbled at her back again, grabbing at her dress buttons. After frustrated minutes, when only one button loop had surrendered, he tore the material away in a savage jerk. In response, she dug fingers into his shirt front and ripped until a broad ribbon of dark torso lay naked to her touch.

"My God." He curled a delicious smile as he said it. Before Gaby could grin back, he swooped her off the floor and onto the bed. The plush counterpane and blankets billowed as they plummeted together, dipping into the fleecy folds like morning birds on Highland clouds.

Nothing permeated that downy heaven for several minutes but the rasps of more tearing fabric. He took two rips to dispatch her dimity bustle. Three for her foulard petticoat. It took five jerks and an exasperated oath to wrench her corset free. Gabriela accidentally tore his breeches, pulling the flap the wrong way in her haste to set his erection free.

When she did, his shuddering moan took the place of her embarrassment. His swollen length fell into her grasp, overflowing the span of her fingers. Gabriela was instantly fascinated. She began exploring his long, velvet flesh, her exhilaration tripling when his head fell back in ecstasy. His hair gleamed ebony and gold in the lamp glow, features such a flawless study of tight anticipation, she expected Michelangelo to materialize any moment for the privilege of carving him.

And she knew the time was right.

She gazed up at the beauty of her midnight lover, despite his continued inflexibility not to return the stare. She glided her hand to the taut muscles of his torso.

"Now," she whispered. "*Now...*"

He said nothing in return—in words. But his touch... *oh, God.* Silken, sensual fingers that stroked her. Lips that worshiped her. Hands that guided her hips to an intimate position around his until he pressed over her, his whole body quivering with tension, a taut-muscled slingshot ready to snap. His hands moved to either side of her face as he kissed her deeply, then he burrowed his straining forehead into the hollow of her neck.

The tip of his sex parted the first folds of her womanhood.

"Gabriela," he grated. "Ah, God…"

"Don't stop." She kissed his neck, twining her fingers in the damp waves of hair at his nape.

"I don't want—to hurt you."

"You'd never hurt me." Knowing intimacy warmed her voice. "You told me so yourself. Remember?"

"Sometimes—" He slid in farther. A strained huff escaped him. "Sometimes I do things I don't—I can't—control."

"Good." Instinctual femininity replaced the gentle tone. Gabriela lowered her hands to the curves of his straining buttocks, and squeezed.

He moaned. Rock-hard heat prodded further into the core of her. She relished her victory, arching into him, opening wider for him. He moaned again, deeper. His legs quaked.

Clearly, the man had made up his mind to be slow and gentle.

Gabriela didn't want slow and gentle.

So she gave him no choice in the matter. Following instinct older than Antigone, she thrust her hips up to meet his, gathering his body fully into her own.

They both gasped.

She steeled herself for the pain. If she'd learned anything at the orphanage besides table manners and bread making, it was that loving also meant hurting, especially for a woman. And yes, the brief tearing of her flesh came—but not before the joyous completion. Not before the profound knowledge of oneness with this man. Her heart. Her love.

The feeling surpassed happiness. Exceeded tears. Her

throat constricted, barely allowing her sparse gasps, let alone spoken words.

Yet words existed. Spilling from deep inside, translating themselves into heartbeats that spoke directly to the powerful presence above her, around her, inside her.

Marcus...

Gabriela. Dear God, Gabriela.

It's wonderful.

I've not hurt you?

For a moment. It's gone. There's only you now. Only you.

I've waited so long for you...

I know. I don't know how I know that, but I know.

Forever. 'Tis been forever. You feel so good...ah God, don't stroke my thighs like that—

You don't like it?

I love it. Too much. Sweet heaven, I'll lose all control.

Gabriela set about making him do just that.

She just didn't expect him to take her on the journey with him.

She never imagined the breath-stealing strokes his hips answered to her thrusts. Not once, even in the fathoms of her fantasies, did she dream of the magic his hands rendered to her body. He discovered her...then exposed her.

And *never* did she dream of the forces he'd unleash in her body. The feeling, so intense, so insane, built to such a crescendo that only her impassioned cries filled her ears.

But when she opened her eyes to let her lover see his effect on her, only a hot silver glow filled her gaze, bathing the whole room in a hypnotizing, otherworldly light. What on earth—

Marcus!

Close your eyes!

Marcus, what's happening? What is it?

Only the power you have over me. Do you not feel it? Close your eyes, open your senses...and feel me.

I feel your heartbeat...

Our *heartbeat.*

Your body...

Our *body.*

Your desire...

Oh, aye. Oh, aye. Oh—

"Gabriela!"

His outcry shattered the air, primitive and passionate. His roar rippled in time to his release, both filling her, completing her, lifting her senses to the stars. As Gabriela floated gently down from that heaven, she curved a joyous smile...then sent one more thought to Marcus, scooped from the light lingering in her soul.

My love. Our *love.*

★ ★ ★ ★

She awoke to more silver light, but now the luminescence came from the morning haze filtering through the gauzy white bed curtains. Gabriela fingered aside the fabric to peer into the apartment's living room, where the same light bathed everything in hushed gray stillness.

A stillness intensified by Marcus's absence.

Her heart felt that fact before her eyes confirmed it. Yet while vacant in person, her dark lover filled the room in essence. He was everywhere still; living on in her mind's images as she ran fingers over the sheets around her.

She envisioned him as he'd finally withdrawn from her, falling to the pillows, satiated and smiling. She relived the magic of his tender kisses throughout the next hour—then the renewed desire that had stirred them both again. With a growing smile, she remembered the reckless abandon of their second coupling. Marcus had flown her higher than the first time, making her sob with the intensity of her release. A groaning explosion had followed from him.

Her memories reluctantly returned to the more temporal realm of the morning. She stretched and moaned, entertaining the temptation to burrow back under the covers and fall into a sleep made of passionate dreams. Damn the interview she had today with the *Chronicle*. Forget the emergency costume fitting and the extra rehearsal so tonight's understudy could finally get Act Two right.

Marcus. I only want you, Marcus.

Where *was* he?

Only his empty pillow stretched across the other side of the bed as answer. At first, she brushed her knuckles across the white expanse, as if by caressing the few black wavy hairs he'd left behind, she'd conjure the whole man. When the motion only yielded a sharper longing, she gathered up the whole pillow, breathing in his misty, musky scent.

Her eyes popped wide as she looked over the top of the pillow.

She tossed it against the headboard with a hard *whump*. As if she heard the sound at all, as she scrambled across the covers and jerked back the curtain at the foot of the bed. As if remembering to do so at the last moment, she wiped her eyes. Surely she imagined the exquisite sight before her. Maybe she really did need more sleep. A lot more.

They didn't make day gowns this beautiful, did they? Yet she reached up to the garment hanging on the dressmaker's dummy and ran fingers along a velvet polonaise that felt very real…and very luxurious. She traced along the expensive satin of the neck trim, marveled at an eight-layered underskirt of breathtaking écru lace, and squealed in delight at the matching velvet and silk hat, styled in the most elegant current trend. To the side, exquisite leather gloves rested next to a full toilette of frilled underthings. Completing the ensemble: a double-bowed pair of slippers straight out of *Cinderella.*

Gabriela giggled. "Oh, Cinderella…you could only hope to have my Prince Charming."

Confirmation of that statement came in the form of a small card, tucked into the intimate V where the gown would accent her breasts. Warmth suffused her as she grabbed for the envelope and ripped out the card inside.

Only two words awaited her gaze, penned in a script so formal, it appeared medieval. Yet the careful calligraphy made the words more precious, filled her heart with that much more love for the man who told her, simply and solemnly:

Thank you.

She pressed the card against her heart for long minutes. In that silence, she reflected on everything she'd come to love about Marcus Stafford. The kinship of his lonely, seeking spirit. The wordless understanding they shared, manifesting in the magical communication between their souls. And, of course, their mutual love of the theatre…her unending discovery of his natural talent, his unbreaking belief in hers.

Stumbling on *that* thought halted her reverie. God's grace; what was she doing lying around here when priorities lay waiting? Priorities Marcus didn't just encourage her to meet but expected her to maintain. On the back of his note, he'd even penned a reminder about the morning interview and directions on how to get out of the apartment.

And now more than ever, she longed to exceed his expectations.

Now more than ever, she really believed in dreams coming true.

She almost laughed again. Amazing, how she'd once feared Marcus would strip away her aspirations. Instead, he'd stepped into them—then changed them into incredible reality.

For instance, the Prince's Grand Troupe didn't loom as a terrifying icon any more. As she dressed, Gaby admitted she'd come to consider the selection process as challenging, not insurmountable.

And Alfonso's intimidations? She thought on the poor man's ramblings now, and merely smiled. He'd become an amusing story, not a haunting threat.

With Marcus by her side, the world was filled with so many smiles now. With Marcus in her heart, self-doubt had become self-assurance.

With Marcus in her life, what could go possibly wrong?

The answer filled her heart as she indulged in a girlish twirl in her new clothes. She only wished she had a mirror to truly revel in the finery. A thorough search of the apartment's doors, closets and even spacious bathing room didn't yield even a hand-held looking glass.

No matter, she decided. She'd wear the gown again when she saw Marcus after the performance tonight, and let the intensity of the glints in his gaze be her gauge of success.

She'd let her own gaze do a little assessing, too...such as the look she'd level before telling him just how much she loved him. Then she'd *show* him just how much she loved him...

A perfect night. A perfect man. A perfect life.

She could hardly wait.

CHAPTER EIGHT

Marcus could hardly wait.

And now more than ever, he hated himself for that fact.

He hated standing here and shaking in this cold chamber, sitting with the knowledge that as London prepared for its Saturday evening enjoyments a hundred feet above, he could barely breathe.

Not until his dinner arrived from the St. Thomas Hospital's morgue.

A humorless grunt resonated in his throat. He braced both arms against the wall of his crypt, battling his hunger with every coiled muscle in his body.

He had wheeled a fine turn at becoming Hamlet to his Ophelia, after all. Just as Will Shakespeare's prince fell to the blade of Laertes, so his body's cry for blood had destroyed the sublime moments he had known just after awakening tonight.

He'd finally glimpsed paradise...

He could not remember the last time he had slept so peacefully, recalled such paradises of dreams, or smiled at such magnificent memories. For a long while, he had simply rested atop the dirt that had given him slumber, for once grateful for the blackness encroaching on his senses. If he had to sleep in hell, it was finally heaven to be visited by an angel named Gabriela. And when the visions of her came, he greedily remembered every caress, every kiss, every touch...

Then the hunger had taken control.

He composed himself long enough to stumble out of "bed," scrawl a note to Joseph at the hospital's morgue, and summon his favorite street urchin to deliver it. All the while, his mind and soul churned with one name.

Gabriela.

Beautiful Gabriela, giving her body to him.

Precious Gabriela, entrusting her heart to him.

Innocent, unknowing Gabriela, falling in love with a beast.

"Sweet Jesu," he groaned.

What have I done?

But even in his weakness, the answer to that resonated with terrifying clarity. Marcus knew exactly what he had done.

He had fallen in love with her in return.

Nay. He had fallen in love with her a long time ago and simply never allowed the acknowledgment to bear fruition. She was a tree he did not dared to eat from—or so had been his thinking.

But then he had heard Gabriela weeping that night—ah God, that fateful night—and his senses fell prey to the same beautiful spell she cast over the rest of him. He had comforted her even as her tears watered the tree, coaxing the branches of his soul into bloom. She nourished the tree in return with her smiles and laughter, tempting him more each day with the forbidden fruit of her love.

Selfishly, Marcus had finally devoured the bounty. Senselessly, he ignored the laws of decency, of man and maybe even of God.

Stupidly, he had taken a heart he had no right to claim.

He had to give that heart back—no matter if he would prefer handing over his own arms and legs, instead. But he felt dismembered already, knowing the torment which lay ahead... knowing the pain he would have to pound into Gabriela's stubborn skull in order to transform the amber flecks in her eyes to shards of hate.

But her hurt would heal—in a shorter time than she expected. Her heart would mend. Her world would continue, she would know more loves and laughter, sorrows and hardships, before the peace of a mortal end. In time, she would rediscover the comforting cycles of life...and death.

He was not so certain about his own heart.

Perhaps he was dying now. Surely that was the meaning of this agony ripping across his chest. As he slid to the ground from it, the grate of an opening stone door resounded through the chamber. A chilled wind hit his hunched back. A man's footsteps followed. The steps scuffed to a stop a moment later.

"Guvnah?" came a coarse voice. "Hey, guv, ye in here?"

"Aye."

He barely managed the word. He didn't bother to rise or offer his exact location. Joseph did not care As long as the hospital's morgue keeper received his generous compensation for these twice-weekly deliveries, Joseph remained a staunch guardian of the stranger—and his vile secret—living in darkness beneath Drury Lane. Even ten years ago, when Marcus had finally trusted the man to bring his "packages" directly to the subterranean vault, Joseph had glanced around the crypt then simply said, "Don't give any answers and I won't ask any questions."

Since then, only Marcus asked the questions. Even tonight with his stamina cut in half, he forced himself to wade through mental marshland and bring the necessary words to his lips.

"A recent arrival?" His jaw shook around each syllable. Sweet God, he hated this. He asked about a human body like a fishwife haggling over a plucked duck at market.

But Joseph might as well have been on a Sunday picnic in Hyde. The man whistled a bawdy version of "Good Luck to the Girl Who Loves a Sailor" as he plunked his burden down on the stone slab.

"None more recent than this," he boasted. "Fetched ye a blighter straight off the hospital's back porch. Never even made it inside before he passed on, so I didn't have to waste time on his papers. Not that I'd get anywhere with 'em, anyhow. Just another gutter duck; couldn't remember his own bleedin' name. Anyhow, he's still warm. I think ye'll be pleased."

"And...he has no family?"

An exasperated sigh blended with the first drips of rain down a distant drainpipe. "No. No one."

"'Tis crucial, Joseph," Marcus growled. "I cannot take someone's father or brother or—"

Or lover, his mind added. For the first time in his life, mortal years included, he comprehended what a precious word the term could be. And what a curse.

"Like I told ye, guv, he's nameless." The man emitted a phlegmy, uncomfortable cough. "I got a gander at him meself before he passed completely on. And the blighter's eyes...well, he cashed out o' life a while ago, if ye catch my flounder."

"Aye," Marcus replied in a relieved murmur. "Aye, I do." He folded his arms, enduring renewed shivers brought on by a fresh wave of hunger. Fulfillment lay close now. "M-Many thanks, Joseph," he stammered. "Your recompense will be delivered to the hospital tomorrow."

"Ahhh, thank *ye*, guv." The mortal made his way back to the door with a lighter step, his burden now deposited. "Always a pleasure."

Marcus only answered with another grunt. This was anything but a pleasure.

"Health and strength to ye, guv. Good evenin'."

Not a dot of mockery punctuated the man's remark as he took his leave, which dragged out another derisive snort from Marcus. He had time to issue little else. His body drew on dangerously dwindling reserves—and the coming hours would demand all the strength he could get.

He owed Gabriela the dignity of saying goodbye to a man who at least seemed normal.

★ ★ ★ ★

Gabriela wished the curtain call would just end.

As instantly as her mind courted the thought, she begged heaven's forgiveness for it. Though never officially *thou-shalt-notted* on Moses's tablets, surely it was a minor sacrilege to wish oneself finished with a five-minute Drury Lane standing ovation complete with armloads of roses and outcries even from the private boxes.

All the private boxes except Marcus's.

Though she couldn't actually see the box past the footlights, her heart confirmed Marcus's absence as if a spotlight blared upon the space. She still didn't understand the amazing mental connection they shared, nor did she think it vital to, but she knew their physical union had strengthened their psychic bond tenfold. So powerful was the link, her emptiness without him equaled her fulfillment in his arms.

That made the emptiness bloody near unbearable.

She dipped a pair of last curtsies then nearly tripped over her skirts as she hastened off stage. Surely theatre business detained Marcus from attending tonight's show, but she swore she felt him awaiting her in the upstairs apartment now.

That brought her a clandestine smile. The waiting had been torture but inspired her body to a hot hum of readiness. Every second of the separation would be worth the agony once she stepped into his arms again...once they became a single heart and being again.

"I'm coming," she promised in a whisper. "Not long now."

Three steps from her dressing room, her blood sluiced with ice. Her arms dropped, plunging flowers all around her feet. Cloying cologne doused the air.

Cologne emanating from the slick-dressed blade waiting in a casual slouch against the wall.

"Mr. Renard," she stated flatly. "Good evening."

His thin lips quirked in a mockery of a smile. "Darling, I thought we'd agreed on 'Alfonso.'"

"*Mr. Renard*, I really do not have time this evening—"

"You haven't had time many of these evenings." He stretched her nerves with his words on a verbal torture rack before snaking a hand around her nape. "I've missed you so, little Gaby."

"Don't." She jerked back as far as a passing costume rack allowed.

"Don't what?" His well-oiled smile curled again. "Don't miss you?" A soft chuckle. "Impossible. You're a fever. You've gotten into my blood and you won't leave."

A scarf selected that moment to slip and snag in one of the rack's wheels. As the dresser fumbled with the cloth on one side, the forest of costumes closed Gaby and Alfonso in on the other.

The snake wasted no time seizing advantage of the

situation. "Don't say you haven't missed *me*," he murmured. "Don't say you haven't been lonely, rehearsing night after night in this barn by yourself. Gabriela"—when she refused to look, he jerked her chin up with both his hands—"when are you going to cease this nonsense?"

Despite his painful hold on her jaw, Gabriela almost laughed her reply. *I'm never going to cease, Alfonso. Heaven has blessed me with a person you can never hope to become. A man you will never be.*

She yearned to shout the declaration into his cold, sharp face but this wasn't the right time. What she and Marcus had still gleamed like a newly-formed diamond, perfect but unpolished and therefore, still vulnerable. Tonight, she counted it victory enough to step back and pin him with the same silent serenity a director used on an unwanted actor. As the costume cart wheeled on again, she turned and followed it, leaving Renard behind without speaking another word.

Or so she thought.

Two feet from the threshold of her dressing room, her path was blocked once more by the cologne-reeking torso.

Gabriela forced down a measured breath. Another. She stepped to the left. Alfonso countered, bracing an elbow to the portal at the level of her breasts. She didn't attempt the right side. God only knew what he'd do for a blockade effort there.

"Let me pass."

Alfonso clucked his tongue. "But you haven't answered my question."

Gaby's head pounded. Locking her teeth against the frustration didn't help matters. "It doesn't warrant an answer. You know I won't give up until the Prince's Theatre Troupe comes to call."

"And you think your handful of good reviews will bring them running?"

"I don't think it's any of your business. Now *let me pass.*"

Before she could take another breath, she was bodily forced back against the wall. Alfonso clamped both his hands on her shoulders. His fingers dug into her skin. He loomed with quiet, almost frightening calm.

"I think it *is* my business." Poison laced his wine-smooth utterance. "Perhaps you'd be interested to know they've already selected over half the principals for the troupe."

Gabriela jerked her sights up, barely noticing his satisfied gleam at her consternation—and too stunned to care.

But something inside her didn't accept the defeat. From that same place, she pulled a new and bold strength. It even made her smile as she squared herself against Alfonso.

"And how do you come by this intriguing little *bruit*, Mister Renard? I'm not inclined to believe some tidbit whispered during a tryst with your latest willing chorus girl."

"Quick, darling—but wrong. I dined with Davis Webber last night. Rather nice fellow. He's quite excited about the ensemble they've gathered."

Her stomach plummeted. Davis Webber. The creative and casting director for the Prince's Troupe. She didn't think Alfonso knew the man, much less dined with him. Then again, Alfonso seemed to know everyone.

"I still don't believe you," she blurted. "Why didn't I see any notices in the paper?"

"You know Davis. He wants to announce the entire cast at the same time. Make a production out of the production, so to speak. It's all a secret until then."

Bewildered, Gaby didn't say anything. Apparently, that

translated into an invitation for Alfonso to press closer, his touch softening and drifting to her collar bone.

"But sweet Gaby," he murmured, "that doesn't mean *we* have to wait."

"What?" she replied distractedly. "What are you talking about?"

"Darling, you're through with this Prince's Theatre Troupe foolery now. And *my* stage still awaits."

She'd endured the words fifty times before. But as the man's fingers drifted lower over her bodice, a frisson of alarmed instinct pierced the muddle of her mind.

"I'm not through with anything." Gabriela channeled her frustration into shoving from his arms and hurrying into her dressing room. "Except you and your manipulations."

"Gabriela, stop being a fool!"

"Go away, Alfonso."

She slammed the door and twisted the key in the lock. The lout's pounding was inevitable but she barely heard the clamor. It was a dull background to the questions barraging her mind.

Could she believe the bastard? But did she dare not? And if his assertion held any truth, what did it mean for her chance at the remaining Prince's Troupe positions? Short of reading Davis Webber's mind, how did she know if she'd even turned the man's head yet? If her letters of interest had ever crossed his desk?

Or if even now, her dream was no more than a pile of incinerated ashes?

The dream.

Gaby started. Her fingers flew to her lips as a comprehending smile bloomed there. "The dream," she murmured. *The* dream. Not *her* dream, as she'd always known it, but *the* dream...a vision to which she no longer claimed exclusive ownership.

And she realized her soul's declarations to Marcus last night had lacked one important addition.

My dream. Your dream. Our *dream.*

She sat at the dressing table with a soft laugh. She couldn't give up on her goal now if she wanted to. She imagined merely attempting to tell Marcus such a thing. Her mind's eye already saw his gaze flashing at her, burning with one hard silver command. *You're giving up only when I give up.*

She seriously suspected that Marcus Stafford did not know how to give up.

Alfonso pummeled louder. Funny how the beats were perfectly in sync with the meter of her heartbeat, calling for Marcus with an urgency beyond physical or even emotional completion.

Her soul needed him, too.

Her spirit yearned for the affirmation of his embrace, the boldness of his kisses, the magic in his eyes that transformed her into an angel, capable of doing anything and going anywhere her fantasies led.

Her soul needed to know he still believed in the dream, too.

But first, she needed to get out of here.

★ ★ ★ ★

Reflecting on that moment as she scurried across catwalks then down hallways she'd committed to memory, Gabriela granted herself another tiny laugh.

She couldn't help it. No playwright would attempt such a scene for fear of being laughed out of business on grounds of unrealistic content, yet reality it had been.

There she'd stood, mouthing oaths at Alfonso as he'd charmed the key to her dressing room out of the wardrobe mistress in the hall. As the two of them fumbled with the lock, Gaby had paced in desperation—until she looked to the movable panel in the wood behind her dressing table. Marcus had shown her the room's feature a few weeks ago. At the time, Gabriela had rolled her eyes as he commanded her to use the hiding space if she had to, adding on something about monsters popping up in the strangest places in this city—but tonight, she was bloody grateful for his paranoia.

Just when she'd stepped into the niche then slid the panel tight, Alfonso had pounced into the "empty" room. An oath escaped him to make a dock thief blush.

Remembering the creative cursing now made her let out a longer giggle. But she fell silent, heart racing and senses thrumming, when approaching the carved wood door of Marcus's apartment.

She pushed on the slightly opened portal, and saw him again. And felt him again.

Dark power. Deep aching. Profound love. For *her*.

"Marcus." It came out a joyous sigh. She swept to where he sat on folded knees in the middle of the plush Persian carpet. She dropped and molded herself to his back, reveling in the feel of his broad shoulders, the muscles pushing against his silk shirt and satin waistcoat. She buried her nose in his hair, reveling in the masculine smells of fog and rain and an earthier scent she couldn't identify. Then she kissed the back of his neck in greeting.

In reply, his shoulders tensed.

Then nothing.

Fear nibbled a small part of her chest. "I—I'm sorry I'm late. The curtain call took forever, and then—well, then, Alfonso was waiting outside my dressing room—"

His shoulders constricted harder.

"It's all right," she soothed. "He didn't do anything. I hid in the secret closet you showed me." She laughed into his ear. "I wish you'd been there, actually. It was quite funny. I learned a few new colorful colloquialisms, if that's a bright side. But he took forever to leave. I came straight up in my costume, though I so wanted you to see me in the new gown. It's beautiful, Marcus. Thank you—" She kissed the valley behind his ear, secured her arms tighter around his chest. "Thank you."

She nestled her chin on his shoulder, awaiting at least an obligatory "you're welcome."

He raised one hand and wrapped slow but strong fingers around her forearm.

Then nothing. Again.

Something bigger than fear bit off another piece of her heart.

"I got up here as quickly as I could," she rambled faster. "I was worried I'd kept you waiting so long. I didn't want to anger you."

That incited a reaction. "Anger me?" His voice resonated with a strange laugh. "I am not angry, Gabriela."

"Well." She underlined the word with determination. "Good."

At that, she swung herself around and into his lap, forcing him to either hold her or let her plop to the carpet. Gabriela wagered he'd battle as hard to prevent this half-foot fall as he had her thirty-foot plummet to the Drury stage.

Sure enough, he caught her without a flinch of effort. The strength of his embrace brimmed a smile to her lips. She beamed the look up at him but just in case he didn't get the message, she reached along the path of their invisible bond and told him again, with her soul.

Nobody has ever made me this happy.

She knew he heard—and understood—by the way he traced a slow finger over her lips. With each space he covered, a thick silver sheen materialized in his quiet gaze.

Too quiet.

Her smile faded. Swiftly as the last rays of sunset drowned by night, she opened her senses wider to him—

And was instantly flooded with sadness.

Her chest cramped. Fear made an outright feast of her heart.

"What's wrong?"

She didn't play coy with the query. Her expediency made no dent on Marcus. He let a long moment fall beneath heavy silence—while his stare darkened like she was exhuming his soul.

Finally, a lonely word spilled from him. "I—"

"What?" she urged.

"Gabriela—"

"*What?*"

He said nothing. But upon the taut strings of her soul, a faint chord of words strummed.

I love you, too.

Gabriela tumbled to the floor on her own will. She rolled to sit before him, knee to knee, while grabbing both his hands. Marcus resisted so savagely, her fingers stung from the friction of it.

She reached again. Curled one hand into the front of his shirt. His muscles tensed beneath her touch, though he didn't shove away anymore.

The victory—though why she even fathomed such a word right now was baffling—was small. Marcus slammed his eyes shut. A shudder rippled down his rigid frame. His head dropped. "I...think you need to go now."

"*What?*" She almost laughed. "Darling, I—I think I must have misheard—"

"You misheard nothing. I love you, Gabriela...I do. Which is why you must leave me and never come back."

She fumbled for his hand again. "All right, come now, grump...what on earth is this really all about?"

The only thing she comprehended between one blink and the next was being hauled to her feet, wrenched to stand face to face with him—and being sliced by the dark pewter ax of his stare. There were no more silver lights for her to ponder. No more emotion in his soul to match to them, either. He gave her nothing now, except one ruthless chop of a growl.

"Must I repeat myself?"

"Perhaps you should." She flung it as unthinking retaliation. What the hell was wrong with him? This truly had to be a mistake. Her mind simply had to have sorted his words wrong—or some dark, horrid stranger had taken over *him*.

Gently—dear God, so gently, it made her nauseous—he loosened his hold and took a measured step back. "I said... 'twould be wise for you to go now."

"You think I'm going anywhere now?" She planted her own stance with arms jammed to her sides. "You don't get another a step from me, Mr. Stafford, until telling me what's going on."

He took a hard breath. Pinched the top of his nose. "God's blood, Gabriela. I am overtired of this."

Her nerves scattered like a frittering chorus girl. And heaven help her, she looked exactly like one while chaining her hands around his neck. "If you're tired, then let's go to bed."

But neither his body nor spirit twitched to meet hers. He reached back, covering her hands, squeezing in preparation to pry her loose. "You do not understand."

No. Every cell in her body screamed it. *No. I've been good this time. You* love *me. Your heart just whispered it. I heard it!*

"Marcus," She was unable to secure the tightrope her voice wobbled on. "Marcus, I know this won't be an easy situation. You're Drury's owner. I'm just a developing actress. We'll have to be discreet. I know that. I *do* understand."

His fingers constricted around hers. "You understand nothing."

"You're wrong."

"Nay." She'd heard milder growls from lions pacing in the zoo—and imagined she'd be thrust away from one of them with less vehemence. "You do *not.*"

She fell into one of the high-backed chairs, unhurt in body but spurred in anger. "Do *not* tell me what I am capable of comprehending or not. I know what I'm doing. Last night—"

"Was a mistake."

His head came up on a smooth snap. Which was a complete deception, because then his gaze found her—

Striking her world with lightning all over again.

Lightning. Yes. This had to be what a hilltop tree felt when shot through with a bolt of silver fire, destroying its roots of existence. She really had thought him jesting with her—until he'd turned on her as a complete stranger.

Still, she accused, "You—you don't mean it." She reclosed the distance between them in two strides, grabbing his hands again. "Marcus, you don't mean this."

But his second snarl drowned her last word. The sound, low and vicious and bestial, erupted from a place so deep inside him, it bit into her fingers and clawed all the way up to her shoulders.

He thrust her away before wiping his palms on his wool-covered thighs—as if she'd soiled him. She gulped back a tide of bile and tears.

"God's teeth," he muttered. "You are not going to *weep*, are you? Oh, Gabriela." He gave a condescending click of his tongue. "Gabriela, last eve was wonderful. Do not think I did not...enjoy you. We both had a bit of nice bed sport, and—"

"Bed sport!" It was her turn to stumble back. "No. *No.* I don't believe you, damn it. Why are you doing this? Why are you *really* doing this?"

At that, for a shining hope of an instant, a shadow shaded his gaze. Muscles flinched in his legs. It was as if the physical essence of him couldn't ignore her pain. Gabriela used the moment of vulnerability to reach out to him with spiritual arms, as well.

Go away. Get away from me.

She reeled and fell to the floor from the psychic attack. But he didn't stop there. His mental fingers gave chase, constricting around her soul like talons. She gasped as her soul fought for life. She looked up to see the silver force of his glare, hovering around her like a vast storm.

On her hands and knees, shaking from head to toe, she turned to face that storm—vowing somehow to conquer it.

She looked up, taking in the powerful set of his legs,

unmoving save for those violent spasms in his thighs. Clenched against them were his hands, bound to forearms with pulsing veins. The ties on his shirt had fallen loose, exposing the twin planes of hard muscle atop his heaving lungs. Incredible. Even in his dark rage, he formed a hypnotizing sight.

When she looked to his face, that conclusion rang more true. She found her way past his sweat-soaked hair to his glowing, glaring eyes. In them, she saw everything: loathing and love, agony and adoration. Her soul couldn't match what his emanated, yet she didn't move, couldn't turn away.

"Leave me, Gabriela." Now his command came on shuddering breaths. "I pray you, leave me the hell alone."

Tears scalded her eyes. What was this creature who'd taken possession of him? No other explanation for this torment possibly existed. "Is that what you really want?" she finally managed.

"That does not matter."

"The bloody hell it doesn't." She scrambled to her feet and stalked toward him. "Dear God, Marcus! After all these months—after *last night*—don't you fathom it by now? I'm not just in love with you. I am bound to you. Your feelings"—she jammed a finger to his chest—"are my feelings. I don't just sympathize with your pain. I *feel* it."

"Nay." He spun away, dragging both hands through his hair. "'Tis not possible."

"I don't care what's possible. I know what I feel. At this moment, my heart's hammering so hard it hurts, just as yours. My eyes see out that window you're glaring through. There's a ship on the Thames, and you're wishing you could sail away on it."

He swung a shocked stare at her.

Gabriela lifted a bittersweet smile, more potent tears rolling against her lips. "Don't you see?" she said. "I know you better than I know myself."

"Nay." He whipped back to the window. Lowered shaking fists to the ledge. "Cease this absurdity, Gabriela. You do not know me at all."

"I know your strength and your pride," she persisted. "I know your patience and your love."

"You still—you do *not* know me."

"What else is there?" Like a tide pulled to the shore, an inexorable force moved her to him again. She spread her hands along his shoulders, pressed her cheek to the bunched sinew there. "Tell me."

His whole body quaked, as if his mind vacillated on the edge of a precipice. "You do not want me to do that."

She pressed tighter. "Untrue. I want to know all of you."

"You do not."

"I love you."

"Cease this!"

"No."

His countering roar shook the window. He burst from her, rising and twisting with a glare she hadn't seen in his most enraged Hamlet.

"Damn you!" He seized her shoulders, jerking her like a sawdust mannequin. "Leave me be!"

"I won't." Gabriela questioned her sanity with each rasped syllable, but an execution squad couldn't have stayed her. "I can't. I won't leave you, Marcus. Not until you tell me what's going on."

Her stomach clenched as he let out a morbid laugh that bared his locked, gleaming teeth. "So that is the game, then?

You want to know 'what's going on'?"

He laughed as if she'd begun a joke but only he knew the funny part. As he threw his head back and enjoyed the jest, Marcus dragged her across the apartment. With every step, he twisted his hold tighter around her arm.

"Marcus—you're hurting me!"

They reached one of the apartment's walls, covered by a gold brocade drape. Her mouth dropped as he flung back the drape, revealing it didn't cover a *wall* at all. It concealed a second door to the apartment. The portal was small, narrow, old—

Eerie.

Her half-monster captor kicked the door back into an unrelenting blackness. Though Gabriela cringed back, Marcus yanked her forward, flattening her body to his long enough to smash her lips with a punishing kiss. "Still hurting you, darling?" A cruel grin curled his lips when all she could do was choke in reply. "Ohhh, you have no idea what I'm capable of. But perhaps 'tis past time to show you."

As he began hauling her into the blackness, Gaby tried fighting him again. "M-Marcus? Where are we going?"

"Isn't it obvious?" He jerked her hard, showing her no mercy with the clasp. "Come. Follow me to hell, little fool."

CHAPTER NINE

Blackness. Ugliness. A twisted, furious maze, plummeting deeper and darker toward disaster.

His mind, or the passageway ingesting their steps into the earth's bowels?

Marcus had long ceased knowing the difference. Had long ceased to care.

The little idiot loved him despite his relentless rejection, did she? She refused to be a normal female, and reward his insults with a clean slap and a handful of sobs? She did not believe he could be such a revolting bastard?

Then damn her, he would simply show her the truth.

Indeed, as he wrenched her down a flight of spiraling stairs, through the thick oak door in Drury's foundations and finally along the dim passageway, he ceased pretending to have human breaths. His own wolfish huffs echoed in his ears. An animal's pulse raced harder through his veins.

He tried to care about Gabriela's effort to keep up with him. He searched for concern about her pained whimpers at every harsh jerk he meted. He desperately sought anxiety for *himself*, clawing for a vestige of horrified reason to turn him back from this ill-fated stunt.

But when the beast possessed him this time, it came to conquer.

And seized his humanity as first prisoner of war.

They finally arrived at the second door. The menacing

oak portal, bound by hinges of black iron, had never looked more a hated enemy to him. Unfettered by thoughts of decency or control, Marcus tore away the lead lock along with its mounting plate. He tossed the wreckage against the stone wall. A clatter roared through the passageway but rapidly faded, leaving behind the scratching of night creatures and the weeping of underground moisture.

"M-Marcus?" The dim awareness came of Gabriela's trembling voice at his shoulder. "What's going on? Where are we?"

The beast answered her with a jeering laugh. Marcus's debilitated psyche felt the responding rip in Gabriela's heart. He ached with her hurt and confusion.

Nay!

He repeated that soul's cry with a primal bellow. He'd promised to show her hell but now wondered how she'd see inside his mind. How she'd see this abyss of hating himself so much...

Of hating her, for making him go through with this atrocity.

With that hate, he shoved back the door and flung Gabriela into the chamber.

She stumbled, feet tangling in her costume, making her flail for balance—but he knew clumsiness was not the root that finally tripped her to the ground.

She fell when she saw his open crypt.

And robbed him of even more sanity as she did.

As she crouched there, shoulders shaking, eyes wide with glimmering copper confusion, she had never looked more touchable or beautiful. Sweet God. His cock actually leapt for her. His heart raced to his throat and throbbed there.

He wanted to take her there on the packed dirt floor. No,

he wanted to fuck her. Hard and fast and wild.

He could never touch her again.

The wick of his soul sputtered a last effort for life then snuffed out. It couldn't kindle any reaction at all—no more rage or hate, not even more arousal—nothing remained but a sense of artificial propriety that he carried out from habit more than anything, dipping a bow so low, it bordered on caricature.

"Madam, I bid you welcome to my realm."

He felt Gabriela raise her stunned stare. He lifted his head enough to meet her eyes—and the pools of horror forming in them. Soon, so very soon now, she'd finally begin to hate him. *Thank God.*

"What is this?" she hissed. "What the *hell* is this, Marcus? Your idea of a sick joke?"

A slow grin escaped the beast's guardianship. "Is that what you think?"

Jesu. What a glorious storm she made. Anger twisted her features into a raw and stunning sight. Her skirts billowed with her advance, mesmerizing as squall clouds. The force of her step shook her hair free from its combs, cascading it down her bodice as she skidded to a halt before him.

"I think," she said past quivering lips, "that you're afraid, Marcus Stafford. You're so terrified of what we shared—of what we still share—that now you're trying to frighten me, too." Sable ringlets whipped across her cheeks, drawing his sights back to her tear-filled eyes. "Well, guess what? I'm not scared. I'm not scared to love you! I'm not scared of your silly mausoleum, or the difference in our status, or the difference in our age—"

He could not control the laugh he bellowed. "The difference in our age," he growled. "'Tis a rich humor that you spin tonight, sweet."

"Stop it!" He felt the infuriated heat of her breath with the retort, indicating how doggedly, how *stupidly* she followed him. "Speak *English*, damn it, not your poetic gibberish!"

He halted to laugh at that, too—but this time, the sound didn't echo back a note of satisfaction. His mirth died somewhere deep in the cavern of himself as his sights fell upon the leather-bound book he kept stored in a nook next to his ancient writing table.

As usual, a lone candle stood vigil over the book, the sole object once capable of restoring a dim sense of identity to his homeless soul. Now Marcus saw the journal for the illusion it was in this sham of his life. Its pages carried no more reality than the scrims, props, and costumes waiting in the wings of the theatre far above.

"Poetic gibberish," he murmured. "Oh, Gabriela. 'When a man's verses cannot be understood, it strikes him more dead than a great reckoning...'"

"Very good." Her sarcastic sniff still came excruciatingly close behind. "*As You Like It*, Act Three, I believe. Now do you want to explain what's really lathering you?"

He sighed. Once. But somewhere between the overture and final curtain of that breath, a chill of resignation whispered across his soul. The gust rendered the winter inside him complete. Only a flicker of heat remained because he stole it from the ignited fury of her spirit. Gabriela's incredible, undaunted mortal spirit...

He drew on the last ember of that flame to pace closer to the nook—and the journal. The old leather binding let out a protesting crackle as he opened the front cover; the aged pages filled the air with dry soughs as he turned them.

He stretched a beckoning hand to Gabriela. "Come here."

She wasted no time in meeting his request. Her fingers slipped between his, warm and slender and strong. He closed his own around her hand, still amazed at the flawless connection even their hands shared.

He had to find the strength to do this to her. *For* her.

"How old do you believe me, Gabriela?"

As he expected, only her impatient sigh flickered the candle as reply.

"'Tis what I thought." He curled his other arm around her shoulder and pulled her toward the book.

"Marcus," she grumbled, "It doesn't make a diff—"

"Read it." He pointed to the exact line he wished even as he slid his burning eyes shut.

"I can't," she retorted. "It's written in some sort of archaic script. As a matter of fact, grump, it looks much like the way *you* write."

"Look at it again."

"Where is this getting us?"

"Look at it again." He ordered it from locked teeth. "And take your time."

He opened his eyes in time to catch her achingly adorable grimace, her painfully innocent huff. But she obeyed his hest, bending and focusing on the yellowed page.

After a moment, she began to read in unpracticed but articulate segments.

"On this sixth day of June, in the year of our Lord fifteen hundred eighty, we rejoice to christen our beloved son, now three months on this good earth...we have named him Marcus James, after his much-loved grandfath..."

Her voice trailed off. Just before being sliced completely by a gasp. She snapped up wide eyes, filled with bronze fires of intensity. They were the only thing in her face that still possessed color.

Marcus released her hand so he could wrap both arms around her. The muscles beneath his touch shook with consuming trembles. He prepared himself to cushion her faint.

He never expected her vehement shove. Nor her whirl back to the book, slamming it shut as if he'd just made her read an obituary. 'Twas an irony he could have enjoyed if it wasn't so pathetically true.

"I've had enough of this, Marcus. Damn you, enough! What *is* this?"

She emphasized with furious jabs toward the journal. For one moment, Marcus was able to marvel at her in bittersweet awe—before her pain assaulted his senses.

Oh God, her *pain*.

Every step she took pierced her deeply, painfully. Disillusion delighted in twisting its cruel blade in with every move she made. But the worst realization had yet to come. *He* held the next dagger—sited right for the middle of her heart.

"What is this?" He forced himself to shrug as if she merely asked after the location of his bath linens. "'Tis my family bible, sweeting. You just read the account of my christening day."

"I—I don't understand."

Of course she didn't. Had he really expected her to take in this bizarre spectacle, assimilate it all then pop out the most hideous conclusion she could dream of?

"Gabriela, I was born in Shropshire, on a birthing stool in my mother's bedroom, on a spring morning in fifteen eighty-five."

"On a *what*?"

Even through the suffocating pain, he almost loosed

another laugh. It did not escape him that she gaped more at the first portion of his announcement than the last.

He forced himself to go on. "I grew up happy, at least as 'happy' went defined then. We were lucky. It was a time of prosperity for the country, and my father turned a love of Oriental treasures into a lucrative importing business."

He squeezed his eyes shut, grimacing as he remembered Darius Taylor Stafford, so hearty, passionate and creative—and many years dead now. "I...loved him," he murmured roughly. "Therefore, when I became of age and he expressed his dream to sponsor me at court, I never thought of refusing. The day after my sixteenth birthday, I was off to Whitehall."

In the continued fires of her eyes, he watched her wage an inner battle between the safety of logic and the insanity of believing him. "Whitehall," she stammered. "Wait. Whitehall *Palace*?"

"Aye," he answered softly.

She paced faster. "Ridiculous. Whitehall Palace was wiped out by fire almost two hundred years ago."

"Aye. Long after my years there."

"Stop." She jerked up both arms, as if his words formed a racing steam train. "Stop saying these things. *Why* are you saying these things?"

"Because," he said, keeping her gaze locked to his, "'tis the truth."

"It's impossible!"

He reached for her hands, spidering his fingers through hers. "Not for a vampire."

Despite his grip, she wrenched free.

Like a flood, her disbelief doused his senses as she stumbled backward. With what little psychic force he could summon, Marcus argued back his truth to her. But her soul did not listen. Her mind whirled in too much chaos to hear.

"Gabriela." He closed the distance to her, and reached to her again. "Look at me."

"No."

"Look at me," he commanded now, "and think about it. Listen to me—"

"*No*." She staggered backward, searching for balance but stumbling into the plateau of soil that still bore the imprint of his body. "You're...lying," she stammered, scrambling across the mound until she hit the opposite wall. "No. This is all—why are you lying to me?"

"Sweeting—"

"Don't call me that!"

"*Gabriela*."

He had no choice about his next action. Every time he tried to touch her by mortal standards of movement, she bolted from his range, a maddening Puck in his midsummer night's nightmare. Instead, deliberately not hypnotizing her senses against the sight, he covered the distance between them with the speed of lightning. In the same action, he hauled her against him.

She deserved the truth. At all cost or explanation.

"Listen to me," he continued tightly. "I thrived at Whitehall, Gabriela. I loved it there—too much."

She nay issued even a blink of retort. Sweet God, he had not wanted it to be like this. This explanation possessed all the warmth of a military briefing. But there was no more time for tactful grace. The instant he had pulled her close and she turned her eyes up to him, those sienna depths sparkling with piercing grief, the ramparts of his control corroded. Only a few minutes likely remained before his battlements completely collapsed, sinking him into despair beyond the reach of words.

Only a few minutes left to finish breaking her heart.

"In only a matter of months, my desire to please my father turned into something more," he rushed on. "The craving for success became my obsession. Status was *everything* at Whitehall. A man either had it or he did not. He was either somebody or nobody."

He shook his head and snorted in self-deprecation. Hearing himself tell the story for the first time just confirmed the grand farce about it all. What did any of that status mean now? All the pomp and glory, the titles and ostentation; they reflected the honor of nobody and were remembered by none but little London historians and their little librarian wives.

And one lonely vampire who lived in the sewers beneath Drury Lane Theatre.

"I wanted to be a somebody." Marcus turned from her as the memories pulled him tighter. "I wanted it more than anything. I wanted the preferred seats at Will's performances. I thrived on the reverent nods as I walked the court halls. And I liked being watched and admired and listened to.

"And yet, it wasn't enough," he grated. "Can you believe it? I wanted *more.*"

He clenched his hands until they shook, hating the next words—and images—he dredged from the muck of his soul. "That 'more' came one night in the form of a surprise guest to Whitehall. Her name was Raquelle de Lanya. She was exquisite. And mysterious. And magical. And she stole my mortal soul in the space of one shared bransle dance. By midnight of the next eve, she stole my immortal soul, as well."

Only a tearful sniff and an audible swallow gave him any

indication Gabriela hadn't given in to a faint. "So—you're telling me this—this *Raquelle* just threw you to the ground, sank her teeth into your neck, and didn't stop until you grew massive incisors and raced off in search of a sleeping virgin?"

"Nay," he countered.

"Nay?" she spat. "Nay *what*?"

"She came nowhere near my neck," he said slowly. "Raquelle found her feeding more satisfying...when it came straight from her lover's heart."

He felt her laugh bubble through her senses, disoriented and disbelieving, before she bounced it off the stones at him.

He also felt that mirth die as he ripped open his shirt, pulled at her fingers, and guided them to the pair of puncture scars in his chest.

"I know." He answered it to her soul's silent perplexity. "They are not very big. Not the boon one expects when visited by the undead, aye? Yet they were not much different two hundred and eighty years ago."

Her face reflected a dozen shadings and sensations during the two steps she jerked away. But she never lowered her hand. "Two—hundred and—"

"Aye. A little more than that now. Raquelle took me in the year sixteen hundred."

"Then why—" Her voice caught. "Why are you bleeding now?"

Marcus looked down to his chest. Just as she said, a spattering of black-red droplets littered the V where his shirt hung open.

He did not wipe the mess clean. The effort to raise his head and give her an answer yanked the last stones from his soul's foundation. "'Tis not my blood, Gabriela."

She laughed again. High, hysterically. The sound mingled with her tears, a play of heartbreaking music. Marcus had ceased traveling to Italy a near century ago, cursing the opera for the agony of its arias. Now he damned himself the fool, presuming he ever knew what agony was before this moment.

"Oh, of course," she whispered. "Now you're going to tell me—"

"That I fed tonight, and happened to get a little slovenly," he finished.

She dropped her hand. And her smile. "I don't believe you."

"I know."

Marcus dragged in a heavy breath. He said nothing else as he watched the doubt creep fully over her. The quiver of her chin. The rise and fall of her chest on desperate breaths. Her refusal to look at him anymore, her stare raking the crypt's confines with the dread of a Gertrude just told she had swallowed poisoned wine.

"Who—"

"Nobody you know. Nobody *anyone* knows. I have a... friend...at St. Thomas Hospital. When there is a body with no name or identification—"

"Don't." She labored harder for breath, sagging against the wall. "Don't say any more." Her face contorted as her shoulders seized tight. "Damn it!" she rasped. "This isn't true. I cannot believe this!"

"But you do."

"No!" She turned and wet the cold stones with her hot tears.

"'Tis no use to deny me, sweeting. You said it yourself. We are bound. We know each other."

She whirled, back on her feet in one motion. "Know you? You monster! I don't *know* you!"

She jerked forward as if to strike him but at the last moment, swerved toward the door. "Don't say that again," she uttered, "*ever.* I don't know you—whoever or whatever you are. I never knew you."

Aye. Here it was. The moment he'd worked for, furiously driven them both at for the last hour. Success, at last. The truth, finally known. The ordeal, done and over.

Then why did the torment in his heart rage beyond any pain he'd ever imagined?

Why did he stagger to her again, reaching out an entreating hand, instead of just letting her go then falling into bed? Why did he not declare the chit good riddance and sleep off the heartbreak for three days?

He'd never know. He'd never know anything again but the black agony when she spun around, raced past the door, and slammed it behind her with a terminality unequaled anywhere but the depths of hell.

★ ★ ★ ★

Thank God Donna wasn't home. The moment Gabriela burst into the flat, she crumbled to the floor, unable to step further. As her knees buckled, the sobs came. She let them come until unconsciousness approached, merciful with its shroud. When she woke up, she retched until the tears came again. Somehow she made it into bed, calling herself every synonym she knew for *fool* between her heaving sobs.

You had to start calling yourself the world's expert on pain, didn't you? You had to believe you'd had your quota of lies and heartbreak for one lifetime.

And then you believed Marcus Stafford was a gift from heaven.

The man was a better actor than she dreamed.

Correction to the script. She hadn't been gulled by a man. She'd believed the grandest deception in the world by a three-hundred-year-old—

What?

"Dear God," she whispered. What kind of a beast had she made love with last night? What hellish atrocity had she welcomed into her body, her soul, hoping her womb nurtured life to its *baby*?

And what kind of a creature had he transformed *her* into, that her skin and senses still craved his body's heat? Why did her empty soul still cry out for the union of his?

She shuddered with harder sobs, shaking the bed with them, until somebody weighed down the mattress behind her.

Cool fingers pressed her cheek. "Dove?" came a familiar voice, echoing through the strange fog of sensation. "Saint Genesius, you're burning up. And you're filthy. And what is this—Gaby, you're still in your *costume*. What the bloody hell happened?"

A laugh surged past the dried bile in her throat. The sound reverberated back from some kind of soft surface, high and hysterical, intermingled with words that made no sense. As if the truth would strike Donna as any more coherent. *You see, I've been having this affair with a vampire...yes, that's right... well, I actually didn't know myself, until he just happened to let it slip...why didn't I notice that he talked like a scholar, dressed like a pirate and referred to William Shakespeare like a best friend? Because I'm an idiot, that's why. An oblivious, obtuse idiot.*

Then the abyss completely swallowed her.

She had no idea how much time passed as she traversed the violent chasm into the pit. When sleep came, she woke up screaming from a recurring dream. She and Marcus made love on a downy cloud, two dark angels in a world of light, only when she turned to kiss him, he met her with burning eyes and gleaming teeth. At the end of the dream, he grinned while pulling her off the cloud, into a darkness full of stars...and eyes.

Damn it.

She still loved him.

And hated him.

And feared him.

God help me.

Somehow, the Almighty heard that feeble appeal. After a week—or so, she reasonably guessed—in a morning already too mucky and muggy for its own good, He sent her an effective if questionable angel.

"Up," Donna barked, throwing back the bedroom curtains, ignoring Gaby's moan at the invading flood of light. "You have breakfast in a half hour and rehearsal at ten."

She braved the glare to shoot a glower across the room. "I have what?"

"You heard me." Her friend clunked a teacup to the nightstand. "You have some catching up to do. Augustus made some major revisions to Act Two."

She rolled back into her pillow. "I don't care."

"The bloody hell you don't." Donna jerked the armoire open. "It will probably rain today. Do you want to wear your wool pinstripe or the blue walking dress?"

"I. Don't. Care."

"Yes, you do. The walking dress, I think. It'll put some

color into your complexion. God knows you need it."

Gabriela crossed both arms over her torso. "Donna, what are you doing?"

The woman, already impeccably coifed and powdered, tossed stockings and a corset at her. "Saving your career, if you must know." Donna set hands to hips. "No sense hiding it," she muttered. "Adorable little pet, Drury's abuzz about you—and the rumors *aren't* nice. Half the ballet's convinced you ran away with a Swedish duke, the stage crew is betting Alfonso has you tied down somewhere in Saint John's Wood, and the rest are divided between looking you up at Bedlam or writing you off to opium."

She choked on a sip of tea. "Opium!"

"Now do you care?"

Gaby looked away, repeating the question to her benumbed heart. She didn't know what she cared about any more. Or who.

Or if she could ever care again.

She pronounced the only certain conclusion her contemplations delivered. "I can't go back there."

But as her friend stalked off to check on breakfast with a colorful curse, Gaby wrestled with the impression that she wasn't going to have much choice.

★ ★ ★ ★

The moment Marcus awakened, he knew she had returned to Drury.

Even interred by the stretch of rock between them, he felt the instant change in the air, the very walls around him. He vaulted out of the crypt, senses crackling with her nearness, pulse pacing itself to hers.

He battled not to invade her mind but within a moment, that choice was ripped from him. He experienced it all. The last week filled with her heartache. Her thrashings in a sea of confusion, so lost and helpless. Hating him. Loving him.

He slammed him to a stop.

Loving him?

He scraped numb fingers through his disheveled hair. He was not sure what to call the feelings whirling through him, so conclusive he had been about never feeling anything again. But here they were, a deafening symphony, not about to let him have the silence he longed for...the peace Gabriela deserved.

The night was a torturous eon, though he glared at the clock marking the passage as only three hours. He heard the odd whispers and giggles that were her "welcome" back to the theatre, envisioned the gawks she must be enduring with them. He heard her sigh, bravely preparing for the night's performance, nonetheless. And of course, he heard the din of the audience along with the curtain's opening rise; another when the lights came up for the evening's interval.

As the clock finally knelled nine hours and twenty minutes, the symphony of his senses was unbearable. He wrenched back the door, ran up the stone stairway, and spun right at the first landing—toward his private box.

He had to see her again. Just once. His honor be damned.

Bloody hell, his soul already was.

★ ★ ★ ★

It was nice to be back, Gabriela admitted. Nice but nothing more. The smoke of the stage lamps and the busy sweat of backstage slid over her with a musty familiarity. The motions of getting into costume—Louis somehow had her Act Three ensemble replaced without question—and of applying her "stage face" to the rhythm of Donna's chatter were a comfortable salve to the gaping wound where her heart once lay.

But they were surface repairs. Nothing more.

Act One elapsed with relieving swiftness. She defied Donna's command to eat some apples and cheese during intermission. Merely looking at the food brought back images of a magical midnight, seemingly so long ago now, when she'd last eaten the fruit...and Marcus had first tasted *her*...

She barely held in the little food that *was* in her stomach.

Standing in the wings now, listening to the French diva emote her way through Augustus's new Act Two monologue, she employed the same will to focus away from the hollow in her gut and the fuzziness in her head. She needed to listen... blast it, which line was her cue again?

A terse cough from center stage snapped her head up. The diva's flaming glare declared that the cue, whatever it was, had been delivered. Twice.

Gabriela gulped. And rushed on stage.

And felt Marcus in the very air she breathed.

His gaze, unblinking, followed her every step. His pain, mingled with hers, enwrapped her body. She knew his power and presence everywhere...outside, inside.

She heard the gasp she emitted, echoing over an expectant audience to the back of the theatre.

To the private boxes.

She looked there. She looked to him, her soul screaming at him, her heart sobbing for him. Wanting him. Needing him. Calling for him.

But only darkness returned her cry. It fell over her senses like a black bridal veil.

A moment before that nuptial knew consummation, she heard a woman's scream signal the start of audience-wide chaos:

"My God! She's fainted!"

CHAPTER TEN

Marcus vaulted to the ledge of his box and leapt over without stopping. Neither did he pause to care about the dozen witnesses on the ground floor who gaped as if he were a vulture of Ares come to life, this stranger in black who had plummeted into their midst from fifty feet above.

Yet for the first time in his undead days, he wished the beastly comparison true. He yearned to take flight over the throng he plunged into, all pushing as violently as he shoved, their curses mingled with their jibes about what force had clipped the wings of the fallen angel on stage.

Their slander, easily inverted from all the praise of a week ago, fueled the terror in his veins to a protective fury he'd never experienced—a need to show them that wings or no, *this* angel was avenged by a nightmare from hell. His chest heaved with the burden of breathing, of feeling, of loving.

And the snarl in his throat exploded into one tortured word, filling the theatre to the rafters and beyond.

"Gabriela!"

But the crowd only heeded him with more laughter.

"Poor man," someone giggled.

"Hopelessly smitten," said another.

"Poor *Gabriela*," quipped another, answered by a cloud of chuckles.

Not even Louis paused, in the middle of giving his terse assurance for refunds to all, before scooping the angel up and whisking her behind the closing curtain.

Two hours later, his fury burned to a new degree of frustration. Marcus paced the catwalks until they shook, his steps echoing in the cavern of Drury's now-empty spaces, peppered by his growls of every profanity that knew its vogue within the last three hundred years.

He had once likened himself addicted to her like opium. He wondered if he now endured the torment called withdrawal.

He stopped only to hearken for any sound from the green room or dressing rooms. Anything, *anything*—

Nothing. Aside from the brief moment he had felt her snap back to consciousness, a lead barricade had slammed shut on their invisible bond.

But with the rest of his preternatural functions still intact, Marcus heard everything else. The whispered gossip of the ballet as they prepared for their suddenly free evening. The way their sibilances swelled at the arrival of the company physician. At last the rasp of the paper as Louis sent a note off to Augustus, requesting a morning meeting to discuss candidates for Miss Rozina's permanent replacement...

Then, for well on the last thirty minutes, nothing.

He paced harder. His imagination took the ballet's wild little stories and added terrifying embellishments. She had fallen into a coma. She was dying. She was already dead.

He shook his head like a wild animal. *Do not give the thought existence, damn it. Not one second's worth.*

The physician departed, shaking his head. The last of the crew left, lasciviously eyeing some of the ballet. Louis rumbled out, wearing a scowl worthy of any soliloquy in the *Hamlet* script.

Marcus stalked faster. Swore in different languages.

Kicked a chunk out of a dusty corner in the theatre's wall. Where was she? What had happened to her? God's teeth, had they all left her in that dressing room to die?

He was forced to a desperate crossroads. Go to her or tear apart every inch of Drury's interior with his bare hands.

He snarled one more oath as he hurdled the catwalk rail and unloosed a length of scenery line. Without stopping to reconsider the command of his heart, he descended to the stage in an effortless sweep.

At the bottom of his descent, he nearly collided with a wrenchingly familiar figure wobbling from the green room door.

Even at his near miss, Gabriela cried out in surprise, stumbled back, and lost balance. Driven by pure instinct, Marcus caught her before the fall, sweeping her close. He dropped back against the wall with the sweet, wonderful weight of her. Treasuring the moments before she realized the identity of her savior then cursed him a demon anew, he crushed her yet closer.

No sound sliced through him except her sob.

Her sob?

Aye, 'twas indeed her *tears* soaking the front of his shirt. But did they denote her joy or her agony?

"Marcus." Confusion resonated in her rasp, giving him no more explanation than before. But she locked her arms around his nape as her tears coursed harder. "*Marcus.*"

"I had to," he confessed, "just once more—I had to see you." When she gave a soft nod against his shoulder, he threaded his fingers into her hair—just once. "I should let you go. I *have* to let you go."

"No!" Yet she followed the protest with a large step back,

her gaze fixed to the ground. "I—I mean—yes, you're right, of course." She burst out with another sob. "No. No, you're—oh, I don't know what's up or down anymore! Oh, Marcus—"

"I know." The words broke along with his heart. Against all the forces of his logic, he reached for her again, hauling her crumbled, crying form to him. "I should not have come," he stammered. "God's bloody teeth, I have only made you miserable."

She looked up at him, doused the silver intensity of his confusion with the copper flames of her own. Like forest fires at midnight, those blazes raged against unreadable horizons.

"I think I was going a little insane," he admitted. "I could not sense you anymore."

"I know."

He felt his left eyebrow drop. "You do?"

"I tried to reach you, too." She glanced away, fingers tugging at the top button of his shirt. "I cried out for you—"

"You did?" He lifted a finger beneath her chin, coercing her gaze back.

"I called to you from inside—from my heart." Her whisper was soft—and beautiful—as morning mist. "I was frightened. I've never been so disconnected with my body before. I didn't know who else to turn to. But the doctor gave me some medicine. It muddled me. I knew you couldn't hear." She emitted an awkward laugh. "Believe it or not, that made me more frightened."

She added a handful of his shirt to her tremulous grasp. But Marcus curled her fingers loose, cocooning them in his, instead.

'Tis all right, he sent his soul to whisper inside hers. *'Tis all right. I hear you now.*

He did not lie. The captivating angles of her face showed her comprehension of it. Her lips lifted into a smile. More shining tears slipped down her cheeks.

Marcus...I cannot help myself. I love you so much.

Ah, God. The knowledge of it and the saying of it...such a minuscule, monumental difference. His senses reeled with wonder. His heartbeat thudded in every nerve ending.

"Are you sure?" he whispered.

"I'm sure that I have never known another man like you, nor will again."

He snorted. "*That* is undisputed truth."

"I'm not teasing about this."

"Nor am I."

His concise, clipped tone sank into him. Nay, this was *not* a silly script turn. This was not a script at all. This was the crossroads of a real life. Gabriela's. It was time for terrifying questions—and potentially anguishing answers.

Knowing that, Marcus tilted her sights back up to him. He leveled the full force of his vampire's gaze into hers. He gripped her shoulders with all the strength—and violence—he dared unleash in his body. "So what *do* you want, Gabriela? Am I a monster or a lover? A demon or a dream?"

Against his most strident vow not to, he quivered through the following, eternal pause. He knew she saw his dependence on her answer in every inch of his face—and he did not care.

Finally, she nodded. Slowly. Silently. Just once.

She sighed. Slowly. Silently. Just once.

In the breathless pause after, she molded each inch of her body to every inch of his. Lifted both her hands to the sides of his face.

And then kissed him.

Ah, God, *she* kissed *him,* right on his monster's mouth. She wet his monster's cheeks with her soft, salty tears.

She declared her love again into both of his monster's ears.

Every moment a new gift. Every touch an incredible prize. And with all of it, bringing a realization that dizzied him with its impact.

He did not feel a monster anymore.

Oh, nay. Quite the opposite...by blissful, burning degrees. His pulse raced with very mortal urgency. His blood heated, all-too-human and hot, as she caressed his shoulders and chest. His head clouded with joyous masculine awareness of her skin, her hair, her perfume, her desire.

He groaned, deepening the kiss. He growled, deep and low, when she succumbed to the slick invasion of his tongue. Sweet Jesu, the effect she had on him...conscious thought went incinerated in the madness from her touch, her kisses, the longing mewls in her throat. She seared him so deeply, he began to wonder which one of them had truly spent the last fortnight writhing in sleepless fever.

The ramifications of that thought penetrated his brain. Marcus broke off the kiss with a determined jerk.

"We must desist." But between his hard breaths, he could not cease his hands from roaming the graceful contours of her back. It had not escaped his attention that she'd shorn all her costume save a lace-topped chemise, covered only by a frothy white dressing robe. "You have been ill..."

She only responded with a seductive smile. Her arms slipped around his waist while her lips found the most sensitive spot on his collarbone. By all the saints and sinners, how did she know about that spot?

He fumbled to catch her hands and set her away. But she

had the advantage. She reached through the aroused tangle of his psyche to move thirty seconds ahead of him, easily slipping away before he found her, each time finding a new place to enflame his body with her caresses.

"I'm not ill anymore."

Marcus shook his head. "You fainted."

"If I do it again, you'll catch me."

He loosed a husky chuckle. "Little vixen."

She brazenly pouted. "So you *won't* catch me?"

He bore his stare into hers. "Any time," he vowed. "*Every* time."

She replied by kissing him again. Openly. Ferociously. A brand of pure possession, snapping away the crutches of his polite concern as ruthlessly as she tugged apart the robe herself and offered the treasure beneath in a knowing slide of soft curve against hard vulnerability.

His cock sprang with lightning while his senses flooded with need. Instinctively, Marcus slammed his eyes shut as molten silver surged his brain. At the far edges of that blinding heat, he felt Gabriela's mouth at his jaw, her fingers at the ties of his shirt.

So good. Bloody damn, she felt so good that he had no idea how they'd slipped from the wall to the floor, presenting a new angle of sensual danger. If the flywheel of his control slipped by one more notch, the curtain would furl free...this play of passion would know its crescendo.

But crescendos backlashed into disasters if not all players knew their purpose on stage.

With heaving breaths of effort, he hauled back his desire long enough to grab her and pin her, letting his eyes fly open along with his determined growl. "You know not what you're doing, Gabriela."

"The bloody blast I don't." She looked straight up at him—into him—beholding the depths of his condemned soul and not cowering an inch. "How can you say that, when you know the hell you put me through?" She reached up, cupping his face again, her eyes shimmering. "Don't you see? For the first time in my life, I know exactly what I'm doing. I know exactly where I belong—right here, on stage, with you. I've found my heaven." Her fingers twisted into his hair. "*Our* heaven. Please..."

She pulled him into a supplicating kiss. If his faculties reeled before, they capsized now. Sweet God. Was this *her*, begging *him* for deliverance?

Though Marcus accepted her kiss, he was afraid to move, to shatter whatever miracle she had wrought to give him in this perfect star of an instant. His soul exploded past the confines of this wretched world, glimpsing a place of light and life.

"Heaven," he rasped at last. "Sweeting, I do not think I can believe in the place."

"Of course you can." Her answer was like the brush of an angel's wing. "I'll show you how." Her touch slid down his neck, beneath his shirt, pressing warm and strong over the cadence of his heart. "Don't be afraid. I'll show you the way...if you'll let me..."

He gave her his answer—a kiss as much surrender as command, equal part domination and submission, pleading for her guidance even as he felt her body tremoring at expert lover's touches he'd thought forgotten a century ago. She shivered and arched for him; she whimpered and sighed; she answered the strokes of his fingers and the heat of his movements with a guileless sensuality he had never thought possible in a woman.

With that purity, she proved good to her word. She led

him out of his darkness on a stairway of kisses and softness and passion—and at the top, she cleansed him in the nirvana of her goodness and love. Marcus's soul burst with amazement. His lungs struggled to breathe as they pumped with arousal. He clung to her, yearning to climb inside her for the forever of his days, so he should never hate or hurt anymore.

Somewhere in the silver-white glory of that heaven, her lips found his again. They drank each other greedily, reveling in the communion they'd soon become. And while their mouths intertwined in desire, her heart wound into his with a plea that stopped his breath in its fervor.

Don't make me go away again. Please don't make me go away.

He answered with every straining inch of his being. *Never. I promise.*

She rendered him incapable of any words, spoken or spiritual, after that. Marcus hissed in amazement as she slipped an eager hand over the hard ridge between his thighs. Light and heat and arousal spread from her magical fingertips, turning his balls into hot coals and his penis into a solid poker of need. And then, dear God, when she started to knead him there—

He withstood the torment for thirty seconds—a phenomenon for his superhuman capacity—before forcing her hand against the floor, over her head. As time burned away the next minute, he slammed both her arms to that arousing position, her two wrists captive beneath his grip. His other hand yanked her chemise over her hips in urgent fistfuls.

When he unsheathed the vortex of her sexuality, he slid his fingers down and in, moaning when his touch met a hot, silken pool. Gabriela unleashed a primal sound that shook all his male instincts. He growled and replaced the caress of his hand with the swell of his need.

She responded by lifting a sleek leg around his waist.

He grabbed the curve of her thigh and pulled her harder against him. "Little wench," he accused, his mouth hot and heavy against her ear. "Naughty, lovely little wench...with such a perfect body for me to fuck."

"Yes, Marcus...ohhhh, yes."

He freed himself at last. His cock swelled before he drove up inside her, far and full and complete. He dropped her hands in order to brace both of his, making her ride each lunge of his desire to its longest, hardest extent. Her cries coincided with each thrust of their bodies, pleading and urgent and perfect.

"More, Marcus...please...I want more. *More!*"

He gave it to her. He gave her all he had. All he was.

Perhaps, all he would ever be.

★ ★ ★ ★

Later, he cradled her until she fell into a peaceful sleep—most likely, her first complete rest in days. Wrapping her back in the robe, he climbed back into the catwalks and ascended Drury's silent heights toward their apartment hideaway.

Many times during that climb, Marcus looked down at his swaddled angel. Aye, tonight he had no less than taken a shard of light from the domain of day. How long fate would turn its back and feign ignorance on his sin, he knew not—nor cared anymore. For now, he and Gabriela would make the night their new heaven, the dark their new discovery. And love their sweet, stolen scrap from the claws of time.

Stolen time...

It was more than he had ever hoped for. More than he had ever dreamed.

He was euphoric with the gift. Grateful. Satisfied.

He only wondered how long Gabriela could be.

CHAPTER ELEVEN

"Gabriela, we must talk."

Gaby emitted a slow sigh into Marcus's chest. Ten minutes ago, she'd awakened here with a smile on her face and a wish that time would stand still. For now, she chose to ignore the impossibility of such a thing. For a while longer, she'd rather believe the same clock which had ticked through a few hundred years to bring this man to her would halt at seven minutes after three o'clock on this dark May morning, and let her stay with him forever.

She should have remembered Marcus wouldn't stand for that. The man she loved did not consider forever a blessing.

"There are matters we must discuss before the dawn comes," he persisted. "Before I must...go. Important matters."

Gaby suggestively kissed her way over his heartbeat. "Are they truly that important?"

"Aye." Not even her ruthless attack on his collarbone altered his tone—though the twitches of his thigh muscles maintained her hope of attempting another incursion.

"Very well." She pulled back with a pout. "My ears are yours, grump."

Marcus turned to his side and pierced her with a gaze more somber than his tone. "I did not think we were jesting about this."

"And you're in the wrong act, Mr. Stafford. That was several hours ago."

Marcus clamped a hand around the back of her neck, forcing her to accept the diamond brilliance of his gaze. "We will have no more lies between us. You *must* consider the truth of our situation from now on." He pulled his stare away, as if repenting for his outburst. "You must realize," he murmured, "I am not just a—a grump. I am—"

"I know." She pressed two fingers over his lips. "You're a vampire. I know."

He opened his eyes again, and now their surreal silver depths vacillated—as if her words both healed him and killed him. "Do you?" he murmured, low and tentative. "Do you *believe* this, Gabriela? Do you accept it?"

She couldn't help a little laugh. "What do you think I've been bloody near meditating on for the last five days? What do you think occupied every moment of my waking consciousness and invaded any second I managed to sleep? Marcus—" She slid her hand to his jaw. "Believe me, I haven't been able to stop realizing what you are."

He flinched again but Gaby shook her head. "Hear me out," she urged. "When I walked onto the stage tonight and felt you again—and felt *alive* again—I came to a huge discovery. *What* you are is not as important as *who* you are...or what you are to me, or the magic we make when we're together."

She finished with a lingering kiss that started doing things to *her* pulse—but it did nothing to ease the pained creases in his brow. He looked so very much an unsure Elizabethan boy, and her heart lost another little piece of itself to him.

"But is magic enough?" he grated.

"Oh, Marcus." She kissed him again. "It's more than enough."

At last, his frown eased a fraction. Gaby smiled and coaxed

his brows back further with tender tracings of her finger. "But now that we *are* speaking of magic…" she ventured, "I need to know about this bond we share."

His forehead tensed beneath her touch. "Gabri—"

"Please, Marcus," she insisted. "It—it overwhelms me. Sometimes, I swear my heart beats in time to yours. It's unlike anything I've ever felt before."

"Not I, as well." He tilted his head back to catch her finger between his lips, then suckle it in a cherishing kiss.

"Then what is it?" she prodded. "It's *not* normal."

"Nay, 'tis not."

Gray mist darkened his eyes. Gaby almost didn't want the significance of it translated—perhaps the line between the man and the mystery of him was best continued as a blur—but an uncontrollable necessity drove her on. She loved him. Because of that, she needed to plumb his darkness, unravel his mysteries.

"All right," she said slowly. "Then is this some kind of a force you can wield? Sometimes it feels as if you climb right inside my mind."

He answered with a thoughtful tone. "I cannot enter your mind, not physically. I am afraid 'tis too tight."

She reined back a laugh. "My apologies. Suppose I'll have to tidy the place a bit more, then."

A dip of his eyebrow said the humor hadn't been lost on him. But his reply came intent as before. "I can, however, change my own physical dimensions, to the larger or smaller, with a few limits."

Gaby blinked. She believed him, which amazed her as much as the stunner he'd just dropped. "You mean," she finally murmured, "such as becoming a bat at will?"

"If I fancy. But I do not often fancy." He shifted and huffed. "Yet if I am forced to that sort of situation, I prefer to become a wolf. Or"—he shifted again—"a butterfly."

Gaby bit the inside of her cheek. Marcus snapped a glower, discerning her reaction, anyway.

"A butterfly is...nice," she soothed. She got a vehement grunt as retort. "Oh, Marcus," she murmured, brushing the strong line of his jaw. "My Marcus. I'm sorry. I don't know much about all this, except for what they print in the weekly serials."

His grunt turned into a growl. "And heaven help those who nay believe *those* tales."

"Most of them talk about a vampire's ability to hypnotize his victims. Well, is that what's going on?" The words came with more difficulty now—because she wasn't sure she wanted the answer. "Have...you been hypnotizing me?"

He took a long moment before replying. "I tried," he finally answered. "And I was triumphant. Just once. On my second attempt, you found me out. *You* ended up controlling *me*, with your orders to come back and help you with your rehearsals." He shrugged, his Elizabethan boy now graduated to a cocky lad ready to take Whitehall by storm. "I'm afraid my skills lie in sensual, not supernatural, conquests."

Gaby's eyebrows crunched together. "But you still could be using me and I wouldn't—"

"And if I am," he countered, pushing her back into the pillows, "would you be able to see into *my* heart and soul, as well?"

Again, she sighed into his chest, now an unavoidable, broad horizon atop her. The man—and his enticing torso— had a point. But his deduction didn't bring her any closer to understanding the connection they shared. The enigma brought the endless layers beneath Drury's stage to mind. One successfully snapped trapdoor only led to encountering the closed hatch of the next...

To further thicken the muddle, Marcus's voice, loving but uncompromising, came echoing in her head.

Gabriela. Look at me.

Defiance should have occurred to her, if only to protest his invasion of her vulnerable mindset. But in that word, her quandary lie: Marcus didn't invade. He belonged inside her. He always had. He always would.

"I shall try to explain," he said aloud. His gaze, like the brace of his body, was resolute. "What you and I share...'tis common yet not so common."

"*That* cleared everything up," she quipped. "My many thanks."

She expected an equally dry riposte in return. When he just dropped his forehead to the valley above her breasts and shook his head, Gaby buried her fingers in his mussed hair, reassuring him. It never struck her until now...she moved about the world each day, telling dozens of people, "I'm an actress," or "I live on Hay's Mews," or "I love the city at Christmas time." Marcus had lived *millions* of days but before this moment, had never had to put his existence into words.

No wonder it took him a few seconds to lift his gaze again.

"A vampire *is* capable of sharing a mental bond with a mortal," he said softly. "Much like the link we share. The connected couple is able to share thoughts and feelings, even commune with each other over some distances." He dropped back to her side while taking in a long breath. "But the union is usually only gotten through an act called initiation."

"Initiation," she echoed. "When did we do that? Did I know you were doing it?"

He shook his head again. Brushed one big, gentle hand over her forehead. "You did not know," he murmured, "because I never initiated you." A wave of fear rolled across the dark cliffs of his face. "God only knows what would happen if I did."

Gaby felt his frustration. She tried to share it—but nothing came to her except a bemused grin, tugging her lips without mercy. "So you're saying we did this all by ourselves?"

"I suppose I am."

She didn't try to hold back her laugh at that point. Especially as she caught his face on both sides of his adorable glower, and planted an adoring kiss on his mouth.

"Magic," she whispered. "It makes perfect sense."

And then, Marcus chuckled, too. He filled her soul with the sound, a rich rumble of summer thunder precluding the blossoming rainbow in her heart. They laughed and kissed and teased some more, rolling from one side of the huge bed to the other, lovers bantering in a meadow of down and candlelight...

And magic.

A long while later, they lay breathless and content in the tangle of sheets they'd created. When Marcus pulled Gabriela tighter, she didn't resist. He traced lazy circles on her shoulder while she traced similar patterns on his chest.

Halfway through her twelfth circle, she softly ventured, "Marcus?"

"Hmmmm?"

"Explain initiation some more."

As she anticipated, all his muscles stiffened. But he replied in a calm voice, "'Tis the act of feeding, more or less. A vampire takes blood from a mortal, but drains them not."

She nodded, expecting an answer like that. "So does the mortal turn into half a vampire?"

A low chuckle added a velvet undertone to his reply. "Nay. But the blood bond is a powerful link between the pair, so the mortal often tires easily during the day, and is more attuned to the world of the darkness. When the vampire awakens at dusk, they can summon the mortal with a mere thought." His voice transformed from velvet to an uncomfortable burlap. "Very simply, the vampire has complete control over his...disciple. 'Tis not a natural or honorable authority to have. I have seen it abused on several ugly occasions."

"It sounds romantic to me."

"It is *not*."

He threw up a sudden fortress of silence. Gaby respected his unspoken command, feeling him battle the unwanted memories of those "ugly occasions."

Two hundred eighty years of such nightmares. Dear God, what kind of existence had he endured? Would she ever really know? Would she ever comprehend the scope of his knowledge, the breadth of his experience, the depth of his loneliness?

She wanted to. With all her breath and being, she yearned to.

That longing compelled her next question, despite her fear of it. "Did Raquelle...initiate you first? Before she..."

To her surprise, he spouted a harsh laugh. "Hardly. Raquelle was not the initiating sort."

But she surprised herself more. More accurately, her next words shocked the warmth out of her limbs. "Will you initiate me?"

He bolted off the bed. "Absolutely not."

His sudden absence stung like a North Sea wind—bringing

the logic behind her request into ice-sharp focus. What was so wrong about her request? About yearning for an intimacy beyond dreams with the only man she'd ever love?

She wrapped herself in the sheet and rose to her knees. "Marcus. Just think of all we could share—"

"We share enough already." He whipped his shirt off a chair and shoved his way into the sleeves.

"But I love you."

"I love you, too. 'Tis why the subject is closed." He jammed into his breeches just as fast, securing the codpiece with swift strokes.

Gaby climbed off the bed. "Marcus—"

She didn't know what cut off the rest of her words first. His furious whirl back upon her, or the pure silver fire in his stare.

"The subject is closed, Gabriela. Mention it not again."

★ ★ ★ ★

For once, she heeded his behest. Five and a half weeks later, as he sat at his writing nook in the crypt, Marcus thanked the forces of nature which had combined to effect that small miracle.

Gabriela had spoken no more of initiation, though he had felt her desire to on a few hundred occasions. He also surmised she was grateful for the request he *had* granted: to help her learn about other aspects of what she termed his "unique mode of living." But he'd demanded something in trade for it. She would return to the stage and renew her commitment to winning a visit from the Prince's Grand Theatre Troupe.

There was no question in his mind about who had

cinched the better half of the deal. The next evening, the woman threw herself into a performance gleaning three roof-raising ovations, as well as Louis's silence about seeking her replacement. Every night thereafter, Gabriela pushed the role to greater success, reflecting the breakthroughs of awareness and ability she achieved nearly nightly in their after-hours sessions...their rehearsals begun with Shakespeare or Dryden and ended with passion and fulfillment.

Aye, she bloomed beneath his guidance, sometimes beyond what *he* envisioned. Every night, she unfolded the petals of herself as willing student, precious soulmate, and incredible lover...as if she had only needed him all along.

"Christ," he muttered to that, disgusted with himself. *Asinine notion.*

But had he not found himself pushing past the two-hundred-eighty-year-old topsoil of his own loneliness to meet the warmth of her questions? Had he not explored the most disturbing realms of himself to bring back serious answers for her sincere queries about his life, despite the terror that just one of those responses could send her running from him forever?

But Gabriela never ran. She had accepted his answers with quiet attention, as if he explained the secret to playing a perfect Lady Macbeth instead of such useless morbidity as his feeding needs, sleeping schedule and what it felt like to hear every whisper in Drury's house if he so cared.

The only moment he had noted revulsion in her gaze came when he recounted the incident in Hungary with Gertrude... oh, sweet Gertrude, with her big eyes, bigger breasts and, he had learned the hard way, big vampire-hunting village. When he finished the recount, Gabriela had snorted and called

Gertrude a loud-mouthed, dark-ages bumpkin—which had sparked *him* to a burst of adoring laughter.

And hatred? Aye, Gabriela showed him hatred, too—only once. The night she requested the full story of what Raquelle had done to him.

She had listened while he held nothing back, beginning with Raquelle's tickle of a seduction, bidding him to a tryst in a forest glade not far from London at midnight—of course. There was a cave in that glade, one of his mates told him later, where exotic and erotic ecstasies took place...

He had arrived at the glade an hour early, yet Raquelle was already waiting. With one note of her throaty laugh, she had led him to the grotto, then deeper inside with her own clothes as path guides. Before he knew what happened, the temptress had intoxicated him beyond thought with that laugh and her body, and a sweet alcoholic ambrosia she kept plying to his lips.

He almost had not been able to continue then, the words of shame and horror locking in his throat. But Gabriela's touch drew out courage he thought long-dead. So he continued, telling her how he found himself naked and tied to a massive stone slab, staring up at a ceiling of leering stars, the smirking moon, and Raquelle's equally bare body. She'd been insatiable and unreal, draining the milk from his cock before dropping her head to his chest, her teeth into his heart—

He'd halted the story there. The words would truly come no more. Marcus had tried turning away but Gabriela clutched him into her arms, becoming his silent seraphim of strength as the memory refused to grant him mercy. Shaking against her, he'd relived that heinous moment of shock, of helplessness, of raging and roiling, of dying and then living again...ah God, of

Raquelle pressing her sliced breast to his mouth, forcing him to suck from her...

He had blocked his thoughts from Gabriela after that. No way in hell would he expose even the bravest parts of her soul to the two-week torture following his transformation. He could not tell her of his vow to wither away dead before taking the blood of another, only to fail when Raquelle brought the corpse of a sheepherder to the grotto. He barely brought *himself* to recall his wanderings through the forest, pleading God for some respite from the onslaught of perception: of smelling, hearing, and seeing every sound and sight and life within fifty miles. Especially anything with blood flowing in its veins...

But most of all, he would not tell her of the hope.

He did not know why he bothered to call it such anymore. He had long since given up on Raquelle's cryptic announcement of so long ago, delivered just after she had cackled her way through an explanation of what she had done to him.

Ohhh, dear Marcus. You will get used to this. In time, you will even thank me for it. Non? *Well, fine. If you choose to deny the gift, then be informed that I have heard of a cure. No, I do* not *know that much about it, darling; I happen to enjoy being a member of the most superior species on earth. I only have only heard them say it is not instant or easy, and involves a magical spell, or some such* absurdités. *If you care to waste your precious nights seeking something like this, I cannot stop you. Yet neither do I care to play party to it. Too, too bad, Marcus. I thought you would be such fun.* Au revoir, cherie.

He had never seen her again.

Nor had he found the miraculous "cure."

He had searched for it. God, how he had searched. Combed

one end of the world then the next, seeking the deliverance from his wretched infirmity. He toured France with a one-eyed gypsy woman, exhausting every vile-tasting *brasseur de le vampire* in her memory. He tarred his face and crossed a jungle to have a voodoo shaman bless a dead snake around his neck. He hiked the Himalayas for fifty years, inhaling every incense the *lamas* gave him. In the Orient, he let himself be speared by three foot-long acupuncture needles. He tried enchantments, spells, crystals and even simple cold cures.

But in the end, the sun always rose again. In the end, he always felt his skin crackling with the encroaching heat...

In the end, before racing to the pathetic black safety of the earth, he cursed the God who turned His back on an unsuspecting fool named Marcus Stafford.

But in time, he lost the will to curse. That came shortly after he terminated the hope of Raquelle's "cure." Finally, he returned to England, where the sky, the fog, and the cold were a perfect picture of his life's dismal eternity.

By then, Drury Lane was fully constructed and basking in the patronage of a king obsessed with—who would have dreamed it possible—an actress. Marcus's need for extremely private living space suddenly received royal sanction—and if King Charlie ever noticed the dismal creature sharing his special subterranean passageways, the promise of Nell Gwynn's waiting bosom obviously made the matter a secondary concern.

A few times, he considered coming forward to Charles. He had yearned to jump from the darkness, seize the man's shoulders and shout, *You are a moron! She is a viperess disguised in paint and perfume. You are the bloody King of England, and she shall ruin you!*

Now, Marcus was glad he had kept to the shadows. Now, he understood what drove a king to burrow beneath city streets, woo the wrath of the entire court, and defy the expectations of a matrimony-mad country.

Now, he understood the power of a thing called love.

The thought ushered him back to the present, riding on a soft chuckle. *Speaking of mindlessly mooning morons...*

He laughed again, thinking even this damp tomb became brighter at the sound.

A nasal cough vibrated the air behind him. His senses jerked from their reverie and the feather pen slipped out of his hand, leaving a large pool of blue ink on the fragile rag paper.

"Well, damn me," drawled Joseph, standing two paces behind him, "there *is* a first time fer everything. Do believe if I were a snake, ye'd be dead by now, Guv."

Marcus pivoted, a scowl starting to tighten his temples. Instead, he curled up one side of his mouth, delighting in his ability to enjoy sarcasm again. "Not bloody likely, my friend."

He enjoyed another laugh, silently this time, at the blatant wobble of Joseph's smile. On shifting feet, the man grumbled, "What the blemmin' hell do ye want? I almost thought yer note was a mistake. I just brought a fresh slab o' meat fer ye last night; I don't think I can pull it off two nights in a row without anybody noticin'. What're ye doin' anyway, guv? Sharin' the spoils with a friend?"

"I did not say I needed another 'slab'."

Joseph just threw him a direct scowl. Nervous and disconcerted, but still a scowl. "Ye've never asked fer anythin' else before."

"Hmmm. True. I suppose I have simple needs."

"I wouldn't call 'em *simple*."

He did not fault the man his slobbery snort of punctuation. "Nevertheless, I think you shall find this eve's request easier to fulfill than usual. And my gratitude"—he leveled an impenetrable stare into wary eyes— "twice as substantial."

At that, between what Joseph perceived as one moment and the next, Marcus flipped open a "stone" in the wall, clicked access to the wall safe beneath and brandished a handful of solid gold sovereign pounds, each still bearing a perfectly-pounded likeness of Queen Bess.

Joseph's grimy beard dropped open. "Jesus, guv."

"We can do business, aye?"

"Indeed, we can."

Marcus slipped the coins into a cloth pouch. "Good."

"And I know just the place to get ye the goods. Little place over in Belgravia, believe it or no. Finest in London, I hear 'em say."

Marcus found it his turn for a perplexed stare. "Finest in—?" He shook his head. "You do not know what I need yet."

"The hell I don't." The man cuffed a slap to Marcus's shoulder. "Aw, there's no need fer airs around me, guv. I'm even proud o' ye, now that I tinker on it."

Marcus's left eyebrow dropped. Joseph only deemed a few of life's subjects worth "tinkering" over. He did not knew if he should even fathom a guess which vice the man had imagined for him.

"C'mon," Joseph prodded. "There's only one thing this kinda quid gets rolled fer. Women. And *this* kinda quid'll get ye—"

"A dozen raspberry tarts with fresh cream."

He slammed the payment into Joseph's hand and turned before any meaning but the obvious be taken. Nonetheless, he felt the mortal's confusion swirl through the musty air. He sensed Joseph peering at the pouch, his puny brain actually wondering if he had missed a vital section of the conversation.

Marcus didn't prolong his dilemma. "You need but pick up and render payment for the pastries," he confirmed. "I already ordered them."

He had actually done so a week ago, after Gabriela brought half a dozen of the little pies up to the apartment and devoured the lot in a half hour. As Marcus watched her lick the bright pink filling off her thumbs in near-carnal ecstasy, he had instantly started planning tonight's surprise: a candlelit welcome for her, beginning with the tarts and a bottle of 1598 Chablis. The evening's second course would consist of fruit, cheese and bread, which she would devour while giving him an act-by-act detailing of the night's performance. Course three: a new silk gown and matching peignoir set, leading swiftly into course four, in which he would show her how delicious raspberry filling could taste on places other than thumbs...

God's sweet mercy. He could hardly wait.

"You shall go here," Marcus charged, scribbling the street and number of Athena's cottage on the edge of town. "She is a friend who takes special orders for me, so do not look for a baker's shingle." Athena had reluctantly taken down her sign in 1817, after "neighborly" whispers mutated into suspicions about the beautiful pastry chef who never appeared after the early morning bread rush, created beautiful birthday cakes for everyone but herself, but never seemed to have a birthday herself.

Joseph looked at the address and shrugged. "Seems like a big fartin' faldoral just fer a dozen bleedin' tarts."

"*Raspberry* tarts."

Joseph cocked a knowing grin. "All right, Guv. Who is she?"

Marcus managed an indignant snort. "She?"

"Ohhh, aye." The croon floated across the room on underlines of certainty only attempted by witless mortals. "I shoulda called yer horse the second I walked in. Here ye are fritterin' about like a rangy school lad, wearin' fancy velvet clothes I never knew ye possessed, sittin' in such a lovesick moon that I bloody well could have sneaked up and—"

"Joseph—"

"And quite the testy lad, too."

"*Joseph.*"

"Awww, c'mon," Joseph pressed. "Just a hint. Ye really care about the chit, eh?"

Marcus surprised himself by sliding back a long, slow smile. "Aye," he said then. "Aye, I love her."

"Well, bleedin' hell." Adding to the strange turn of their exchange, Joseph's voice vibrated with something close to fatherly affection—no matter that *he* could be the man's grandfather three times over. "Well, that *is* wonderful, Guv. Wonderful."

"Uh...many thanks." He was uncertain what to do about the first honest attack of *awkward* he had experienced since thirteen.

That was before Joseph opened his mouth again. "So. How soon 'til ye got 'er on the back and full-in-the-belly?"

He forgot all about *awkward* in a second. He dismissed Joseph rapidly, turning his full attention to the newer sensation. 'Twas too crucial to be ignored, for it carried a vision that burst in his brain with staggering possibility.

The impression of Gabriela, round and ripe with his child.

Nay. Impossible.

But vampiric offspring *had* been known to happen. 'Twas rare, usually only when vampires coupled with gypsy women, or were gypsies as mortals themselves. Still, there were the odd incidents throughout the centuries...

Terribly, highly impossible.

He heard the results varied from disastrous to joyous.

Unthinkable.

A dream never to come true. A reality never to happen. A life he'd never have.

CHAPTER TWELVE

Life, he resolved, only existed of tonight. All it *could* exist of. Marcus had forced himself back to the hard reality of that, despite the few seconds of joy he'd indulged at Joseph's innocent comment. Perhaps in a few hours, a hope of tomorrow night even might start to glimmer as possibility, but beyond that, the future belonged to the darkness of the unknown.

Truth be known, the mantra was something he committed himself to quite often these nights—but this eve, it carried extra importance. He yearned to transform the next few hours into diamonds and adorn the queen of his world with every one of them. Maybe, if he paid worthy homage to his sovereign, if he loved her hard enough and strong enough, the future would battle time for him, and stay locked in the sweet ecstasy of this night.

Now, he only had to make everything perfect.

After Joseph departed, Marcus sprinted back to the apartment. On his way, he honed one ear toward Drury's stage. Everything was running on schedule; Gabriela had just made her Act Two entrance. He wore a satisfied smile by the time he reached the upper rooms.

He lit the last of the candles around the sitting room, dozens of the tapers glowing from ornate candelabra that he interspersed between towering urns full of dark red roses. He pulled petals from another dozen roses then scattered them in a path leading to the bedroom. The trail ended at the foot of the bed, where an ivory lace gown and peignoir lay glowing in amber radiance against the coverlet. He sprinkled some petals across the bed pillows, as well. Gabriela's hair would smell even sweeter with the hint of rose in its silken bouquet. God, how he loved her hair. And how she wrapped the tresses around his body when he was inside her, teasing the backs of his thighs with the soft, silken tendrils...

As usual, his cock began to pound at his breeches, officially bringing his wait into the realm of excruciating.

Yet, he waited. He made one more critique of the room while running anxious hands over his face, his hair, his never-worn-before clothes. He had found the black velvet doublet and soft leather hose in Mother's cedar chest three days after her death, eighteen years after she had presumed him dead.

Marcus instantly knew why she had kept the finery, anyway. The pieces were to comprise his wedding attire.

My Lady Stafford, he prayed fervently, *if you could only see your fidgeting groom of a son now.*

"Christ's foot," he gritted as he rushed back down to meet Joseph. They only now dropped the curtain on Act Two. As he carried the warm tray of tarts to the apartment, sugar filling his nostrils to match the sweeter thoughts in his mind, Marcus decided "anticipation" was an overrated concept.

Still, he waited.

At last, the thunderstorm of final curtain applause surged through the building. Another mob of Londoners had fallen to the spell of Gabriela's beauty, magnetism and talent.

He waited some more.

Thirty minutes. An hour.

He reached out to her with his mind. There was no response—though he still felt her presence in the building.

What the bloody hell?

He confined a knot of dread to his gut with a clenched jaw and coiled fists. But a herald of hideous logic rose from a place deeper than that, intoning its ruthless conclusion.

You knew this was coming, Stafford. You knew this would be the bridge to cross in the end. You told yourself to be ready, told yourself not to dream of holding her forever—

"She is coming." he gritted, starting to pace. "She is coming back, damn it."

Acid ate its way across his stomach through more eternities of minutes. He stopped keeping track of how many when he crushed the clock with a quaking fist.

★ ★ ★ ★

Gabriela paused, breathless, in the apartment's doorway. She'd sprinted all the way from the catwalks, not an easy feat in the emerald silk and cream lace production of a gown she'd hastened into.

But her first sight of Marcus made the extra twenty pounds of corset, petticoat, and heeled shoes well worth the ordeal. She leaned against the door frame for a long moment, simply absorbing the candlelit glory of him.

She would never tire of this sight. Ever.

She took advantage of his rare unawareness of her, thanks to his closed eyes, position on the couch, and the mental partition she'd deliberately erected between them for the last two hours.

Two hours. It felt like two lifetimes. Her heart caught and her knees puddled as if it had been. His sculpted torso and long, elegant legs were the material of her most illicit fantasies.

He was her beautiful, black-clad angel...and such an important part of why tonight's incredible events had happened at all.

How many times during those proceedings had she yearned to simply envision him? How many moments had she yearned to summon to him, feeling his smile join the growing triumph and joy in her heart? But she'd resisted the urge. She'd called upon every ounce of willpower despite the pull of Marcus's repeated calls, telling herself this moment would be worth the wait. Oh, yes...

Gratefully, finally, she let the bonds on her senses slip free. Immediately, she stumbled back. Dear God, after just two hours, the renewed flow of his presence hit her like a tidal wave.

Then his eyes snapped open.

And lightning joined the tidal wave.

"Marcus." She rushed toward him on the joyous whisper—but stopped short when another flood of feeling struck her.

Pain. A black, deep chasm of it.

She knew this sensation. She'd experienced it before. The night they'd first encountered each other, he'd spun and damned her for making him feel it. But that night, Marcus had whirled on her like a wounded beast, raging against his injury, fighting it. This was different—to the point of panicking her. This creature before her was the image of defeat. And his aching, bloodshot stare told her why.

He hadn't thought she was coming back.

And part of him, a very large part, was prepared to lay on that couch past dawn because of that conclusion.

"Marcus." She dropped to the floor at his side, lifting her hands to his face. "I'm here."

His eyes slid shut then squeezed hard, as if her touch brought both dream and nightmare. She burrowed her fingers into his sweat-tipped hair and angled his face for her soft kiss.

He froze. Held his breath. His hands rose slowly, curving around her shoulders. At first, he barely touched her. Then his grip turned fierce.

"*Gabriela.*" It was a growl of gratitude, of possession. He drew her unresisting body atop him, but not prior to tearing free the ties and buttons of her petticoat. He yanked the stiff framework from beneath her skirts and hurled it across the room. The next long minutes were savage in their silence but Gabriela didn't need words. Her heart listened to his soul's cry, wrapped warmth around the core of his chaotic spirit—though doing so swept more amazement through her own senses.

This man had lived hundreds of years. He'd danced with a queen and shared an underground abyss with a king. He'd traveled the world dozens of times over. He'd shown her the treasures he'd saved from his favorite places: a jade elephant from the Orient, a seashell playing a Caribbean ocean song, a friendship bracelet from a Sioux Indian boy on the western American plains. Undoubtedly, he'd known women in those lands. Exotic women, well-versed in the language of pleasure, all too eager to tutor a silver-eyed stranger with the touch of an angel and the body of a god.

It couldn't possibly be that his heart shared so much of what filled hers. This bone-aching, heart-tearing need...

Could it?

For an instant, she allowed herself to believe the answer yes. It was the moment Marcus slid his hands up her nape and into her hair, his guttural purr betraying his gratification. Then when their gazes locked again...the hooded intensity of his stare as he traced fingertips over her temples, her eyelids, down the bridge of her nose, over her parted lips; exploring her, learning her.

Yes.

In this minute, she believed even the impossible true.

Yes.

It made her greedy for more. *God, just one more minute of this joy. Just one more moment of forgetting the odd little Italian girl in place of a woman who finally feels cherished...*

She laughed in soft delight when heaven gave her its compliance in the form of Marcus's more urgent caress. His hands descended to the V of her bodice, dipping beneath, cupping her with bold strokes. Her nipples budded beneath his questing fingers; a sheen of silver mist swirled in his eyes. He pressed his lips together...hiding his teeth from her.

"Sweet Jesu," he said tightly. "How I've missed you."

"Marcus...oh!"

Her adoring sigh shot into a gasp when he jutted his hips, urging her to straddle the evidence of how *much* he'd missed her. As she formed the hollow of her body to the hardness of his, Marcus's fierce hiss joined her breathless song. Only the cambric of her drawers and the leather of his breeches held the crescendo of their opus at bay.

The concerto climbed a gradual scale of passion, the loving strings of their hearts melding with the drumbeats of their bodies. Each measure played inexorably into the next, a beautiful tumble of notes, beats, and trebles. She sank against him again and they kissed hard, mouths fusing, tongues tasting, desires swelling, pulses pounding.

"My love," she told him, "I missed you, too."

She expected a responding smile. Instead, Marcus's muscles tightened. "I tried to reach you." His voice was damn near a plea. He raised a hand to cup her face. His remembered pain again threaded a needle through her heart. "So many times, in my mind, I called for you, and—"

"I know." She pressed herself tighter to him, yearning to close out all his fears and uncertainties.

"Then...why did you not answer?"

In reply, Gaby conducted their concerto into a new movement. She sent him a smile slow and illusive as the undulations she began with his lower body. "Sometimes a girl has to have her secrets, Mr. Stafford."

Marcus gulped. His eyes slid shut. His head fell back over the couch's arm, displaying the labor of his Adam's apple as he attempted to speak. "S-Secrets?"

"Mmm hmm." She said it with pouting lips and demure eyes while trailing her hands down the ebony velvet encasing his chest. Such a heavenly contrast...plush softness against hard definition; the color of midnight swathing a vista stark and magnificent as the moon. She raked fingers lower over that wonderful, muscular surface until alighting on the codpiece of the historical breeches. They fit him so blessedly well. With two deft tugs, she opened the restraints between his thighs.

"Yes," she emphasized, slipping a hand into the juncture, mingling her gasp with his. "You see? Secrets can be splendid when you finally get to share them."

Marcus's chest rumbled with another bestial growl. It was a breathtaking match for the paw-like grip he clenched to both sides of her waist. "I am afraid you have unearthed every shred of my secrets tonight, lady. I am quite...bare...to your mercies."

"Oh no," Gaby countered. "It is *I* who lay open to *your* benevolence." She finished with another gasp, her words validated when his erection found the slit in her drawers and nestled against her intimate curls.

"Oh, aye...I remember. We were...speaking of your naughty secrets."

She loosed a husky laugh. "Not naughty. Just...secret."

"I protest," he murmured. "*Very* naughty." As if to emphasize, he pushed up harder against her arousal. He was relentless, rubbing her with the taut crown of his sex, back and forth...

Sinuous torture. Unequaled heaven.

"Marcus!"

"Confess it to me," he ordered, gripping her hips tighter. "Tell me what roguery kept you from my arms, from my heart—" His brow tightened and his lips flattened. "Tell me, damn it, what kept your light from my soul."

She thanked Providence that she didn't carry *England's* imperial secrets. They'd never be safe the moment she looked into the molten gaze of this man, entrapping her with the power of his very soul—and instantly pulling the words he demanded from her.

"Louis called me to his office after the performance tonight..." She trailed into a soprano'ed sigh. Sweet mercy, how this man could move his body. His tantalizing little thrusts were a perfect, sweet torment.

"And?" Marcus's tone dipped lower. Sexier. Gaby attempted to simply breathe. When he reiterated the prompt and she still didn't respond, he slowed his pace and eased a fraction away.

"No!" she whimpered. "Oh Marcus, please—"

"Louis called you into his office . . .?" Still so infuriatingly controlled. He could taunt her with his beautiful arousal all night, and they both knew it. She hated him. She wanted him.

"There—there were two men waiting there—oh Marcus, *yes*, don't stop—"

"Two men?"

Even in her delirious state, Gaby smiled at the jealous growl undercutting his query. "Two men," she clarified, "from the Prince's Grand Theatre Troupe."

He halted. Completely.

His sword of a stare was now double-edged, apprehension and anticipation playing the two sides. His hands tightened on her waist, his large thumbs pressing the bottoms of her ribs.

She rejoiced in the pain. Perhaps he did care so desperately for her! If only for tonight, perhaps her fate was his fate, too. Her joys, his joys.

And her triumph, his for the sharing.

"The troupe producers want to see me," she said, unable to hold back her smile. "They're coming to the *Hamlet* opening night next week, and they want to talk to me after the show."

His reaction wasn't exactly what she expected. Honesty be spoken, it wasn't *at all* what she expected. Two moments of unmoving silence. Three. Gaby's smile faded. For a moment, she almost thought she'd caused some super-real seizure beneath that glorious chest, and had just killed the only man she'd ever love.

But then, Marcus Drake Henry Stafford smiled back at her.

Not just any smile. Not his scampish lad's smile or his sultry lover's smile. Not even his approving mentor's smile, which she half expected even in their current positions.

His lips parted on the biggest, whitest, most powerful smile she'd ever seen on a man's features.

His joy was radiant, as if every star above had heard him wish for this moment. He moved her to tears. The first sob came with his buoyant upthrust, at last joining their bodies in a jubilant bonfire. Their souls surrounded the blaze, taking up the chorus of their passion song, carrying their bodies to the shattering cymbals and crashing drums of climax.

When the culmination came, Marcus ripped open the couch cushion as he pumped his searing flood into her. Gabriela joined his name to the collected tears on her lips. Absolute emotion claimed her senses as absolute ecstasy claimed her body.

Dear God, she yearned, that they could claim this moment as their forever. She looked down, trying to memorize him, so taut and dark and magnificent beneath her. Loving her. Completing her.

At least...for now.

And her tears came softly again, making dewdrops upon the black waves of his hair. Marcus said nothing, letting her shed them.

The feelings of two, released in the tears of one.

Tears of gratitude for this nirvana they had.

Tears of longing for what could never be.

★ ★ ★ ★

He insisted on celebrating. Gaby's pleas to remain right where they were, even coupled with a valiant nuzzle to his collarbone, didn't falter his determination. Neither did her blatant attempt at seducing him into the rose-petaled paradise of a bed *he'd* created. Marcus merely hauled her up, smacked her with a brisk kiss, and ordered her into the lace dream of a gown he seemed to produce from nowhere. "Be ready in ten minutes," he decreed. "We have *much* celebration to attend."

As usual, the man stood by his command to the letter. Ten minutes and five seconds later, he whisked her into the sparkling London night, the air kissed by enough of summer's approaching warmth to imbue their adventure with a caress of magic. With his rogue's grin firmly in place again, he offered a hand to her, carrying a beautifully packed picnic basket in the other.

And then he gave her a more staggering gift than his smile.

As they walked down the deserted city streets, he sang to her. Softly, lifting just a whisper of volume...yet opening her world anew with his soul-deep breaths of bass that soared into heart-held prayers of tenor. It was a world where knights still fought for the favors of princesses, where explorers crossed half the globe for their queen...and lovers faced death for each other. A world where honor was more than a word and love was a treasure instead of a toy.

"Like lovers do their love," he continued to tell her in song, "so joy I in you seeing. Let nothing me remove...from always with you being."

The rest of the courtly ballad took them down St. Martin's Lane, across Trafalgar Square and into the moonlit beauty of St. James's Park. Marcus continued to hum the melody as they followed a path along the park's largest lake, skittering tree leaves now his accompaniment.

But he severed the song on an abrupt step as they emerged from a bower of willows. Gabriela instantly knew the reason why.

Along the opposite bank of the Thames, they beheld the stately silhouette of Whitehall.

She felt his thoughts coil away as his fists curled at his sides. But he couldn't shove away all his revelations from her, not after how intimate they'd been tonight. She glimpsed his battle between memories of a lifelong past—and the lust to destroy what the fire of 1698 hadn't.

To make complete cinders of the site where Raquelle had taken him on the first step toward damnation.

"God's wounds," he finally rumbled. He dropped his head and emitted a rough cough. "I walk past here all the time. The bloody place never affects me anymore."

The argument to that was blatant—and she let her logic hurl it.

But never two hours after a nervy mortal has all but ripped your insides asunder, Mr. Stafford. Never after you've been drained of so many defenses, or stripped of so many barriers.

Marcus didn't hear, let alone respond. His physical withdrawal mirrored his mental retreat. Gaby could only stand and witness both in helpless silence.

Determined courage gave her the perfect cue for alternative action.

Gently, she disengaged the basket from his fingers and set it on the knoll behind them. She lifted her hands and scooped up both of his, purposely standing with Whitehall behind her.

"Marcus," she whispered, "I understand. And yes, I hurt sometimes, too, when I think of all the muck of the past. But I don't let the hurt win. I summon the *good* memories. Remember all the beauty and happiness you found at Whitehall. Remember the *good.*"

She held her breath for an eternal pause—until he gathered her close, pressing his lips to her temple.

"You are right, sweeting. I nay think Good Bess would be kind about the remainder of her good halls being torched to the ground."

Gaby pulled back enough to look in his eyes. "You really knew Queen Elizabeth?"

To her surprise, he chuckled. "Everybody knew her. She was a beloved and respected sovereign; generous with her wit as well as her rage."

She tilted her head, studying the reminiscent haze in his eyes. "Tell me more."

To her exhilaration, Marcus smiled wider. He drew her near again, drawling into her ear, "Ye want to know of Elizabeth's fine court, do ye?"

He broke the contact, but only to spin her into a courtly pirouette while dipping his gallant bow. Gabriela couldn't help a giggle as he bent and brushed her knuckles with a courtier's kiss. That laughter stuck in her throat when he lifted his head back up. The teasing glints in his eyes had become an eddy of silver swirls, heating her with a contradicting message to his mannered chevalier. Her breasts tingled. Her most secret core turned hot and wet.

"Court's unwritten rule number one," he told her, voice thick, "the more chaste the kisses, the more lecherous the man."

The whirlpool in his stare deepened. He drew her in closer. Gabriela willingly let him. Yet when just a whisper of night separated them, he spun her around again—an action she'd have taken as a snap of anger, if not for the increasing need she caught in his starfired stare.

He yanked her back, shoulders against his chest, head in the crook of his neck...her bottom against his arousal. He began to rock her, sinuous and slow, dragging her pliant form with him into intense slides of motion. He surrounded her, hard and irresistible. He possessed her, body and mind. He was passion barely reined. Animal barely tamed. Darkness barely dimmed.

His voice came again at her ear, mesmerizing and melodic.

"The days of Elizabeth's court were a wondrous time. Many called all of us the center of the Renaissance...the rebirth."

"I wonder why," Gaby slipped in on a sardonic breath. She felt a newborn herself in this spellbound moment, her body clumsy and weak against the fluid force of his.

"'Twas much to learn." He suggestively nipped at the hollow of her neck. "Aye, we all felt as babes each new day, discovering new beauty and knowledge about the world then sharing it in song or poetry, or perhaps by paintbrush or sculptor's spatula."

Gabriela pout. "Was that *all* you did, sir?"

His grip tightened, almost as if scolding her for the thinly disguised innuendo—until his other hand descended to her abdomen. His fingers, long and magical, pressed the flat of flesh, bringing tighter against his heat and power.

"Nay," he growled, his voice vibrating into her nape. "'Twas not all, my curious maid. 'Twas not all by far."

Gaby's eyes slid shut. His voice drugged her, a spell of his desire. "Go on," she whispered.

"Well..." His tone gained the wistful warmth of remembrance. "The evening's revelries always began with the feast. Dear God, the endless feast...but I always did enjoy the toasts more than the food." She felt him indulge a small smile. "Jesu, how we all vied to come up more grand and eloquent ways to salute Bess. One eve, Sir Walter—"

"Raleigh?"

"The one." He said it as if merely confirming the name of his horse. "Now, Sir Walter delivered this toast" —he gave an annoyed grunt— "by the time he finished, the bloody wine had become another vintage."

Gabriela laughed—then smiled as she really saw that

magnificent hall, candlelight casting a rich glow on silks and satins, velvets and furs, pearl-draped breasts and hose-encased thighs. Thighs like Marcus's, solid and powerful, in full view all night, endlessly enticing a woman, forcing her thoughts down wicked paths...

"And after the feast?" She wondered if he heard the tension in her tone—or comprehended the heat that prompted it, pulsing stronger in her core by the minute.

"Ahhh." Ohhh, yes. He *knew*. "The after. My favorite part. In the after, my fair lady, we had the *dance*."

More clearly than the visions behind her eyes, the music began in her head. The dulcet blend of recorder, dulcimer, drum, and tambourine made her feet move without thinking, without caring. She didn't know the name of the dance and didn't care; she only accepted Marcus's mental tutorial with open joy. She'd longed to know of the world which had created him but had never expected to become part of it.

Of all the gifts he'd given her, this was the most precious.

They moved with each other in the moonlight, uncaring about time or place, stepping, dipping and circling in time to the song flowing between them. Every time Gabriela glanced to him, a mysterious smile filled his face...and a thickening stare. Amazing. As the courtly choreography dictated, they only touched at the hands, but with each brush of fingers or clasp of palms, Marcus stoked a warmth that grew in her center...an odd, almost frightening heat, like watching a bonfire through mullioned glass. She didn't know whether to welcome it or run from it. To surrender or fight.

They danced on. Prismic dew drops sprayed off her sweeping skirts. Deepening night urged the wind higher, lifting Marcus's black waves off his face, redefining his jaw into more formidable angles. Soon, Gaby couldn't pull her stare from the sight of him. Their glances became a fusion of gazes. Fleeting touches became longer hand clasps...then daring caresses to waists, to faces...to eyes and cheeks and lips...

When the music faded to a stop, Marcus took the single step remaining between them. And, strangely, dropped his arms to his sides. Gabriela's arms followed. They stood, both breathing hard, the tension thick and sweet between them.

It was torment. She wanted to touch him...everywhere. She longed to push that soft velvet over his hard shoulders, slide those sinful breeches down his long legs then run her hands over every defined inch of him...

But that yearning was also the emotional steel in the invisible shackles around her arms. What if she broke those bonds and showed how deeply she needed him now more than ever? What if she whispered that the producers' visit had showed her the lines in a new script, called *petrified insecurity*? What if she told him how terrified she was about coming so far with the dream, only to fail now? Only to fail *him.*

She forced her lips around safer words. "What did the court do when they finished dancing?"

For a long moment, all she received as response was the whir of a cicada. Marcus still stood, motionless and mesmerizing, his stare darkening by the second. Her apprehension threatened to become dread—until he beamed a smile of full joy for the second time tonight. That perfect, powerful smile razed the most frightened corners of her...

But before she could recover enough to smile back, he switched the look again. It turned suggestive. No, it was outright risqué.

"Who says we are finished dancing?" he murmured.

Maybe she was worried too much about smiling—when there were much better things to grasp for. Gaby proved her instant approval of that by locking her arms around his neck. Pulling hard. And guiding his damnably sexy mouth directly onto hers.

Marcus groaned, sealing the surety of his readiness for her. The bold plunge of his lips and tongue swiftly reestablished his domination of their dance during their new positioning of the "steps" to the grass below them. They gasped and kissed, bodies twining and heating through the sweetly torturous confines of their clothes.

The earth embraced her from below. The sky careened overhead, a vast fabric of stars and wind and moon—and Marcus. He molded his body into the crux of hers, rocking against her in heated imitation of the union they craved.

She sighed. He moaned. They writhed harder and faster, night dew and night wind whirling around them, through them. She slid her hands around his thighs, urging him to thrust harder—but he suddenly broke his lips away on a guttural groan. The sound echoed into her, eliciting a strange combination of intrigue...and terror.

"Marcus?" she uttered. "What's—"

"*Stop.*" He stilled atop her, a shudder claiming his big body. "Sweet God, Gabriela, take your hands from me. Just for a moment, love—please."

But in that instant, in the raw tremble of his voice, a deep feminine resolve overrode her apprehension. Gabriela didn't move her hands an inch. And that same womanly instinct told her Marcus didn't want her to, either.

"Gabriela. *Fuck.* Please!"

"Why?" she whispered. "Oh why, when I need you like this...need to touch you..."

She squeezed harder. The soft leather felt amazing around his lean, muscled buttocks. She sighed in pleasure. He sucked in sharp air. "Sweeting, I will lose control—"

"But I want you to lose control."

"Nay!"

"Yes." She skidded her hands over his torso, jerking free the ornate ties of his shirt along the way. "Yes."

"You know not what you ask."

She knew exactly what she asked. She knew the wild, unthinking response she sought from him—the unlocking of him in his supernatural glory.

Of course, she didn't know exactly what that goal entailed. And, yes, her spine absorbed a frisson of fear at the unknown valley she approached. But the rest of her body, especially her heart, compelled her forward into the mystery.

She raised her head, pressing her mouth to the irresistible jut of his collarbone. "I want to give you pleasure. *Complete* pleasure."

"Vixen," he croaked. "You incredible little vixen. Look— what you're doing—my doublet is falling apart..."

"Good."

A dark sound, half chuckle and half growl, spilled from him. "Bloody damn, Gabriela. Your lips feel so good there..."

"Give it to me, Marcus." She enticed him without mercy, rounding his shoulder with moist nips, grazing his neck with her teeth. "I want you. I want *all* of you this time."

"You—cannot always have—everything you want." He threw his head back, attempting to escape her merciless licks but only straining the ties across his chest tighter...widening her lips' access to his broad, chiseled chest.

She didn't let the opportunity go unclaimed. And claim

him she did—feeling the moment he let his sanity slip, and using it to lift her legs around him.

"Sweet bloody Jesu." He grabbed for her chemise and drawers but found only the curves of her moist, naked flesh. "You are merciless."

Gabriela didn't deliver her prepared comeback. His big hands, with poetry-filled fingers, stroked magic into her skin and her senses, robbing her thoughts, stealing her lucidity.

"Touch me, Marcus," she finally pleaded. "Don't stop touching me."

He repeated several earthy oaths, Elizabethan-accented phrases she didn't understand, before breathing, "So wet. Oh, love...you are so wet and ready for me."

"Take me..."

His responding growl was the most beautiful music he'd produced tonight. Savage and masculine, the sound punctuated his urgent tugs, at last freeing his magnificent sex. The hard, perfect stalk jutted from the break in his breeches, the drops on its crimson crown gleaming in the moonlight.

The next instant, he was inside her. Gabriela welcomed him home with shameless sighs though she strained as hard as she could to keep her wits as they made love. She longed so deeply to watch him this time. To behold his face in all its otherworldly power as he found his ultimate release...

But the intent faded as quicksilver light engulfed more of her body...as molten silver droplets replaced her blood and tears...as the world became the silver-hot scream and silver-soft sibilance of Marcus.

Marcus.

His hardness, buried in the core of her. His magnificent arms, lifting her off the ground to hold her tighter. His torso, taut with exertion yet not sweating a drop, lungs and heart pumping a wild madness against her own.

It all made her crave more of him. Oh yes, she felt him, every flawless muscle straining against her, every breath resounding through her, but she didn't *feel* him; not the way he'd made her feel his courtly world just minutes past. She wanted to know every degree of the otherworldly heat that gave his eyes the magic of lightning and his limbs the strength of thunder. She longed to touch, smell, and hear the world with *his* fingers, nose, and ears.

Most of all, she yearned to know how her body felt around him, tight and welcoming, drawing out the most precious seed from him...

The scrape of the matter was, she knew she could. That completion was just a prick of her skin away. She longed to be truly one with this man, to share his deepest dreams and darkest nights. And she'd complete the circle by making him part of her—the biggest, brightest part. When he woke, he'd see the sunset through her eyes. She'd give him the dawn to dream of as he slipped off to sleep.

Their hearts inside each other. Their lives entwined.

As the dream filled her mind, Marcus's sex swelled against her womb. His cock beat hard on her walls as he drove hard toward his zenith. With each thrust, he shuddered and growled, losing more of his logic. His heartbeat raged against her breasts. His groan filled her head.

And his mouth panted at her neck—his teeth just inches from her jugular.

The time was right. The time was now.

Gabriela swallowed just once. Then came to her ultimate decision.

She clutched the back of his head. Then pressed his lips to the throbbing vein in her neck.

"Do it, Marcus," she implored, praying the hot salt of her tears would only seduce his hunger more. "Initiate me. Make me yours for the rest of my life."

CHAPTER THIRTEEN

Aye! Marcus's senses screamed. *Take her now. Just one sip. Just one delicious taste...*

The torment intensified when he sipped the ambrosia of her tears. A hungering whine clawed up his throat and resounded through his blood, making way for the beast in him. He licked the salty honey from her skin as he pounded harder into her body, lapping at her from cheek to chin to delicious, quivering breasts.

He dipped his mouth to the pulse in her neck again. Eagerly laved the succulent tastes there. Shuddered as the thirst ravaged his control, drowning him in silver savagery.

So close, so hot. You can taste the rich wine of her already...

"Yes." Her whisper lured him closer to the edge of insanity's sweet abyss. "Marcus, please!"

Nay.

What was this? What was going on? Gabriela, his luminous and fearless Gabriela, now an *ally* with the monster she had vowed to help him fight? Pleading with him to initiate her into a world so opposite her courage and life? So easily betraying herself—and him?

With a roar, he catapulted away.

Through interminable moments, he could not move from his hands and knees. His head sagged as his lungs heaved the pungent grass and dirt his fingers clawed up.

Behind him, Gabriela waged a similar struggle for air. Her

rough breaths gave way to a gulp. "Marcus—"

"*Silence.*" He closed his breeches with furious jerks. "Set your clothes aright, Gabriela."

"No." She lunged for him. Like a night beetle caught in sudden light, he scrambled from her. "No," she persisted, "not until you listen—"

"Listen?" Rage blasted his gut and shot him to his feet once more. "*Listen* to more lies from your fleeceful mouth?"

She bolted to a stance as rigid as his, grass clumps turning her hair into a wild forest, fingers working more creases into her skewed gown.

She looked a mess.

She also looked more beautiful than he ever remembered.

God damn her.

"You think I *lied* to you?"

Marcus spun away. He had to escape the fierce sheen of her stare before it razed his senses anew. But even that was another deception, aye? Copper trying to pass itself off as gold.

"Little thinking had to be done," he returned. "You made your ultimate ambition more than clear, sweeting."

He heard her sharp skip of breath. Then nothing. Then nothing *but* her breaths, coming harder as she paced to him. Hard and fast—the only way she could stay. He knew because he felt every stinging drop of them. *God.* She made sure no mental walls stood between them *now.*

In other words, she took advantage of every manipulating trick in the book.

Well, almost every trick. She stopped three steps away from him—perhaps four on her beautiful mortal legs—yet nay attempted to touch him. "What the bloody hell is that supposed to mean?"

A dark chuckle emanated from his gut. The damnable sound tricked Marcus into thinking he could face her once more. But as soon as he did, he nay knew copper from gold again. He could not discern her pain and upheaval from his own. He could not tell—

Her pain? *Her* upheaval?

God's teeth. The chit really had improved her acting. The wobbling tears in her eyes. The goosebumped waver of her chin. All so convincing. She'd become well worth every pound Augustus paid her.

The thought rekindled enough fury for him to turn and close the gap between them for himself. He stopped sharply, wasting only half a breath before snapping up her trembling chin between two fingers.

He spoke to her in a whisper that emulated her breathy pitch. "'I want to bring you complete pleasure, Marcus. Give it to me, Marcus.'" His tone dropped along with his hand. "Bravissimi, sweeting. 'Twas a performance was worthy of a commission from Will himself."

He expected the brunt of her slapping hand. Mayhap a gasp of genteel fury, followed by tears so false, he would have not a shred of trouble laughing himself deeper into his shelter of wrath. Escaping, finally, the sick ache that crushed his chest.

He did not expect her to keep standing there, clearly fighting for strength to step back but wrestling against chains of fear and fury. "I meant every syllable of those things."

"I do not doubt it," he growled. "Not at all—as long as those syllables reaped your ultimate ambition."

At least this time, she gave him the wide-eyed glare. But the predictability of her reaction stopped there. Where Marcus had expected—hoped for?—overdramatic outrage, this woman once more somersaulted his world with the intensity of her steady stare, unmarred by anything except the harsh stain of her pain.

"Is that what you really think? That the only reason I went along with all this tonight was because I *planned* to beg you for initiation? That I had it in mind all along?"

Damn and demons.

He could do nothing but slam his arms across his chest, wondering why he suddenly felt the one on trial. Worse, ruminating why his treasonous cock hardened so fast for the woman, when *her* only goal looked like his slow and tortured death.

"If that had been my intent," she softly added, "why didn't you feel it in my heart or read it in my mind?"

Finally an accusation easily answered. "You forget, sweeting, that earlier this eve, you adequately blocked me from your mind for two hours."

"So that makes me guilty of it now?"

"It lends integrity to the plaintiff."

"Oh, please!" Gabriela paraded toward the lake, throwing hands up at a gaggle of half-awake brown ducks. "Can you believe this?" she asked them. "Tell this man the moon has robbed him of his sanity!"

He had strived for patience. Her antics damned the effort. She was huffing at him like a wife caught with her hand in the emergency money jar. By sweet Bess's grave, if the situation were only so simple. If only they could spend all night battling about things like the children, the house, her cooking, his nose picking...anything, dear God, but things like her self-control, her self-will—

The fate of her soul.

"Damn it." He reached her side in one resolute stomp. "This is not some glorious game, Gabriela. Your moves count on a very real playing board now. True forces of spirit are at work, with real resonant consequences." He swallowed hard while drawing her close again. Her mortal flesh and bones felt so fragile in his grip, as breakable as burlap and twigs if he so chose. "*I love you*," he gritted. "It would rend me in half to be the one who ever hurt or endangered you. Do you not understand that by now? Can you not comprehend 'tis why I ordered you not to speak of initiation again?"

"But it's a ridiculous order!" Her glare went up in enraged copper flames. "So no, I do *not* understand. I am quite certain I don't wish to, either."

His throat convulsed. Fighting his fury was now a supreme skirmish even for his superworldly senses. *Reckless, foolish wench.* If she comprehended a speck of the slap she dealt, so casually spitting on the words he proclaimed from his deepest heart...the dams of his restraint were strained thin as rice paper beneath vinegar.

"Oh, sweeting." His voice was a vibration of low, broken thunder. "You had better understand. You had better *start* to understand."

"Why?"

In the space of the question, she switched the keys of their embrace. *She* became *his* jailer, her love-filled gaze and her brave-set chin becoming beautiful chains around the felon of his three hundred year-old cynicism.

"Oh, Marcus...I'm sorry. I simply cannot accept the ugliness you speak of. If initiation is half the miracle you say it is, then I can think of no sweeter gift you can grant me."

"*Miracle?*" He snorted. "Gabriela!"

"I want to fuse my soul with yours, Marcus. I want to bind my heart to yours, to make my thoughts become yours so we'll never truly be apart again. What's so wrong about that? What's so horrid?"

"Stop." He yanked her hands into the grotto of his own, holding them between the rapid beatings of their hearts. "*Stop it*. You know not of what you speak."

"Perhaps," she conceded after a weighted moment. "Perhaps I don't know of it all." She lifted her gaze again to his. "But I know I'm not afraid."

He dropped her hands and swung away. "Then you're a damn fool."

He had not stepped away far enough. She darted in front of him again, twining arms around his neck, her entrancing curves pressed to him. She burrowed her lips against his neck like a kitten seeking comfort. "I want to give you sustenance, Marcus. *My* sustenance."

"Dear...God." It grated out of him before he could think. As if he *could* think.

"My heart, beating with yours."

"Gabriela," he warned.

"My blood, flowing in your veins."

"Cease this. *Now.*" He forced her away with shuddering arms. *Stop it before I give in to your heinous seduction, you muddled, magnificent girl.* "Stand away from me, woman."

"Why?"

That word again. Damn her, that soft, beautiful word—the one she knew how to wield with the ruthlessness of a cutpurse. Her body, her words, her taste, her life...

No. Goddamnit, no!

"Why, Marcus?" She repeated it with such subversive

care. Damn her, as if she cut through the chaos of his thoughts and saw how perfectly she embodied his Venus and Aphrodite, his Beatrice, his Eve, his dreams and hopes, his weakness and downfall. "Why stop?" She tunneled long, warm fingers to the back of his scalp. "When it's what we both want? What we both need?"

He tore away by two rough steps. His head fell but only for a moment. When he looked to her again, he knew what she saw, for it seared every corner of his mind first. The full, hellish power of his eyes was a mix of silver and blood that made even other vampires recoil.

"You little fool," he seethed. "'Tis not what we both want and certainly *not* what we both need—because you will give me more than your blood." He held no raging note of his voice in check, either. "Look at me, Gabriela! *Look*. I am not man. I am monster. You will be a mental slave to a beast!"

Damn her again. She did not drop an inch of her stance, indeed holding herself with all the serenity of Aphrodite. "That's my decision to make, not yours."

"God's bloody bodkin it is."

Her frustrated sigh should have come as a relief. Instead, the defeat in her heart jerked on his own like a seven-ton anchor, landing them both in a sea of angry silence.

"Damn you, Stafford," she finally rasped, voice heavy with tears. "I'm not asking you to infect me with the plague."

"Nay, Gabriela," he replied, now weary as dawn approached. "You are asking much worse."

★ ★ ★ ★

Gabriela noticed the change the moment she stepped through the stage door the next afternoon. The little things told her.

A compliment on her hat from a passing stagehand. The way the ballet girls nodded to her instead of giggling at her. Even Louis's gentle manner in giving her a blocking switch for Act Three due to a malfunctioning scenery pulley.

Word had traveled swiftly down Drury's backstage halls. In the wake of the visit from the Prince's Grand Theatre Troupe scouts, she'd finally been relieved from the role of cast cuckoo.

Over the following days, more "little things" added up, increasing the feeling her life had become an amazing dream. "Our living sunshine," said a card accompanying two dozen yellow roses from the orchestra. "A survivor, even of our teasing," came the ballet's note, as adorably awkward in apology as they were strikingly graceful on stage. But the fly crews rendered her favorite accolade. Their catcalls of, "Go win those blokes over, champ!" would live in her fondest memories forever.

Yet the victory rang hollow. The applause, at last begun, fell on her deafened ears.

Marcus had departed her soul.

Oh, she still saw him. Every night, an hour after final curtain to the minute, he materialized from the stage right shadows, leather-bound copy of *Hamlet* in one big hand, tersely reminding her where they'd broken rehearsal the previous night. He answered no questions and responded to no comments except what related to that evening's script section. In all their preceding rehearsals combined, Gaby had never seen him more committed in body or dedicated in mind.

She'd also never reached her senses so far into his, and encountered nothing but locked doors.

She would've started wondering if she'd dreamed the

months of their affair, if the sight of him still didn't incarnate her fantasies so completely. Every inch of him was still complete strength of shadow, desire of darkness...and even without their spiritual link, commanding as midnight. And still reigning over his gaze, so ageless and guileless and endless, was the unguarded longing of silver-tipped morning mist...

"How now, Ophelia?"

The perfect inflection of the words prompted her back to the present. As she turned to where Marcus waited after feeding the cue, she fumbled through her memory. Damn it, she would have to admit she'd been oblivious to his first reminder. Or worse. Admit she'd been occupied with lusty thoughts of him.

"Errrr..." She flashed a sheepish smile and paced across the stage. "Just one moment." She stalled, fidgeting with her gown. "I'll remember, I prom—"

"Act Four, Scene Five." He bit the syllables to shreds. "Nearly your last scene in the play. Is it too much to ask that we get through this tonight, as you open in this tomorrow eve?"

Her memory easily found the line now. But the breath she took to commence the words came out a harsh sigh, instead.

She attempted looking at him. Marcus had already dropped his head back over his script, nose buried between the pages with an intensity having nothing to do with the excitement of the reading matter.

And in that moment, she knew she wouldn't utter another word of that bloody play tonight.

She took three determined steps at him.

He peered up, puzzled by her silence. She took two more as his left eyebrow fell. His hand tautened around the script's aged binding. His lips parted, lending him the look of a cornered panther.

"Gabriela..."

She expected the warning. It actually strengthened her. He still cared enough to get angry.

She yanked the script from his hold.

"Gabriela."

"I know, I know." She tossed the book into the stage left wings. "I open tomorrow night." Allowing no time for his protest, she lowered her hand into his, forcing his fingers around hers. "I'd like to know just one thing." She leveled it in a fusion of whisper and demand. "Are you going to be here to see me?"

He didn't try to release her. Instead, he scowled into the wings, as if wishing to join his script there. "What the hell are you talking about?"

"Just answer the question."

Unbelievable. She finally made Marcus Stafford squirm.

The man took to the experience as well as a flash singer thrown into an Italian opera. "Damn it."

"Never mind." Gaby shoved away. "I suppose I know your answer now." A bitter laugh bubbled to her lips. "I don't believe it," she uttered. "Even three hundred years of existence haven't taught your mule-stubborn brain a thing."

He snapped his sights back at her. His eyes glinted like newly sharpened daggers. "What the hell do you riddle about?"

"No riddles." Gaby hardened her stare but gentled her voice. "Just the truth." Silence. A floorboard creaked in the stage right wings. The building itself strained in the density of their unmoving confrontation. Just as softly, she asked, "You're still trying to make up for it, aren't you?"

A leaden sigh rumbled up his throat. "Gabriela, what the—"

"Your only 'sin.' Falling prey to Raquelle's game. You're trying to earn atonement for it, even now. You're still aching to prove yourself a worthy proxy of the Stafford name." She whirled and laughed again, this time at herself. "Saint Genesius, why didn't I see it before? The court has changed but the rules are the same. Instead of marking your mettle in the chambers of Whitehall, you've taken on the cause of a poor little actress with stars in her eyes." As she turned back toward him, she began to slowly applaud, indeed wishing stars filled her eyes instead of hot, heavy tears. "Congratulations, sir," she rasped. "Father would be very proud of your success."

She didn't know why the swift jerk he gained to his feet came as such a surprise. Nevertheless, she scrambled backward in rapid proportion to his thundering advance.

But just as abruptly, he slammed to a stop in front of her. "My *father*," he snarled, "has nothing to do with us."

"Oh, Marcus," Gaby countered in a whisper, "he has everything to do with us."

Compelled by a force she no more understood than controlled, she leaned closer to him. And resisted touching him. She wasn't as successful at fighting the power of his presence. The sensual, beautiful force he'd never stop having over her...

"Don't you see?" she pleaded. "He has everything to do with anything you do." She gently shook her head. "It amazes me that you've lived this long without the guilt eating you alive, Marcus. It devours every step you take, every action you make."

His deep growl vibrated to her toes. "You—you do not have the right—"

"I have every right. I have every bloody right in the world."

He joined a narrow glare to the growl. "Are you finished? Or are there sweets in store for being even more right tonight?"

"Damn you." She pressed a fist to the center of his chest. "*Damn* you!" she yelled. "Damn you for letting me love you, Marcus; for letting me care about you then shutting me out with less regard given a leper! Why did you even come back, you bastard? *Why?*"

How long the world went away after that, she didn't comprehend. She only knew she could no longer fight back the tight hurt and lost tension of the last fortnight. And the loneliness. When would her loneliness be over? When would she get any of this *right* for once?

After a minute—an hour?—his voice seeped through the fog of her tears. His velvet baritone murmured her name again and again. His long, potent fingers curled around her shoulders. His touch, rough and possessive, pressed the stiff lace of her gown against her muscles in imitation of the rough threads in his voice.

"Gabriela...oh, Gabriela..."

"What?" It was more than a little bitter. She didn't care.

"I pray you to understand. 'Tis not a matter of your guilt or mine. For once, simply, you asked too much of me."

She wanted to react by wrenching from his hold. For the first time in days, she watched Marcus as he probed her mind, deciphering that fact. She thanked fate for the miracle—but even more for the tightening of his grip in correlation to his finding.

"I only asked to be closer to you," she whispered.

"In a manner I cannot grant." He reached one hand up, encompassing the back of her head. "I am sorry, my sweet vixen. I cannot."

"Marcus..." She leaned up to layer fervent kisses along the crest of his cheekbone. "There can be nothing wrong about initiation, if two people both want it."

He sucked in an unsteady breath. "There is our plight, then. Both of us do not want it."

"Look at me and say that."

"Gabriela."

"You can't, can you?"

"*Gabriela.*"

"You can't because you like this. Because you want more of this, just as I do."

"*Gabriela!*"

He meant the exclamation to terrify her. A surreptitious trip into his mind verified that. But her poor, flustered love didn't know he'd just aided the opposite effect. Gaby's pent-up fury and frustration smoldered close to the embers of desire, need...wanting.

His outburst was the ignition on those embers.

Starting an inferno.

As the blaze swept through her, Gabriela clutched his face with both hands.

Then crushed her lips to his.

A stunned tremor took over his body. His arms clenched as his hands pressed wondrous heat into her flesh. Those strokes began as tentative but swiftly spiraled in urgency, flames now fanned by their absence from each other.

His lips parted hers. At the first ram of their tongues, his moan echoed through her. At the first clutch of her hands to his chest, silver fire flowed through her fingers, turned into molten heat through her body. When Marcus aligned her hips with his, her drawers were already wet. His erection was already huge.

The conflagration of their desires felt otherworldly already. And so breathtaking. And so utterly, unspeakably right.

In that blaze of a moment, an astounding conclusion struck.

This is enough.

Yes. Oh, yes. Who needed some silly initiation when she had the completion of this man's embrace, the marvel of his touch, the power of his love? She had more than what most women dared to dream of: a love created by the force of fantasy itself, a lover who held the ages in his eyes and magic in his heart.

Marcus insisted on terming his existence a curse.

In this moment, Gabriela thanked fate for the miracle of him.

She hurled that thought out to his heart, needing to retie the cords of their silent bond as fast as possible. She vowed nothing would fray those connections ever again—

Until Marcus tore free from her again.

Gaby gaped. Attempted to step close again. He kept her at bay with the length of one shaking arm. With his other, he dragged his shirtsleeve across his mouth. His lips curled into a humorless grin, above eyes that peered out from the black spikes of his hair. Their depths had once more turned into a frozen silver lake.

"It seems I now return your congratulations, lady," he grated. "That performance was your best yet. Not even Raquelle could better it."

She went dead inside. All the warmth she grappled to hold for the man, all the joy and all the hope, were killed in one slice of words.

A million drops of her heart's blood spilled out.

And yet that heart continued to torture her with its beat, very alive and anguished, as she paced two steps toward the man. Correction: the beast who still fixed her with a cold and unblinking glare.

Then that heart stopped. Just for a moment. As she slapped his face with all the strength left in her body.

Somehow, she found the stamina to turn and leave him, too, for her next cognizant perception came of her dressing room door. She wrenched it open and stumbled inside. She heard herself breathing, as if her head had separated from her body. She let her body tremble in order to breathe.

She needed to cry, didn't she? But why was she pondering such a stupid thought? Wasn't it fine that she didn't? Wasn't it more than fine?

She backed against the door to close and lock it. The smell of satin, feathers, old dust and new rice powder washed over her with as much comforting force as the mother's perfume she barely remembered, the cozy home kitchen she never had—and now, for the first time in her life, could write that deficiency off as no great loss.

How had she wasted so many years pining for a family, dreaming of somebody to love, when love only brought...*this*? The shattering. The crushing. The betraying.

And after all that, the loneliness. Awful and aching. Again.

She was done with buying tickets to this show. From now on, the stages of the world would be her home; every new audience, her family. Pain would exist only in scripts, experienced only through the safe distance of the characters she played.

Nice words, she thought. Maybe someday, they'd actually ring true in her soul.

For now, she pushed from the door with an exhausted sigh, trying not to reach out her thoughts to discern where Marcus had now gone.

Her lungs squeezed her breath into a sharp gasp. The shadows in the room had given up an imposing figure, who oozed like oil into her path.

"Alfonso," she stammered. Though the recognition allowed her to breathe normally again, she was unable to suppress her perplexed scowl.

"Good evening, Gabriela." His patrician mien didn't falter. His features locked down on pleasant and smooth.

Too smooth.

Trying to ignore the strange, cold frisson skittering up her spine, she bustled across the room. "What are you doing here at this hour?"

She almost reached her chair in front the mirror. Almost. Alfonso's hand shot around her elbow with lizard tongue speed. He jerked her back to him so vehemently, she wondered if her shoulder remained in its socket.

"I think the more interesting question is what *you're* doing here at this hour." With the chilling words, his grip curled painfully into her arm. Gaby fought the urge to laugh at the tactic. Maybe once, the action would have instigated a shudder to her toes and a serious questioning of her self-esteem. Now, she didn't lower her head the width of a pin.

As much as she loathed to admit it, Marcus's love had given her that legacy.

"I have told you a thousand times," she stated, "I stay here at night to rehearse. Now, *sir*, please take your hand—"

His bark of laughter cut her short. As he whipped her around, forcing her to fully face him, his mirth twisted into a vicious glare...an alarmingly real version of a penny dreadful cover. "Rehearse? Is that what they're calling it these days?" He dipped his lips just inches from hers. His breath reeked of heavy vodka and cheap brandy. "Hmmm. Tell me, Gabriela, what do you call it when you screw him? Act One? And when he comes inside you—is that curtain call?"

The skitter down her spine burst into fear. "Wh-What are you talking about?"

But a deep, chilling dread already predicted his answer.

"*Don't* play witless with me, Gabriela." Her head snapped back as he dug his fingers into her shoulder, jerking her again. "I saw you and your black-haired lover. I saw you shoving your tongue down his throat, writhing all over him like the slut you really are."

"Alfonso. Now stop this. This—this isn't you." She wished she could believe the words more.

"You're right," he drawled. "It isn't. But maybe it should have been all along." He threw his head back on a laugh. "All I did was try to *buy* you! What a fucking fool. I brought you flowers and furs, when all you wanted was a little rough play. Is that it, Gabriela? To be shoved around a bit? Does that turn you on?"

He released her—hurled her—with a thrust so hard, she slid across her dressing table and crashed into her dressing table mirror.

And any composure she still possessed shattered along with the glass biting into her face and arms.

"Alfonso." She managed it as he grabbed the back of her head, dragging her across the jars and bottles she'd broken, "Alfonso, no!"

"I can do it just like he does, Gabriela. Just watch me. Just *feel* me."

"No—please—"

"Shut up. Shut up, you ungrateful little bitch!"

"Alfonso! Stop!"

She lost count of how many times he hit her. But somewhere in the middle of that bludgeoning hell, her lips formed around another name, praying God he'd hear her desperate rasps. Praying God for her life.

"Marcus."

CHAPTER FOURTEEN

The torment continued into eternity. And he didn't hear. The grieving thought wouldn't leave her mind alone just as Alfonso wouldn't leave her body alone.

She slipped into semiconsciousness as the barrage of slicing pain and grunting expletives continued. Only her heart kept calling out in soundless despair.

Marcus. I'm sorry. I never stopped loving you. I never will.

She retreated within herself as Alfonso threw her to the floor, thrust up her skirts and shoved her legs apart. She ran to the secret place inside, far away and numb, that she hadn't been since the day Lord and Lady Rothschild took Fiona Warfield home instead of her. But this time, she ran to that haven with Marcus. He sang to her again, and they laughed together one last time.

And she almost forgot Alfonso Renard ripping at his trousers as he fell ruthlessly upon her. She almost pretended she didn't hear his slurred, "Here you are, slut," as he readied his body to invade her.

She almost shut out the scream surrounding her senses after that.

But why didn't she recognize her own scream? Even more strange, why did her teeth still press against the back of her clamped lips?

She forced her eyes open and her head up.

And came to the conclusion she'd started to hallucinate.

Through a sticky, bloody mist flowing from her forehead, she focused on Alfonso's contorted features. The comprehension struck that the scream...had been his. He roared it again while cowering in front of a slavering, midnight-black—

Wolf.

The animal shook its haunches free of splinters from the door it had just pounced through. The bottom Alfonso's trouser leg hung in tatters from its huge mouth. The wolf spat the material away before peeling back its jowls in a long, violent snarl, exposing white, vicious teeth.

Gabriela jerked with astonishment. She scrambled to her knees, swiping the blood and hair from her face as she stared at the beast. More specifically, into its eyes.

Ageless, fearless silver eyes.

When I am, however, forced into that situation, I prefer becoming a wolf...

"Oh, my God," she choked.

★ ★ ★ ★

She had barely gotten the words past the bruises swelling her lips and the shock clogging her throat, but Marcus heard. Ah God, how he heard. In wolf's form, he heard, smelled, saw and felt everything with more awareness than his normal abilities.

But the feeling part—that was the worst. After hearing her first scream as he had stood on Drury's deserted stage, he actually flinched as Renard's first blow drove into her. And when the bastard pushed her to the floor, readying Gabriela for his body's violation, Marcus had thrown his head back into a roar that shattered six stage lamps.

Then, swiftly and methodically, he had cleared his mind of everything but one purpose.

To kill Alfonso Renard in the most terrifying, painful manner possible.

The intent swelled higher through him, invading every hackle and haunch of his being, riding the same feral bloodlust that escalated in the moment between his first crash into the room and Renard's astonished glance up. The moment he had seen the maggot kneeling between Gabriela's legs.

That image carried Marcus across the floor now, stalking steadily, barely holding his fury in check—but enjoying every second of Renard's terror nonetheless. A pleasured growl trembled from his jowls. The bastard's last minutes of life would also be his most horrifying, And aye, Renard's blood would be the sweetest nectar to ever flow down his throat.

"What the hell!" He watched more than heard Renard blurt it. The sounds were a tangled garble against the chaos of anger, instinct, and canine awareness dominating his head.

He snarled again, the tang of the pursuit filling his mouth.

He advanced further, backing Renard into the corner behind Gabriela's ruined dressing table.

"What...bloody hell...is this?" Renard shouted. "Gabriela... call...bloody pet off me!"

Marcus coiled his muscles and snapped his jaws, three seconds away from showing the whoreson just who he could brand "pet," when another voice made its way into his This time, echoing *inside* his senses.

Marcus! Marcus, please, if you can hear me, don't do this. Don't do this!

He wanted to tell her to shut up. He wanted to tell her how much he loved her. He ached to say so much—but his animal's brain grappled to form words at all.

Beat...you, he got out. *Raped...you.*

No, he didn't. You got here in time.

Still—deserves—die.

No! Marcus, please! He's not a faceless beggar from the hospital. They'll search for his killer. They'll search for you!

But if she caused him to consider her plea at all, Renard stole that choice from him in the next moment. A broad grin replaced the man's dreading gape. Before Marcus could make sense why, the moron advanced back toward Gabriela.

"Nice poochie," Renard crooned. "Poochie, right? Ah, Gabriela...nice try...almost had me gulled. Looks...like wolf. Clever; clever."

As he passed Marcus, the bastard raked a dismissive hand across his head, nearly ripping one ear off with the motion. "Run along, mutt. Miss Rozina...me...unfinished business." The same hand dove into Gabriela's bodice and squeezed her breast so hard, she cried out. Renard cut the sound short in her throat by backhanding her. The blow was so violent, her head snapped back.

Should not—have done that—maggot.

Marcus leapt for that hand with every raging instinct in his being. His howl resounded through his ears as he bared every tooth in his mouth. He landed perfectly on his prey, crushing bone and flesh. He tore at everything and stopped at nothing, savoring the scent of fear and the climax of victory.

But most of all, reveling in the taste of blood.

He spat two fingers out and snapped his head around for more. Renard's blood was a fine ambrosia, spiked with the elixir of his terror. The man had plummeted to his knees, shrieking and gaping at his bleeding hand as if he lived a nightmare that would disappear if he blinked hard enough.

Haven't—begun—nightmare, bastard, came the delicious morsels of thought through Marcus's brain. He circled the whoreson again, taking his time with every step of his huge paws, relishing his quest for blood for the first time in his existence.

But he should have known she'd be watching. And listening. And coming after him with her inescapable chains of love and concern. *Marcus. Please. No!*

Go—away, he fired back in a mental snarl.

"What...hell is this?" Renard's sob interrupted them. "My—my hand...my hand! That—*thing* bit off...hand! Kill you... this! I'll kill you...goddamn monster!"

"Alfonso!" came Gabriela's shaking rasp—even now, filled with compassion he could not fathom. "Please, Alfonso," she begged. "Don't...another word. Don't...another muscle!"

Renard actually threw back his head on a demonic cackle. A thick sheen covered his gaze, the alcohol and the blood loss taking their toll on his senses. "Or...hound of hell...finish job?" He lowered a sneer at her. "Don't threaten...again, Gabriela. Not your style."

That decided it. Alfonso Renard had lived much too long.

He lunged. Descended hard. Let Renard's terror, sweat, and blood infiltrate his nostrils. Velvet waistcoat and fine lawn shirt came away with one bite. A scream resounded through his head. *Good,* he answered savagely. *Scream—for life—bastard.*

"Marcus—Marcus, no. *Listen* to me!"

He froze. Breaths still frothing through his teeth, senses still swimming with fury, he watched the white of Renard's eyes disappear as the man dropped, fainting into unconsciousness.

Get out, he ordered her. *Get out now. He just made—easy*

for me. Oh, aye; now it was going to be just the piece of cock sweat and him, only the kill and the blood and the exhausted retribution at last. The victory teased the back of his throat.

But Gabriela would not let go. Her voice swept again in his mind, conquering his concentration with her shaking whisper. She wrapped both arms around him despite her dwindling strength, burrowing through blood and fur to pull him back with every ounce of mettle she still possessed.

"Marcus...please...if murder him...have to run." Her tears spilled, warm and sweet, over the hairs inside his ear. A shiver coursed over him. "Marcus...need you. Need you now. Please... don't run. Please...I...need..."

That shiver became full, freezing fear—as her arms went limp and her voice died away.

Gabriela!

"Gabriela!"

His human bellow rang through buzzing senses. He looked down to his crouching arms, bent knees and blood-spattered chest.

He was naked. He did not care. His sights and senses filled with her. A dark crimson gash ran the length of her forehead. More blood trickled from deep cuts down her neck and arms, and splotched the gown now stuck to her thighs and legs. Her wet eyelashes closed on clammy skin, one cheek swelled twice the size of the other, marbled purple and black. Her ripped gown revealed more bruises that fanned across her breasts, in the pattern of spread fingers.

"God," he choked. "God." He yearned to touch her. He pulled back his hand. He was terrified to touch her. "Gabriela. Gabriela." His voice still sounded like another creature. Lost. Alone. So alone without her.

"Nay!" He scrambled off Renard and heaved her close to him. Cold. She was so cold. A cry of raw rage overflowed the room; he barely felt the force of the sound ripping up his throat. He crushed her closer as he leapt to his feet, sprinted down the hall, and up into the catwalks. He held her next to his soul as he took the stairs to their apartment five at a time.

"Damn you, Gabriela," he pleaded the whole way. "Damn you, hold on!"

He kicked the double doors in and sped with her to the bedroom. When he lay her on the coverlet, he didn't know whether to laugh or cry.

A chill no longer claimed her.

The first beads of fever did.

Dread and fury clashed, turning him into a helpless beast who sat there chanting her name over and over again.

But then her lips moved. With *his* name. She shifted restlessly, writhing against the fiery approach of infection.

"Marcus?"

"I'm here." He captured her flailing wrists, kissed her burning knuckles. *What do you want to hear, love? What do you want me to do, to say? I shall say it. I shall do it. Just tell me. Just hang on. Please, just hang on!*

But the bonfire in her body scorched away her ability to hear him. "Hot," she whimpered. "Marcus, I'm so..." She wrested a hand away to pull at her tattered gown, sobbing when the material refused to give at her feeble tuggings. "Marcus... help me..."

"Aye, sweeting." He ridded her of the ruined clothes in the same two seconds. Of course. *Of course*, he berated himself; he should have done so upon identifying the fever. He should have done so many things. He should not have let her leave the stage in the first place. He should have apologized. He should not have been such an inflexible ass!

The beratement propelled him up, into the washroom and back with a basin of water, a clean cloth and a bottle of alcohol he had only used once—gargled the stuff, after Joseph confessed he had accidentally brought a cholera victim for dinner. *That* memory sealed the resolve not to drag her anywhere near the hospital.

He repeated that journey countless times during the next hours, pouring dark pink floods down the sink every time he returned. But her blood and sweat wouldn't cease. No matter how many compresses he applied or bandages he wrapped, the wounds kept draining.

Draining...her strength.

Her life.

He did not stop. He could not. He ceased thinking, conserving his energy only for the steeled fortitude it took to emerge from that washroom, to look at her lying there, broken and bloody, then go to her again, soothing her with soft songs while he tortured her with the sting of the alcohol.

Close to the hundredth time he settled to the mattress next to her, she flailed out, sending the basin shattering to the floor.

"No," she rasped. "No more." Her eyes slid shut, her tongue swiped at her parched lips. With astonishing strength, she clasped his hand and pressed it between her breasts. The grip of death. Though Marcus raged against the realization, he knew it as truth.

"Lay beside me," Gabriela pleaded. "Just come lay beside me, Marcus."

He hesitated one half a moment. Then blew out the candle on the nightstand.

There, in the deep abyss of that night, in the darkness so like the oppressive weight on his heart, Marcus lowered himself next to her. He lay upon a coverlet puddled with blood and did not fight a single pang of hunger. Grief annihilated any sensation in his body. Fear seized every stronghold in his brain.

"No," Gabriela sighed into the thick blackness. "No, Marcus, don't be afraid."

He rose to an elbow, bolstered by hope. "You can hear me again?"

She forced down a dry swallow. "Not in words. Only the feelings." She let out a high sob, drifting to a soft end. "Oh, my love, I'll always know what you're feeling. You're here, in my heart now. Don't you know that? You'll always be here. Even after—"

"*Stop.*" He gulped, too. "Stop speaking that way, damn you."

He would have gladly faced hell that moment for one slap from her in reply. Instead, several more swallows convulsed down her throat, before she tangled her fingers in his hair and pulled him to her sweat-drenched body.

"I'm sorry," she whimpered. "I'm sorry I did this to you. And I'm so sorry I was impossible all those times."

"Nay." He smoothed the hair off her battered, breathtaking face. "I was such an ass. Ah, God, I wasted so much time on anger."

"It doesn't matter now." Her voice was peaceful. Too peaceful. Her head fell back to the pillow as if she drifted off for a nap. "Doesn't...matter."

"Gabriela!" Ice shot up his arms. He jerked her back to him. "Gabriela, damn you, it *does* matter!"

"It's all right." Her head lolled over his arm, her fingers

soft as mice steps on his chest. "I love you. I will always love you. It's all right."

'Tis not all right. 'Tis not *all right!*

His soul screamed the decree to a heaven which no longer listened to him, but he did not care. He no longer believed in a heaven that floated over a world where angels like this were allowed to die by the hand of beasts like Alfonso Renard. Where this woman's life and light were spat back in her face before she had the chance to share them with the world, dying in a pool of her own blood, in the arms of an undead monster who had received more life than he ever earned?

Dear God, that he could trade one hundred years of his misbegotten life for one more of hers. He would give up two hundred breaths for a sigh, a smile. Surrender the beat of his heart and strength of his limbs that she would live and love again.

Dear Jesu.

His strength. *His* heartbeat. *His* life.

The miracle had been in his power the whole time. The one certain way to save her, here and now, beyond any compresses, medicines doctors, prayers.

He almost laughed. Almost. The little vixen was to get her way with him, after all. No other choice remained.

No other choice but to let her die.

He slid his arm from beneath her, laying her back to the wet counterpane despite her weak cry of discomfort. "I know," he murmured, stretching out beside her again, attempting to reassure her with his size and strength. "It will not hurt much longer, I promise."

She only sighed, softly and seemingly happy once more, as he traced silver-soft kisses over her lips, along her jaw, behind her ear...to the smooth skin protecting the main artery in her neck.

The pulse beneath his lips immediately thrummed faster. *Damn.* Oh bloody damn; she smelled so sweet. So warm and right...

Must not take too much, a voice ordered from his brain. *Just enough...*

What was enough? He had never done this before. He hesitated like a lad fumbling through a first tumble with the milk maid. Gabriela actually attempted to caress him, so weak and clumsy, sighing louder. His senses burned. His own pulse galloped, out of control yet never committed so wholly to self-control in his life. *How much was too much*?

Gabriela stole the luxury of deliberation from him. While turning and capturing his lips in a long kiss, she flung limp, weighted arms around his neck. Every inch of their bodies now fitted together, heating his senses without mercy. Her heartbeat echoed through his nerve endings. Her blood coursed warm and close, so very close, beneath his lips.

His let the feel and the scent of her wash through him. Anticipation flooded him in a wave he had never known so completely, with an ecstasy he never imagined. Pure silver sensation throbbed in his toenails, out his fingertips, along his quivering tongue and throat.

He coiled an arm back around Gabriela, returning her embrace with savage intensity. With the other hand, he shoved her hair from her neck, angling her perfectly beneath him.

He lowered his head and scraped her silken skin with one fast-stretching eye tooth.

"Marcus," came her bewildered gasp. "Marcus, what's happening? What are you—"

"Hush." He licked the skin to keep it moist, warm, ready. "Everything is all right. I am making it all right."

"Wh-What? What do you mean?"

He moaned, shaking with frustration...expectation. "I love you so much. Love me, too. Trust me. Surrender to me."

And in a moment, you will truly be mine.

CHAPTER FIFTEEN

Gabriela gasped. At least she thought she did. But her dry and fevered throat convulsed on a breath that no longer seemed available. Breath that wasn't important, anyway. Not after the joyous rush of Marcus's words in her head.

And most incredibly, what they meant.

"*Marcus.*" She whispered it in a rush of amazement and, yes, a twinge of alarm. But not fearing the process wasn't to understand or appreciate it.

She understood this. And God did she appreciate it. Venerate it. Pause in amazed gratitude for it.

She yearned to thank him but it was hard enough, just breathing...straining to live just one more moment for him. "Marcus—I love you too. I—"

She floated away on space and time as his mouth parted, letting out a long groan. And the gentle suck of his mouth.

And the passionate sink of his teeth.

They both froze as he pierced her deep, hard. They both moaned as he drank deep, full.

Then lightning flooded her world.

Lightning, full of life. Of strength. Of Marcus—oh, Marcus: everywhere inside and outside of her.

Marcus.

She was a little boy running in a Shropshire meadow with a pinwheel.

Marcus.

She was a terrified new vampire wandering alone through a black forest.

Marcus.

She was a two-hundred-eighty-year-old vampire, gazing from the Drury Lane catwalks at a dreamy-eyed actress named Gabriela Rozina, and falling immediately, hopelessly in love with her...

Marcus.

I never knew it would be like this.

You're beautiful.

★ ★ ★ ★

He had told her he did not believed in miracles.

But then she told him he was beautiful.

Marcus reeled in wonder at the memory even now, hours later, as he stretched in the sea of blankets that covered his earthen bed, reeling with satiated bliss—and continued astonishment. Not even dawn's approach fatigued him from shaking his head at the wonder of the thought.

Beautiful.

She had said *that* to the monster who drained the very life from her, so drunk with the taste of her, he barely forced himself to stop. Out of his mind with her. Out of control with her. Consumed by the life and love and brilliance of her.

Gabriela.

He'd become a five year-old girl dropping tear-stained daisies on her mother's grave.

Gabriela.

Then an unsure actress, hoping the director could not hear the growl of her stomach over the lines of her audition.

Gabriela.

Then a heartbroken woman, looking up from where her dressing room floor into the silver eyes of a stranger, and thinking him the most beautiful creature she'd ever seen...

Beautiful.

Gabriela.

How did I earn the gift of you?

Her soft chuckle came now as answer to that, betraying her eavesdropping on his thoughts. She earned herself his pardon with a long kiss across his collarbone. Marcus had to admit he had never envisioned this cavern as the site of a quaint "camping" expedition, but when he had finally forced himself away from her, petrified he had taken enough blood to kill her, Gabriela had pulled him back with a vigor nearing *his* in force. She followed that by all but ordering him not to move two inches from her.

Aye; in the sinew of her muscle and the cells of her blood, initiation had already begun its secret wonders.

But in the sea of her thoughts and emotions, Marcus had stirred a hurricane beyond compare—a hurricane he might have managed, had he not found himself sucked in to that vexing vortex, as well.

As usual, his angel expressed the sensation best for both of them. *I never knew it would be like this.*

Jesu, *he* had no idea it would be like this. He had envisioned himself the strong one after the initiation, patiently helping her with the onslaught of perceptions, guiding her through the labyrinth of her supernatural awakening as easily as he navigated her across a Shakespearean plot.

Nobody told him immortals got initiated, too.

Nobody told him about the soaring completion of his own

body and soul. The exquisite loss of self. The shattering flood of feelings. The lifetime of memories, comprised of so many new thoughts and discoveries. He had wanted to stay inside her forever, knowing her world and the way she viewed it... living her incredible life.

'Twas little wonder that when the sun prodded its fingers over the world once more, Gabriela had wrapped herself around him with a cry sounding like an Indian mourning moan. But unlike other mornings, Marcus had no hesitation about picking her up and taking her with him.

But while she let him lead their descent through the inky underground, Marcus wondered how much her "guide" he remained—and if the change heralded the seal of doom for their love. This maze of emotion was such an unknown path for both of them. It would be a huge, epic journey. Memories and dreams, heartaches and hopes, triumphs and losses. The loneliness of the past. The vulnerability of the present.

And what of the future?

He did not know.

And it had been a very long time since he looked into the face of the unknown.

The last time, he had crouched against the wall of a forest cave as Raquelle de Lanya's laughter echoed in his ears.

With that recall came the freezing talons of fear. Instantly, Gabriela convulsed against him, too. She looked up, inundating him with a stare sparked of dark gold alarm.

In another second, those sparks softened to embers of understanding. "It's all right now," she whispered, spanning his jaw with her fingertips. "Raquelle was a lifetime ago. *Several lifetimes.*"

As she melded her lips with his, she fused the words of her

heart to his, too. *Let* me *be your lifetime now. Please say I can stay with you. Say I can stay always.*

He wished he could hide his answer from her—but inside a moment, Gabriela heard his soul's acceptance. And saw the embarrassing fantasies that lived there, too. Picking berries with her on a summer day. Making love to her as the dawn struck a faraway beach. Helping her give birth to their sixth, maybe their seventh, child. Getting sick with her. Growing old with her. Living and loving and dying with her.

The hopeless hopes of a monster. The unreachable heaven to a creature of hell.

Marcus rolled away, wordless and resigned. Gabriela did not let him go so easily. Her fingers pressed at his nude body, coaxing him back toward hers. Forcing him to see her nakedness, too...not just the burnished skin worshiped by the candlelight. The exposure of her soul in her eyes, heavy with golden tears. The revelation of her heart in her watery smile. And the song of her heart, peeling in his senses like church bells on a wedding day.

Don't you know me by now, stubborn grump? I don't care what *you are. I love* who *you are. I love* you.

Suddenly, he laughed. She laughed. And they kissed. Deeply. Passionately.

And for the first time ever, this dank cavern transformed into a magnificent palace. His army of candelabras no longer waged battle against the dark. They illuminated his love. The plops of subterranean moisture and the sighs of night wind were no longer a dirge of loneliness...but a lullaby of enchantment.

Gabriela succumbed to slumber first. Her breaths evened against his chest, drawing him deeper into sleep, as well. In the moments before his drugged senses followed hers, he stole the time to weigh his astonishment at this woman.

She had accomplished it yet again. Transformed his world. Transformed *him*. When viewed through her magical eyes, cobwebs and clay floors formed a castle. The dirt floor of a crypt turned into a luxurious bed.

A beast became the prince of her heart.

My sweet angel...that I could have you here with me forever...

He ordered the thought forgotten. He also banished the additional thoughts, those musings lying too close to the surface of his conscience. Ready to *annihilate* his conscience.

Ready to tell him that at a word from her, he would not stop at initiation next time his teeth met her neck.

Terrifying him more than anything.

Because for one irresistible, carnal fantasy of a moment, forever did not seem such a dreadful place any more.

★ ★ ★ ★

*F*or*ever.*

Gabriela w*anted to* scream as the word resounded in her head for the five hundredth time. But that night, as she sat like a statue for the Times and then the Chronicle's sketch artists, her heart winced the word three more times. As she made polite excuses to the fawning reporters, citing the orchestra's first tunings as her cue for last-minute preparations, she endured another half-dozen reprises.

As she rushed back down the hall to her dressing room, she let her mind finally cry it out to the rafters over her head— and beyond.

Forever. It's been forever, Marcus. I don't care what you say. It's been forever.

Sweeting, came his maddening, calm response, *look at your clock. We only parted an hour and thirty ago.*

See? What did I tell you? Forever!

His chuckle swirled through her nerve endings as if he only followed a pace behind her, admiring how the sapphire blue silk of her maiden's costume flowed around her hips. She swore she could even hear a wolfish growl of appreciation, too.

Gabriela tossed him a mental huff, stomped into her dressing room then glared at her reflection in the floor mirror. Louis had helped her clean the room's mess from last night without a question, even when she refused to have a new mirror for the dressing table ordered. He'd produced the floor mirror a few minutes later, taking in the nearly-healed gash on her forehead with the same frowning but quiet regard.

Since then, her emotions had ridden a runaway cart of confusion. Up and down. Side to side. Desperation then elation. Galloping farther from her control every minute.

And the only being able to help her find the reins now sat somewhere on high, laughing at her.

She decided she hated him.

You do not hate me.

She closed her eyes and surrendered to a delicious shiver. His voice was such a spellbinding mix of music and masculinity.

"Yes, I do." She fired off the retort before his words could sooth her ire. "Go away."

She'd forgotten the man read her mind better than he knew her body. *Gabriela.* His voice echoed through her being like a damn prayer, intense and unwavering. *Gabriela...*

Her knees gave way to the attack first. She slid to the

floor, crouching into a helpless ball, wondering—yet strangely hoping—if she'd forever be like this without him by her side. She'd used his very marrow to heal as they'd slept through the day. The vitality now coursing in her blood...his. Her muscles and tendons were like new because of the strength she gleaned from his.

The same strength he insisted she use to leave him "an hour and thirty" ago, despite the agony of taking one step from him.

"What?" she finally retorted to him.

This night is part of why you clung to life for me last eve. 'Tis what we have worked for, dreamed for. I will not let—

"*We* have worked for," Gaby retaliated, snapping her sights toward the ceiling. "*We* have dreamed for. Notice a common thread of scripting, sir?"

His sigh echoed in her head. *Sweeting, this is your night.*

"*Our* night. You should be here. This means nothing without you."

But I am with you.

"Ohhhh, no." That gave her incentive to jerk to her feet. "Don't even *try* to go that direction, sir. I'm much smarter about those tactics than you and we both know it."

No "directions," Gabriela. No "tactics." Just you...and me.

She couldn't sling back anything to that. She literally... couldn't. She watched her hand reach for her hairbrush, completely independent from her will or her mind. It was like another entity had taken up residence inside her. Gabriela knew she should be terrified by the possession but a captivated smile bloomed on her lips, instead.

I am here. Right now, right here. Beside you, inside you. Forever, for always. You have only to look for me. To take my love, to use my strength.

"Marcus—"

Ssshhh.

"Marcus!"

Power consumed her as she'd never fathomed, supernatural and super real, convulsing her so violently, she felt the hairbrush snap in her hand before her foot punched a chunk out of her dressing screen. So strange, so odd—why did her leg look the same, too skinny at the ankle and too curved at the calf, foot still encased in dainty pale blue slippers, when she'd obviously become another creature? A beautiful, powerful being; not just roaming the night but in command of its power...

A desperate, aching being...wanting just to love and be loved.

Oh, Marcus.

I love you, too.

She returned to reality by slow increments. She stretched as if waking from a long and restful nap.

Despite Louis's wall-shaking bang at her door.

"Gaby! Five minute call to curtain. You're on in twenty. You bloody well better be ready, missy!"

She only smiled. Stretched again. Then stood.

Then wrapped her arms around herself and spun a delirious circle in the middle of the room—all the while envisioning a black-haired, sinfully handsome someone forced to his own feet on the apartment's Persian carpet, chuckling while following her.

Her smile inched higher as the back of her brain carried Marcus's harried mutter.

Crafty wench.

Not my fault, she countered. *You make me feel too good, Mr. Stafford.*

A determined snort. *We shall see who feels too bloody good by the end of this eve.*

Is that a promise?

'Tis a fact. Especially if my instinct proves correct.

Instinct of what?

Of Davis Webber himself leading your standing ovation.

Gabriela laughed and yanked him through one more dizzy spin.

She'd never been more ready to be on stage in her life.

Or more excited to be alive.

★ ★ ★ ★

So this is what it felt like to be alive.

Marcus contemplated the conclusion as he hurried down the private hall to his box. The velvet of Mum's handmade finery rustled in time to the echoes of his polished boots—and the unstoppable thrum of sensations coursing through him, all courtesy of Gabriela. So this was what it all meant...this was real emotion, manifested in real physical reactions...

Sweet Jesu.

He felt her steps as she moved through the stage wings to await her cue. Anticipation, dipping skin back and forth between hot and cold, a brief, sweet insanity before the escalation of her heartbeat. Certainly the entire building heard *his* now, too.

His sights kept following hers, narrowing in focus toward the scene the stagehands now pumped with a fine "Denmark mist." He felt her suspended breath as the curtain rose, the audience stilled, and another Drury Lane production began its opening performance.

He did not move. This was it. His Christmas Day, his World Exhibition. The state of being alive. The experience he'd waited several lifetimes to know again.

The thought had just pummeled his brain when her tiny but joyous whisper wafted through his head. *Oh, Marcus. Isn't this exciting?*

Exciting. If one considered the transformation of their gut into a coal-heavy lump, appetizing as the pit it came from... well aye, then...exciting.

He made a quick mental note to avoid all future contact with "exciting."

He adhered to that contract, as well—for a whole quarter of an hour. He adhered all the way up until the moment Gabriela appeared on stage.

And lightning struck his world.

Her performance transcended their expectations. She knew it, as well. Marcus felt her exhilaration as the scene progressed. He also felt her seeking the memories he had shared during their trip to St. James's Park, using the images to transport herself to courts replete with Hamlets, Horatios, Claudiuses, Gertrudes...and tragic young heroines named Ophelia.

She was entrancing.

He selected the description well, if the audience had any say about it. When "Ophelia" exited from her sole scene in the first act, a rare wave of spirited applause broke out to follow her.

Marcus did not watch the act after that. He leaned back in his seat, closed his eyes, and let a wide smile spread as he raced back to her dressing room with her, accepted the accolades along the way with her, pressed hands to her joy-flushed cheeks with her.

And let his heart fill with the breathless, beautiful words from her. *Thank you, my love. Thank you.*

Her lengthy scene in Act Two elicited the same crowd response, resulting in an intermission full of more backstage cheers and adulation.

"You're so beautiful!" three ballet chits chorused.

"You're so *good,*" Donna seethed good-naturedly.

"Will Shakespeare himself couldn't have played it better," Louis stuck his head in to murmur with pride.

In response to it all, she shared the same secretive smile with him.

A hypnotizing version of that smile accompanied her entrance into Act Three—but beneath her poised chin and beautifully-turned expressions, she reached out even more for him, pleading for the ongoing surety of his presence. Every time, Marcus answered by twining his strength, his assurance, his very soul tighter to hers.

The performance progressed to a scene that many deemed the true test of a magnificent "Ophelia." The sequence not only followed the famous "to be or not to be" speech but involved Hamlet and Ophelia exchanging a bordello's worth of double meanings. Subtlety was essential and timing completely critical.

To tighten her pressure, Gabriela had no stage full of other performers to render reactions or offer forgotten lines. Shockingly, Augustus had not written in any swordplay or moving scenery to dilute the audience's scrutiny, either. Gabriela had to trust only her instinct, her talent and her heart—and, God willing, the equal portions of each in the

"Hamlet" across the stage.

Marcus experienced every drop of her worry, though he did not share it. He had bloody near commanded Augustus to award the production's lead to Sean Smythe, a young actor he had met while brooding along the south bank in January. Those were the months Marcus had brooded much, lamenting over a sable-haired angel named Gabriela who, at the time, had no idea he existed. Upon ducking into the Vic music house for a respite, he found poor Sean playing a forgettable role to an unappreciative mob with highly *un*forgettable dedication. Sean would be a perfect Hamlet for this production.

He would also complement Gabriela like fine velvet beneath a fresh rose.

Marcus had been resoundingly right on both counts.

Now he leaned forward, hands braced to knees and sights riveted to the stage, to absorb every moment of Gabriela's ultimate victory over tonight's crowd.

She stepped to her place center stage as Sean temporarily disappeared into the wings—another of damn "renovation" to Will's original script. According to Augustus, the new blocking moves created longer audience interest by keeping the actors in motion, allowing Sean to add a black cape to his costume, guaranteed to make him the object of tea salon swoons by tomorrow afternoon. Marcus had to confess, a sliver of his anticipation lay in finally seeing this renowned cape.

But after a notable pause, neither Sean nor the cape appeared.

Murmurs rippled through the crowd.

A furrow danced on Gabriela's brow. She smoothed it just as quickly. Seemed there was a backstage snag though Marcus discerned not a flutter of panic from her. She turned a page in the "poetry book" she held, acted an amused laugh at something she "read," and executed a winsome pirouette, enough to show the women her grace and the men her legs.

The audience murmured again, this time in approval.

Sean still did not reenter.

A deeper furrow etched Gabriela's brows.

A heavy thunk sounded from the wings.

The audience jumped. She did, too. She pressed a hand to her chest, darted a glance toward his box. *Marcus. This isn't right.*

Ssshhh. I am here. It is likely Sean fumbling with that bloody cape.

I know, but—

Keep moving. Keep thinking.

But in that instant, she ceased to move. She ceased to think. He knew it because in the second her gaze turned back to the wings, her mind snapped away from him like one of the midnight icicles that fell from Drury's eaves.

Marcus lurched forward, physically shadowing his need to jerk her back, but he might as well have tried to hold a real icicle. He fought to enter her senses, met by bone-chilling cold. Only one sound echoed in his ears. The pound of her heart, harsh as the pummels from a hail storm.

Gabriela. Damn it, talk to me. What is it?

In response, the frozen shell of a woman on stage shivered. Just once. From head to toe. Very hard. Very violently.

Just before Alfonso Renard emerged into the gaslight, dressed in Sean's costume.

CHAPTER SIXTEEN

The book slipped from Gabriela's hand and thudded to the stage. The impact resounded in her head as if she'd dropped a block of iron, instead.

But the ensuing echo barely registered against the clanking shock Alfonso clamped around her mind, her limbs. She was his prisoner, chained in place by the black malice in his eyes and the steeled menace in his stance.

Locking everything from her mind but the certainty he'd come back to Drury for just one thing.

And the dread that this time, he didn't plan to let his prize go.

As one fist coiled harder at his side—the fist consisting of soiled bandages and only three quaking fingers—Gabriela wondered if he planned to let his prize *live*.

"Oh, God," she heard her parched lips rasp. "Oh, God. God help me."

And someone else. She should be calling for someone else, too. Someone who helped God. One of his angels? Yes. Yes, her *guardian angel...but oh God, what was his name? God help her, what was his name?*

Her brain clawed at the sudden amnesia in vain. Alfonso choked her memory with his gaze, murdered her last lucid thoughts with the force of his grimace. His stubbled jaw spasmed around sweaty lips and seething teeth. He wheezed down breaths from nostrils distended past their aquiline familiarity.

This had to be a nightmare. Please God, this was only a nightmare. She'd wake in a moment, safely ensconced in that place where night protected all and she slept in the strong, sure arms of her angel...

She didn't wake up. She knew that fact because then, the nightmare truly began.

Alfonso stepped toward her.

Gabriela didn't move.

Couldn't move.

Couldn't speak. Couldn't cry out. Couldn't breathe.

And in half a minute, he'd loom over her again. He'd yank at his trousers. Call her those vile names. The whole world would play witness to her degradation. Then the lamps would turn back up and the world would rise, murmuring things like, "Thought she had such a future," and "Who'd have guessed; a whore behind that sincere face?" before they moved on to more pleasant subjects over their soufflés at the Berkeley.

Her crumbling composure twitched a grin to life on the monster's face. It ignited his cocksure advance, booted feet thudding the floorboards, glittering stare sweeping over her body.

Until suddenly, that stare was snapped wide. It appeared like some outside entity jerked him back, like a dog on a leash. Alfonso stumbled, nearly falling over his feet. That same powerful force flung his sights to the floor. His smirking lips plummeted into whispers mingled of The Lord's Prayer and some very creative cursing.

Through the ensuing pause, thick and taut, Gabriela concentrated on maintaining her own stance. Gratitude razed her, dizzying with its force. *Thank you, God. And thank you, my nameless, fearless angel.*

Only after Alfonso staggered back toward the wings, powerless as that same dog caught sniffing where he oughtn't, did she realize the lightning had nothing to do with gratitude.

The lightning.

Marcus.

Here, inside her mind and her heart once more.

Marcus!

She stared, stunned and breathless, toward the depths of the wings. Blinked past the mist of her tears and the flood of her joy. Her senses reached for him. Her heart ached for him.

Then she found him. Barely managed a shaking breath at the sight of him, a manifestation of the shadows themselves. He was towering and assured, dark and intent, one hand raised toward Alfonso with fingers extended in powerful perfection.

Watching him, Gabriela now understood the pull of his hypnotic command over Alfonso, but was amazed by her own immunity to the force. She still didn't move, marveling at Marcus's discipline in narrowing his power to only one mortal in this small space—especially the mortal he hadn't initiated. The mortal who didn't know the extent of the fury sluicing his veins and clouding his sights in crimson. The mortal who didn't see past that rage and into his heart, forcing back sobs at the magnitude of his love for the trembling woman across the stage. The mortal who didn't have to relive the moment that the incarnation of her nightmares advanced at her. That was before he'd confronted a terror of his own, dissolving himself into a mist for the first time in his existence, before streaking toward a backstage corner. When he rematerialized again, Sean Smythe's unconscious form was his only witness.

Gabriela swayed from the force of his wrath. Beneath his imposing exterior, his muscles clenched and strained against giving the audience a real murder on their playbill tonight. She even overheard the fatally calm murmurings of his brain to his heart.

You will not even have to touch him. Just a flick of your wrist, Stafford, and his neck is snapped. The whoreson is done.

She felt the violence of his battle. The desire to at last use his dark curse to do the world some good. Gabriela searched for the *hurrah* she should give him for the idea of finally meting justice to the monster, but all she longed to do was vomit.

The floorboards spun beneath her. Without the reservoir of Marcus's strength and belief, she was still weak as a curbside lace girl. And thrice as helpless on this stage.

She stumbled and grabbed for a support, *any* support. It would be her first movement in God knew how many minutes, though she supposed Davis Webber or any of his entourage in the first row could tell her the precise count. They were murmuring enough about *something*—a something, she readily concluded, *not* related to her further consideration for the Prince's Grand Theatre Troupe ensemble.

She fell to the bench at center stage, bowing her head while waiting for Louis to render the notice for a dropped curtain—and a ruined production.

"Damn," she whispered, licking tears off her lips. Fleetingly, she wondered if Sean might put in a word for her at that music hall on the south bank. "Bloody, bloody damn."

"The fair Ophelia. Nymph, in thy orisons be all my sins remembered."

Her breath caught as the audience's did. But she didn't look up. She didn't have to. Every inch of her body tingled with the same summer storm magic as the first time Marcus had fed her that cue.

As the tingles dissipated through her toes and fingers, a polished black boot shifted into her view, bracing its heel against the bench. Gaby tracked her gaze up an attached shin and over a powerful knee, where two magnificent forearms crossed with roguish ease. The limbs led to epaulet-accented shoulders, which blended to a high chest encased in embroidered black velvet. The top of that ornate doublet was brushed by the feather curling down from a black rogue's hat.

Which framed the night-hewn features of her own perfect Hamlet.

The audience immediately agreed with that assessment. The approval buzzed across the main floor and up through the boxes. As the sound swelled into a wave of warmth around them, Gabriela looked up into his eyes.

His glowing eyes...washing her anew in his transcendent strength.

Marcus. You...didn't kill him, did you?

He cocked his head with a scoundrel's infinite insolence, sparking female sighs through the building. All that before he bestowed *her* with a private smile.

Marcus. God, how she wanted to touch him, right there along the half-smirking edge of his jaw. How she wanted to kiss him, show him this constituted the greatest gift he'd ever given her. *Thank you.*

Madam, came his cocky rejoinder, *I know not who this 'Marcus' be. Prithee call me my Christian appellative, Hamlet of Denmark, if thee are to call me at all.*

He signed the statement with a flourish of movement, strutting downstage left with, indeed, all the conviction of a Danish prince. Of *any* prince.

That same prince who now cleared his throat, executed a

graceful pivot back toward her, and delivered her cue line one more time. *The* last *time*, he silently commanded. *Ophelia, I believe it is* your *line*?

She yearned to shoot him a long eye roll.

Stafford, you've gone truly bedlam this time.

Instead, she raised her head—and issued the line he awaited.

At least she thought so. The words seemed the syllables and inflections she'd rehearsed the last six weeks—yet in an incredible way, they weren't. The sounds didn't erupt from her memory but from her heart, impromptu words that flowed with fervency gained only from the sense she'd never spoken them before. As if she and this rogue didn't perform a scene, but simply carried forth a conversation with several hundred witnesses.

As if she were really an infatuated court maid called Ophelia.

Somehow, through the next super-real minutes, she *was*.

It was Marcus. It had to be. Gabriela kept snapping amazed stares to the man across the stage. At first, her gaze took in the same outward vision as the audience: a Hamlet eyeing her like a demoness incarnate. But in her spirit, he filled her. Surrounded her. Possessed her as none could or ever would, wrapping her in a cloak of confidence and courage until nothing else existed but this, the world where only they lived, a prince and maiden yet also just a man and woman, playing out shades of truth and conflicts of meaning as timeless as the Cheviots, as universal as the Proverbs.

And beyond. The magic went beyond even that exquisite fusion, connecting their very breaths and bodies, their thoughts, their actions...

They'd never run any scene in the play together like this, unstopping like a live performance, but no rehearsal took the place of the bond they knew and the completeness they shared. Gabriela saw every move of his body before he commenced it. As she delivered her lines, she already heard the inflection of his reply just by looking into his eyes.

Perfect balance.

Sublime harmony.

A perfect duet. Felt as one, played by two.

She only knew the beautiful enchantment had ended when his presence departed her in a sudden rush. From where she stood in the darkened wings, Gabriela let out a gasping protest, but his voice cut her short, echoing a loving whisper in her head...

Later. Come to me upstairs. We shall celebrate. I love you.

"Marcus!"

But she reached at thin air with the desperate whisper. *Marcus?* She lifted her sights—and the silent plea—to the rafters. *Marcus,* she beseeched, *celebrate what?*

He didn't respond. As a matter of fact, she sensed him stepping back, now completely pulling his cloak from her again—

And allowing the lights of the next hour to show her that answer, instead. The light of the house lamps, turned up as she took her curtain call, illuminating the audience's surge to its feet. Then the lights on the police wagon, their stark yellow glare highlighting the transformation of Alfonso into a snarling monster as a now-conscious Sean identified him, and they hauled him away.

At last, brighter than all that luminescence combined, there was the light from the smiles waiting in her dressing room. The throng was headed by Louis. At his side was a beaming Augustus Harris.

"Ahhhh!" Augustus boomed to the satin and silk-clad contingent. "Here's our lovely little star now!"

Gaby stopped short of the threshold. Had someone knocked down a wall somewhere when she hadn't looked? Or had her box of a dressing room magically stretched to accommodate this small mob?

"Don't be shy, Gabriela," her producer urged. "Come in, come in."

Augustus bounded forward and curled her hand around his arm. He waggled his big brows in the same rhythm he used before informing casts he'd added a horse stampede to Act Three.

"I believe there's somebody here you've been waiting to meet," he pronounced.

Funny that she'd contemplated horse stampedes. Surely a thousand thoroughbreds galloped through her belly as Augustus swept her into the throng to stand before a gentleman she somehow needed no introduction to. Like the waters making way for Moses, the crowd deferred to this figure in his cutaway evening coat, well-fitted trousers and dashing white neck scarf, topped by chiseled features and eyes that missed nothing.

Augustus cleared his throat with calculated drama. "Miss Rozina, it is my honor to present you to—"

"Davis Webber," Gaby blurted. As the crowd chuckled, she bit the inside of her cheek in embarrassment. "The honor is all mine, sir," she hurried on, wishing the room's secret wall panel had a companion in the floor she could use right now.

The guest of honor didn't seem to share the group's mirth.

For a long moment, Webber said nothing, as well. Then he held up a finger.

The crowd fell silent.

As they did, Webber's face widened on a very full smile.

The intake of female breaths created a tangible vacuum in the room. He withdrew his upraised finger so he could lower that hand to hers. He lifted her quavering knuckles to his smirking lips. But his eyes never left her face.

"Sir?" he finally echoed back at her. "Miss Rozina, if we are to be working together for the next year, I suggest you start calling me Davis."

The crowd broke into approving applause. Augustus gave a whoop worthy of Cody's Wild West Show, actually swinging her off the floor in an ecstatic embrace. Several dizzying spins later, Augustus plopped her back down while inviting the whole room to the Savoy for champagne, his treat.

Gabriela didn't want champagne. Her head fizzed with joyous bubbles already; the world swam in a haze of delirious disbelief as she and Mister Webber—*Davis*, he reminded her with his mock scowl—agreed to an appointment for her first read-through and costume fitting in six weeks, when *Hamlet* finished its run and she'd be officially free to sign with the Prince's Grand Theatre Troupe.

The Prince's Grand Theatre Troupe.

She repeated the words in slow disbelief after the colorful contingent left her alone to change. "I'm dreaming," she finally whispered. "I must be dreaming."

But when she gazed into the mirror, the reflection in the glass gaped back with eyes consumed by real shock. When she pressed palms to her flushed cheeks, her skin emanated an inferno of real exhilaration.

And when she glanced to her dressing table, a solitary calling card still answered her stare, in real gilt lettering:

Davis Webber
Creative Director, Co-Producer,
Prince's Grand Theatre Troupe
Headquarters: West End

No, she wasn't dreaming.

Just drunk.

Drunk with happiness. Intoxicated with triumph. Inebriated with victory.

She did *not* need champagne.

She only needed Marcus.

Augustus would just have to understand. *So sorry, Mr. Harris, but the headache came on suddenly. You understand; the strain of the performance and the pressure of the situation. A doctor? Oh, no, just a good night's sleep and I'll be fine. Thank you for your consideration...*

Then a short climb, and she'd reunite with her love. Together, basking in their glory. Together, knowing their triumph.

Together...simply together.

Was it possible they could banish hell with the sweetness of such a heaven?

She couldn't wait to get out of here.

★ ★ ★ ★

Marcus couldn't wait to get out of here.

He didn't bother to light any candles other than the single taper he carried, moving to the crypt in a tiny circle of flickering light. He required naught else but to collect a pail of dirt then be gone...

For when his next sleep came, he vowed, he would welcome it upon white perfumed sheets, draped around the woman he loved. The soil, a necessity dictated by too much folklore to disregard, was the last element he needed. Long ago, he had assured the apartment's wood shutters served as more than decorative fancy, in case any unforeseen accident led him to sunrise in need of a resting place closer than this cockroach's hole.

But from tonight forward, crypts had no place in his life. He no longer wallowed in darkness or cowered in subterranean seclusion. To do so would sentence Gabriela to the same lot, for asking her not to follow him down here would prove useless as exiling Juliet from her balcony. And claim as she did to love this *cavern*, his lady deserved more than stone walls for inspiration and water beetles for company—over and above the infections waiting to seize her from the chamber's cold air.

He paused before scooping the dirt into the pail. A grin touched his lips. So the unbelievable had come to pass. Despite the campaign he had waged otherwise, despite his furious fears and his most terrifying apprehensions, the remarkable little wench had finally gotten her way. Gabriela Angelica Rozina, damn and bless her at once, had bound herself to him, worked herself inside of him. Conquered his mind, consumed his heart.

Became the center of his life.

Their life.

In strength, in weakness. In happiness, in sorrow. In sickness, in health...

Until death do them part.

He lurched back to his feet.

Th*e sh*arp ding of his boot against the pail made a deafening clang through the chamber. Even so, he barely heard it. The container tumbled across the floor and collided against the black-shrouded wall.

A blackness impenetrable as *death*.

Nay.

He willed his brain to repeat the command as he grabbed the candle and pursued the bucket. De*ath* had no reserved solo on tonight's program. The bastard would have to wait a while for a slot, as well—another fifty or sixty years, to calculate it precisely.

Until then, Marcus vowed, he would make Gabriela Rozina the happiest, most well-loved woman on—

"Marcus? Marcus, is that you?"

The rasping voice came from everywhere yet nowhere, insinuating itself through him with the same terrifying intimacy. For a moment, he was paralyzed. A breathing statue, praying it was nothing but a trick of the underground wind . . .

The voice had other plans.

"Marcus..."

Again, the sound whispered all around him. Again, a cold presence slithered inside his mind. Desperate as grief. Cold as the grave.

"Marcus...over here."

Like a horse forced to follow its tether, he wheeled to the left, toward the alcove where Joseph usually dropped his deliveries. Oddly, he welcomed the candle's irradiation of the massive stone slab, with its stains of old and new blood. An expected sight. Nothing unusual. Everything in its place. Nothing wh*ich ha*d spoken to him before.

The voice was a delusion.

Thank every damn saint.

Could he be blamed for the imagining? Tonight had measured far from normal, even after his hundreds of nights. He had barely stopped reeling from the impact of initiation, when forced to take his first expedition in mist form. Three minutes after rematerializing, there came the strain of hypnotizing Renard in front of a sold-out theatre, then performing the last three sc*enes of Hamlet* from memory.

He eased out a long breath.

Just as a small, ghostly figure shuffled into his sights.

Marcus instinctively stepped back. But the decaying, decrepit...*thing* advanced by another step. It reached to him with bony white arms that poked from limp drapes of what used to be, as far as he could fathom, an ornate crimson ball gown. With each of those slow slides, slivers of that unreal skin peeled loose, swirling to the ground like snowflakes in a child's winter fantasy globe.

Only when they met the ground, they melted not to slush.

They dissolved to ash.

Marcus gaped at the mounting pile of soot at the thing's feet. He was like every pathetic killcow who stopped to watch the wounded taken from carriage accidents. Revolted, yet riveted.

He searched for luci*d thou*ghts but found only mute shock. He scrambled for the strength to glance away, but realized he could not feel his body beyond his neck.

The wraith began to laugh.

A dark, deep, throaty laugh.

And in that moment, halting his retreat, freezing his blood, comprehension invaded. Catapulted him two hundred eighty years into the past. Threw him upon a cold stone slab and lashed him there, helpless, lifeless—only one word slicing past his clenched jaw and hate-twisted lips.

"Raquelle."

CHAPTER SEVENTEEN

He still prayed imagination had merely bested him. Surely he'd identified the wrong vampire. Better yet, nothing truly stood there before him. A blink, and the apparition would disappear...

She shattered that hope with an ironically serene lift of her *he*ad. A pair of eyes glowed out at him. Glowed. Their pupils were drenched of pure blood red, upon fields of gray no more alive than graveyard fog.

But between those two realms, a third, thin ring of color entrapped Marcus's notice. It gored his soul with sick recognition. The color was violet. The most fathomless, unforgettable shade he had known. The violet of royal velvet, of wizard's crystals.

Of fatal seduction.

"Marcus." She made a valiant attempt at the purr which had once turned him hard as stone in seconds. She also tried to smile, but brown, broken teeth took the place of a smile that had dazzled half of Whitehall. "Darling Marcus. How are you?"

With a flood of relief, he found himself capable of movement again. After dropping the candle, he swung away on furious steps. "I am not your love."

A torturously familiar cluck came behind him. "Whatever you wish, crab apple."

"What the hell do you want, Raquelle?"

Even turned away, he damn near saw the woman's sultry pout. He almost laughed again, though the sound would be born of bile instead of bliss. Some things never changed.

"What the hell do you want?" she answered, mimicking his growl. "Oh, Marcus; for shame. After all this time, I have bothered to come see you. I have taken this time, and the only amenity you afford me is 'what the hell do you want?'"

"Sorry," he snarled, bracing hands to the wall to still the shaking of *his* hands. "The butler has the night off."

Raquelle took care of the laughter for both of them. Well, tried. The sound deteriorated into a hacking choke. She did not stop for several minutes. And Marcus did not move. He battled not to hear the pathetic sounds. He told himself the sight of her, the reek of her, the desperate weakness of her meant nothing to him. Not a shred of concern or a twinge of pity. And certainly did not terrify every bone in his body.

His body, so like hers.

His mind rebelled at the thought with a silent scream. His soul recoiled with less restraint, its hiss exploding past his lips.

Then his body ran with every supernatural drop of strength it possessed. Toward Gabriela. Toward sweet *forget*fulness of this nightmare, of this demoness who had haunted him so long. Too long.

But as he lunged for the door, his doublet was snagged in a death grip. Even in her decrepit state, Raquelle had a hundred years' more strength on him. She dragged him back and pinned him to the wall with fingers that had turned into skeletal talons.

"Marcus." It was a snarling plea. Jesu. He had never heard the woman beg before. The two syllables of his name came between her frantic scrabblings over his chest. "Marcus, please help me. I need you!"

He fought to summon one shred of sympathy. It remained a distant stranger. "Nonsense, darling. You have needed nothing since the night we met."

"Please!" It was a desperate whine. "Marcus, I have *not* fed in two weeks—"

"Truly? I had not noticed."

"Damn you, look at me!"

Despite every protesting cell in his being, he did look. Perhaps in stupid, stubborn rebellion to those cells. Perhaps because he was a pathetic idiot.

Perhaps because he had secretly yearned for this moment over the last two and a half centuries. Revenge over Raquelle in one of the most exquisite ways he could imagine—by watching her die in the dark, *path*etic and ugly.

But as his gaze met the horrific stare at his chest, as he took in the strands of mossy hair drooping over her hag's face and the viscid skin hanging upon her thin limbs, he felt no elation, or even pity.

He felt nothing.

"Damn you," Raquelle croaked again. "Damn you, you have no right to stand there in Peter's judgment on me!"

Correction: he felt one thing. Disgust.

With the realization, he pried her loose and shoved her away. As he backstepped again, he wiped his hands down his thighs, ridding his skin of her scales and her stench.

"I have no right?" he repeated with slow, almost surprising softness. "Darling, that line is more creamy rich than the thighs you once spread for half of England."

"Bastard!" she screeched. "Our accounts are not settled, Marcus. You are mine. Damn you, I made you what you are!"

His fingers curled at his sides. His pulse throbbed, a

relentless dagger in his jaw. "Worry not, lady," he snarled. "I have not forgotten."

Raquelle rolled her eyes. "Spare me your noble martyr trattle. I have a little piece of news for you, darling. You were a pitifully easy duck that night. My Lord Stafford, you craved immortality more than all the other dullards in Whitehall put together. 'Twas written on your face more blatant than a baudstrot's smirk."

She cocked her head, her decaying smile inching by a calculated degree. "You saw the dream without even knowing you saw it, Marcus. You simply required a little guidance to aid your perceptions."

For another extended moment, Marcus did not answer her. "Guidance," he gritted at last. "So that is how you phrase it." He adopted a steeled version of her head-tilted pose. "Such a fascinating way of saying you murdered me."

He should have expected the witch's reaction. Should have known Raquelle would find his tragedy the best entertainment she had known in years, judging from the delighted scream of laughter she sent echoing into the night. Oh aye, he should have expected it but did not—and *that* rendered him impotent of anything else but standing there, senses roiling and heart aching, while this creature finished degrading him once again.

Raquelle's thinning lungs finally reduced her mirth to a handful of labored breaths. She looked up again, and Marcus admitted a jolt of shock at what he now saw in her eyes. More accurately, what he did *not* see. The rings of violet, still confirming her scant humanity, were now nearly nonexistent.

"Murder, my love," she rasped in a voice as frail as chandelier glass, "would have been to leave you in that cave after I had finished, rotting to your death. *You* were certainly not hastening to help yourself." She started to quiver. "I cared for you, Marcus. Whether you believe me or not, I thought I gave you what you truly desired."

He pulled in an unsteady breath. She was right. He did not believe her. Oh, her performance was exemplary—but that was the point. *Her performance.* 'Twas an exterior display, easily donned as costume and face paint, and shed just as thoughtlessly.

And yet...she had spoken the truth. She had kept him alive through those first horrifying weeks. Every night she sauntered back into the cave, proudly dragging her new kill, laying the pitiful heap before Marcus's hunger-racked body with a queen-of-the-beasts smile.

It disgusted him to think of those nights now. But without them—without Raquelle—he would have never lived to know Gabriela. To know the light of her smiles, the healing of her touch, the sanity of her love.

And for that, he was forced to concede one more truth to Raquelle.

Their accounts truly had not been settled.

Though the winch in his gut stretched into his chest, he willed himself to turn, scoop up the candle, and carry it to the alcove filled by his desk. Subterranean wind threw the flame's glow into wild white and yellow patterns across the paper that accepted his missive. Without waiting for the ink to fully dry, he folded the note in thirds, scrawled the words, *Joseph Berger, St. Anthony's Hospital Morgue* across one side, then sealed the flap with a wax seal imprinted with a single *S*.

"Rest yourself, Raquelle." He growled it in weary resignation while releasing the weight on Joseph's delivery door. "You shall feel yourself again soon." *God help us all.*

He thought she actually wept in thanks. He'd never be certain, for he barely heard her overacted soliloquy of gratitude beyond, "Oh, Marcus; Marcus, you *angel!*"

Angel.

His spirit roared into his mind, drowning all else as he sank against the wall. He dropped his head into the claws he dared call hands, and fed the echoes of Raquelle's adoration to that roar. He was not surprised when the mixture exploded past his lips into something between a sob and a snarl.

Angel.

'Twas fitting that the one time the name was bestowed to him, 'twas in the ravings of a half-dead demon. Old Will Shakespeare would have waved his quill in glee at the poetic irony. As Marcus's heart swallowed the comprehension, his fingers dug harder against his skull—longing to rip out the brain now agonizingly capable of such pain.

The pain you knew damn well to expect. The price you readily agreed upon when you returned that first apple-sweet kiss, when you knew Gabriela's first embrace. The contract you signed the moment you reached for the gold. For the joy.

The joy. *Aye, remember the joy. Remember the fleeting bliss of touching mortality again. Remember the fear, the fulfillment... and the deep, secret seed of hope...*

Oh Jesu, the hope.

The hope of one day gazing into Gabriela's eyes, and seeing the reflection of an angel.

Who the hell are you gulling? You are no angel. You will not ever be.

He was the same kind of monster as the wretch who sprang to life as soon as Joseph arrived with the new delivery. The same kind of beast racing to the stone slab like a tiger on a feeding frenzy. Ah, God, he was the same kind of creature which ripped open the dingy sack Joseph had dumped there; sinking her teeth into the corpse's chest with a mindless sob of satisfaction.

He was a being doomed to continue his life by draining it from others. Unnatural. Unholy.

Undead.

He turned, unable to witness Raquelle's garish feeding. As if that mattered, when the candles hurled hideous shadows, anyway. Their undulations taunted him. *Unnn-dead. Unnn-dead. Unnn-dead.*

The shadows moved with the rise of a head, no longer covered with haggish strands, but a queen's thick mane. Raquelle purred in pleasure as her shadow raised a long-fingered nail to catch a drop of blood along her neck. She sucked the stuff off with enough graphic intent that even her shadow was enough to bring a priest to a halt.

But Marcus only saw only the silhouette of a monster.

A monster he had helped recreate.

And all he heard was a cold voice from within, whispering a grotesque truth.

It was easy, aye? So pathetically, mindlessly easy. And consider this, you bastard: if it was so easy to help the witch you loathe, how much easier will it be to transform Gabriela?

His fists began to shake. His head filled with seething silver.

How long until you give in to her pleas? Maybe you shall succumb tonight while thrusting into her. One simple act, and it will be done. One painless bite, and she'll be your own little vampiress, forever. You see? You are capable of being a good monster.

His roar conceded no longer to the shackles of his chest. The sound ripped up his throat and across the chamber, screaming into every crack and corner as he stumbled, dizzy and desperate—

And damned.

Damned to do what he should have that first moment Gabriela looked upon him—even then, beginning to love him. Even then, sealing his love for her.

Their love. The greatest and only gift heaven had allowed him to unwrap.

Their love. Just the memories of the precious joy trumpeted through his senses, heaven's own choir.

Their love. The only light he would carry back with him to damnation's depthless abyss.

Alone. Again. Forever.

CHAPTER EIGHTEEN

Gabriela wondered why Marcus started when she sneaked up to the doorway of the apartment's bedroom and greeted him a quiet, "Hello, my prince."

She grinned. She'd *never* been able to startle him like that. The effect was adorable.

Unable to resist any longer, she slid up behind him, circling arms around his muscled waist and reveling in the rich feel of embroidered velvet beneath her fingers. He didn't return her caress, but his indrawn breath and reflexive shiver bespoke his reaction clearer than a Samuel Phelps monologue.

"Sorry I took a while," she said, readily acceding to the tranquility between them. The calm air was nice after the pellmell storm of tonight's events. "I tried to sneak away after changing but Louis found out my game before I reached the green room door."

She smiled again, flattening her hands against his stomach. A sensual image of the defined ridges beneath slid into her mind. "I told him I had an imperative assignation to keep with his boss." The smile sneaked into her voice. "And he didn't believe a word. So I talked *them* into a compromise: one glass of champagne in Louis's office."

Now that she pondered it, the libation *had* been nice. The bubbles still tingled up her spine, danced through her limbs— and emboldened her fingers to explore lower as she ventured, "Did you miss me?"

She felt Marcus's deep swallow. Heard him attempt a measured breath, which emerged more a faltering sigh, before answering, "I shall always miss you when you are not near." He hissed a little as her fingers cupped his crotch, already firming for her. "Oh, sweeting...always."

"Mmmmm." She snuggled her cheek to the plane between his shoulder blades. "That's good." A fraction of a frown interrupted her reverie. "For a moment, I thought you were... well...afraid to see me."

"Nay." He cleared his throat before shifting from her touch and reaching for something on the bed. "Nay...just busy."

"*With* what?" Gabriela popped up on tiptoes, trying to see over his shoulder. She instantly laughed at herself. Her brow barely cleared his nape. Instead, she swung around him—

And almost found herself taking a dive into a large leather satchel on the counterpane. There wouldn't be much room for her, however. First, she noted several books, including his beloved leather-bound Hamlet and the volume of Middleton comedies he'd reenacted for her at least three times—naked. Peeking from beneath those was a stack of letters from her, all tied in a gold ribbon, as well as several pieces of official-looking correspondence. After that—

She frowned. The bottom of the heap seemed a twist of every shirt, waistcoat, or other piece of fashion history he'd accidentally left behind up here. She knew the articles because she'd been lovingly compiling them in the bureau's upper left drawer—which, she now observed, lay open and empty.

And then, stuffed against the side of the satchel, she saw the picture.

It was a framed likeness of her, sketched by the Drury artist months ago. Months before she knew Marcus existed.

Augustus had commissioned the small portrait for the public*ity posters* in the city squares and theatre lobby, demanding she be made to look like "Galatea herself come to life." Gaby never knew if the result, a captivating swirl of mountain greens and autumn coppers to match her nymph's costume and dramatic hair, ever fulfilled the man's requirements. But she remembered Augustus's *tantrum when Alfonso had offered a king's sum for the objet d'art, which went missing. She also remembered thanking heaven for the culprit.*

Now, she raised a puzzled stare at that culprit.

As she pulled the portrait out, she swallowed against an odd cramp in her stomach. She forced steady modulation over the syllables of her soft question. "Marcus, what is this?"

He shrugged. Shrugged, as loose-limbed as a dandy on the town. Ironically, it exposed a tension in him that she couldn't fathom. A tension that was suddenly terrifying.

"You find me guilty as charged, madam." He used *that* shrug again. "I took the portrait the day after I saw your first dress rehearsal. I could not stomach the thought of Renard possessing—"

"I don't care about the portrait." She shook her head, hoping the action would clear her thoughts. Instead, her mind was lost in a deeper murk of confusion. "I'm glad you have it. But...all of your things...why are you taking all of your things? Marcus?"

She shook her head again. Why did her heart suddenly thud in her throat? And why did he play cat-and-mouse with her on wielding his own stare?

He took the portrait back, and shoved it into the satchel. Then took a breath that expanded his whole chest.

Still not looking at her.

"I must go away for a while, Gabriela."

"Away?" She sounded like a bad soprano with laryngitis. She sounded lost and desperate. She sounded—

The way she hated sounding.

"What do you mean, away?" And jealous. She sounded jealous—and stupid. But she couldn't stop, struggling to reconcile this announcement with the promise he'd given her just an hour ago...

"But you said to meet you here. You said we'd celebrate. You said it inside my mind, Marcus..." *Inside my heart.*

She threw back the shutters on their spiritual bond, preparing for the blinding rays of his. Once their souls reinitiated to each other, he'd cease this talk of just leaving, just like that. Because he just couldn't do that. They were bonded. They were one.

Marcus? Angel? Can't you hear me?

Her heart's outcry disappeared into blackness.

No. Worse.

His psyche answered hers with nothing.

To her spirit's outstretched arms, inexplicable silence. To her searching stare, Marcus didn't turn once. He only shifted uncomfortably while throwing a longing look at the door.

"Gabriela."

She shivered. His tone conjured Parson Reeves with its mix of pity and patience, the he used when calling her to the orphanage office to be told she wasn't the little girl the Fairchilds or the Hardwicks or the Rhynes had in mind.

She stepped back. Dropped her stinging stare to the floor. Beat at her thigh with one white-knuckled fist. "*What?*"

"I shall only be gone a little while."

"No, you won't."

Her voice shed the laryngitis for a more painful alternative. She spoke with a calm that froze her from the inside out as she received a sliver of *something* from his soul. It wasn't emotion, of that she was sure. It was more like a shaft February morning light: blindingly clear, unfeelingly cold.

"Gabriela, it—it is business. I cannot simply—"

"You're lying." So simple. But so bloody certain, as the fissure inside him widened. No matter how her heart yearned to turn back from it now, she experienced the coiled ache of his gut, the burning weight across his chest—the whole torture chamber his body had become with the burden of betraying her.

"Why, Marcus?" She began kneading her gown's tablier into wrinkled knots. "Why are you lying to me?"

"Sweeting..."

"What kind of a game is this? Is this what you're really about? Seducing pigeons like me, training them to fly in your private little show, and then when they need you most, breaking their hearts and waiting for their wings to follow?"

For the first time since she'd entered, he emerged from the shelter of his hunched shoulders. He raised his head, deliberately met her gaze—and sucked out half her breath with the bleak, gray misery of his eyes. And cleaned out the other half with the low grate of his voice.

"You do not need me anymore, Gabriela."

"The bloody *hell* I don't." She hated the harder quiver in her retort. She hated *him* for making her stand here once more, trying to erase the visions that assaulted, yet again...

Child, do not be so sad. The Fairchilds just had someone more like Elizabeth in mind.

Now Gabriela, ye mustn't cry. The Rhynes liked you; they really did.

Next week, Gabriela. More folks will come next week.
Someone will love you someday, Gabriela.
"Gabriela."

She flinched, struggling between the cold echoes of memory and the freezing truth of the present. For a boggled moment, she feared the two inextricably meshed—until he touched her. Just there, at the top of her shoulder; a penetrating cool, a haunting warmth. Flourishing from nowhere, filling her everywhere. And, oh God, so real. So beautifully, horribly real.

"Gabriela, listen to me. You grew those wings with your own heart, your own purpose. And now, sweeting, you shall fly on them with the same. You shall fly to the ends of the earth, and show them the beauty of all your Ophelias and Juliets and Cleopatras—"

"N-No." The word emerged more a sob than a sound. The same agony shot down her arms, helping them to thrust him back before she staggered to the sitting room. Gabriela felt him follow her. The cruel, continuing power of his presence... the ruthlessly beautiful pull of him... "Nooo!"

"Gabriela—"

"I said *no!*" She stretched out a hand, fingers spread and aching. "They all lied to me, and now you are, too!" The world keeled as she shook her head. "What is it, Marcus?" she rasped. "What did I do wrong? I—I've been good, haven't I? Marcus... haven't I?"

For a long heartbeat, he stood immobile, ethereal and unreadable again. But then a shaking shadow crossed his face. Conflict contorted his features. He stared at her—*into* her—and his soul glowed from his eyes once more with silver pain, miserable gloss of rain, the dry tears of a frightened boy locked inside an accursed man.

He took a heavy step toward her. Another. Gabriela jerked her hand higher, muscles trembling, warning him away. It didn't stop the beautiful bastard. He reached up, so gently, so intently...and encircled her hand beneath his, using one long, magical finger at a time.

He dragged her into the consuming crush of his embrace. Only then did he let one phrase escape, guttural and grating. A verbal Golgotha bell.

"My love."

And only then could she see all the way into his mind.

A shocked cry tore past her lips. She scratched away from him like a cat about to be tossed into the Thames—certain she'd prefer that ordeal to this drowning torment.

"Oh, my God. It's her, isn't it?"

Again, fathomless silence. But a royal decree's worth of confirmation ignited his eyes before he wheeled away. "What are you talking about?"

"Stop it!" she lashed. "Damn you, just stop it! I saw her, Marcus. I saw!"

"You saw the bloody hell what?"

"In your mind! Stop pretending such penny novel innocence! I saw her. I saw that woman—"

Another explosion of comprehension blasted her. She bent over to gain breath. "Raquelle," she heard her lips choke—and her heart scream. "Oh, my God. It's Raquelle. *She's* Raquelle."

The certainty flooded her mind and churned her stomach. She folded to the floor as the image assaulted her again, her accusation unleashing every detail out of Marcus's mind and into hers. Shadows made alive by candlelight, outlining full, mesmerizing hair that cascaded over voluptuous breasts, nipples erect. Hips that promised sleek pleasures. And her moan, full of sensual satisfaction and carnal mystery, just before she uttered words that seared Gabriela's soul.

You are mine, Marcus. I made you what you are. You are mine forever.

A sound escaped her. It was beyond a sob; more annihilating than a scream. A quivering, aching sound as her heart was ripped out, one agonizing scrap at a time.

Through the misery, she could still feel Marcus's stare. It was a tangible presence around her, though never inside her as before—as if he willed his gaze to reach out like his embrace, only to be held back by invisible prison bars.

Of course, her soul agreed. *Of course he's in prison. The "prison" of Raquelle's caresses. No wonder you found him packing in such a hurry.*

"It was so easy," she uttered, "wasn't it? So easy to forget your sorry little mortal slut when the great Raquelle invited you to her bed again."

Marcus barely moved. He swallowed, rippling the cords of his neck, as his eyes glittered bright as gashes of glass.

"Is that what you think?" he uttered.

"Is that what I—" She jerked once more to her feet. "For God's sake, Marcus, tell me what else I'm supposed to think!" She lunged at him, curling her furious grip into his huge shoulders. "Damn you, tell me I'm wrong, then. Tell me I'm more lunatic than Marx then kiss me senseless to prove it!"

Her fingers traveled down to his doublet, where her fingers snagged in slashes in the fabric—slashes the distinct width of feminine fingernails. Still, she gritted her teeth and pressed her forehead to his chest, openly supplicating to him.

"Just—just tell me I'm wrong," she whimpered. "I'll

believe you, Marcus. I swear I'll believe you."

She waited. Held her breath. But his hard, heavy sigh twisted her belly with cold, despairing fear. She strained to hear past the thunderous throb of her heart for the corresponding beat of his own but there was no sound. She felt even less.

"I have nothing to tell you, Gabriela."

Her arms clenched with the lust to beat him. Instead, she unfurled her fingers. Stared at their trembling tips against his broad chest. "You're really certain about that...aren't you?"

His own grasp slipped up around her shoulders. "Aye." His hands were steady, mocking her with their strength. "I am going. I *must* go."

"You mean you're leaving." She turned each word into a venomous slur. "For her."

He circled his thumbs around the tops of her shoulders. "I am *not* going to her, damn it."

"You're lying." It was a complete guess. Since he'd closed her off from his thoughts, she had to do this the old-fashioned way. "You're lying and you just want to do this the easy way."

"Gabriela." He sighed the word, as if wearied with a disobedient child. But he still didn't let her go. And she refused to capitulate to the magic of his touch.

"If she wants you, then she'll have to fight for you."

Marcus huffed. Correction: growled. "By God's bollocks—"

"Tell her," she countered. "If you can envision her—and we certainly know *that's* not a challenge—then you can call her to your side. Do it, damn it. Summon that witch and tell her *I'm* willing to die for you. She can even do the deed herself. I'll bet she'd like that. Ask her, Marcus. Damn you, ask—"

Her gasp finished the decree instead of the glaring

gauntlet she'd planned. Marcus's broadsword of a glower, and the head-snapping thrust he gave her shoulders, guaranteed that.

"Damn *you!*" He jerked on her again. "Damn you, Gabriela, desist making this such an agony for me!"

Then and there, as he sliced his whole countenance at her again, as he stared *through* her, Gabriela stopped struggling. Who was this creature clutching her? The last time he'd been such a stranger had been the night they'd first met, and he'd shrouded her head with mist. He'd hypnotized her so completely, she'd bloody near forgotten who she was, never mind the journal and reticule she left behind. But even that night, he hadn't paralyzed her with a glare of such deep wrath, a grimace of such deep pain . . .

Oh, dear God.

Hypnotized her.

Paralyzed her.

The fog. In her head. Again.

"Go to the couch, Gabriela." His voice came through the fog, *part* of the fog, just like before. "Go to the couch," he repeated, "and sit down."

He dropped his hands from her. She turned in harsh spurts of motion, openly trying to protest to his supernatural push. Her arms trembled with the effort to spin herself back around. She tossed her head back and forth against his mind's foray. But she slid an inch closer to the couch with every passing heartbeat.

It was the initiation. He said you'd surrender him all, and he was right. He said you could—possibly would—regret it.

And he was right.

She whined at him. Cried to him. But she couldn't even

lift fingers to wipe her tears away. "Damn it," she snarled. "Marcus...please...don't!"

"I must." He used his hand as a mesmeric wand now, lowering it slowly. The motion was a direct command, coercing her knees to bend around the couch's cushions. "Forgive me," came his haunting, consuming whisper, "I must do this."

She only had one weapon against him now. Her tear-streaked glare. Marcus's hand faltered a fraction, pivoting inward atop his wrist. Then nothing.

"I hate you for this."

"I know."

In that darkness of a moment between them, she knew he did. The recognition inspired her to one last flash of defiance. She coiled determined fists into her skirts, planted her feet, and stood—one last burst of strength to try breaking his unholy spell.

Two seconds later, she plummeted to the floor, thrown down by an overwhelming mental blow. Though she only fell to her hands and knees, they instantly buckled beneath her. Gabriela didn't care. The Persian carpet dampened beneath her drenched cheeks. Her lungs heaved against the boards beneath the rug.

"I...am sorry." A hard inhalation intersected the words. "Gabriela, I am so sorry. But you do not understand. You do not *want* to understand."

She had thought her fury spent. Her heart proved her sanity wrong. An enraged inferno blazed through her senses, gusted into the sights she raised at him once more. "I. Understand. Perfectly," she seethed.

"Gabriela, *cease!*"

She knew he wouldn't let her stand, at least not while he

remained, but she shoved to her knees with all the dignity and determination left in her muscles. "I shall never cease," she spat. "You convey that to Mistress Raquelle, as well. You tell her to get prepared, Marcus—because she might have taken the battle tonight but we'll see who takes the bloody Waterloo.

"You tell her I shall surrender the breath in my body before I cease loving you."

★ ★ ★ ★

Damn her, the woman truly meant her little declaration of war.

Little? Marcus clawed through the mire of his mind to make the amendment. He was more successful at that, however, than uncoiling his body from the subterranean crevice he had called a bed the last three days.

Three days. Could it have been only that fraction of a fortnight ago that he'd attempted to set her free? Could only three moons have risen since he'd fled after casting her into sleep, rather than endure another second of her molten stare or a moment of her beautiful love?

But most unbelievable: could it have been only three nights since she awakened from that sleep, only to find her stubborn, *stupid* way to the London underground?

It had always been his damnation, this shadowed, wretched place—but now it was truly his hell. For endless hours, its tunnels carried her sweet voice everywhere. Echoed with every soggy step she took down passages *he'd* barely navigated for want of light or sanity.

Which resounded once more with the sound of her.

Marcus froze, listening to her distant calls. His knees went to rubble. He plummeted to the cold earth, dropping his head to it like the sewer scum he had become. But true sewer scum could thrive in blissful ignorance of the voice calling down the twisting tunnels to him. Holy Mary, so full of life. Bloody hell, so full of pain.

"Marcus! I know you're down here. I can *feel* you here, damn it. I can feel you trying to hide, but you can't. Marcus... your walls aren't high enough. I love you. I love you..."

With a guttural growl, he clamped both hands over his ears. How was this possible? How did he still feel all this? How did he still fathom every moment her feet touched the slime-covered rocks, every breath she took of this weeping air...and every sob she matched to it? Why did his heart still shatter with each word of her aching cries, echoing through the darkness at him?

"I told you I wouldn't stop. I told you I'd *never* stop, and I won't. You can't hide behind *every* wall, Marcus."

Something between a laugh and a sob escaped him. It contorted on his lips, taking over his whole body. Strangely, he remembered a voodoo ceremony from his rainforest days. People jerked at his feet like they had the falling sickness, apparently possessed by demons. Marcus had glowered on them, questioning the power of spirit over sinew, blood and muscle. He now cursed himself the idiot.

The idiot who would be possessed by his spirit's pain for all eternity.

Do you hear that, Gabriela? I am a creature of hell for eternity. *We cannot change it.* You *cannot change it.*

But she trod on. Marcus trembled harder with the effort of sustaining his mental barricade against her, sensing her follow an "intuition" down a narrower passage leading closer to his cavern.

Dear God, Gabriela. Don't come any closer!

"Marcus!"

She shouted it with renewed, reverberating strength—in the most horrifying sense of the words. He spun toward the wall, feeling the warmth of her through the bricks separating them. His strength waned like butter against the sunshine of her life and intensity. The resulting paste of his body slithered back to his crevice bed. He did not dare even a glance back. The slightest slip of composure would instantly betray his awareness of her...every fiber, every breath, every drop of precious blood.

"Marcus." Her voice was thick with tears. "You're so near. I feel you so near. Why won't you answer? Marcus...I love you..."

He slammed his hands into the ground, burying them to the wrists and twisting them. The clay dug deep under his fingernails, bringing on welcome pain—but it wasn't enough. *Damn you. Stop loving me! Stop tormenting me!*

"Marcus...please..."

Go away!

And, unbelievably, with thanks to whatever force of the universe still listening to him, she did.

And then, finally, came the reprieve of penetrating silence.

Or so Marcus convinced himself for the next week.

Then the next. And the next.

He kept telling himself that eternity would not always seem so...eternal. That mere fortnights would not always seem a century and minutes would not always tick by like hours—

That he would not always wander the city with his head filled solely by one name.

"Gabriela."

He allowed himself to say it just one time each night. This time, the echoes of his worshiping whisper floated down from his perch on Blackfriars Bridge before twirling into the gathering mists off the Thames. But a surprising wisp of early spring wind suddenly brushed the water, erasing the fog—robbing her name from the night too fast.

He growled at the wind. It moaned softly back.

Just before he made an equally mutinous decision.

He could not live like this. Not when the only thing he kept remembering were her outcries from the caverns, haunted and desperate. She did not deserve that place in his mind. She did not deserve to be framed for all time in *his* misery. She warranted the honor of filling his mind with her golden smile, her burnished gaze, her sun-bright presence.

He had to see her again.

Just once.

All he would do was look. She would not know he was there. It would just take one moment. One more time to bask in her beauty again, ensuring she had left the tunnels behind for where she belonged: on the stage. The little dreamer needed to concentrate. Did she not begin rehearsals with Webber and the Prince's Troupe next week? God's codpiece, Marcus suddenly wondered, what day *was* it? More questions flew at him after that, which his mind dispatched with an alertness he had not known since playing Hamlet to the most beautiful Ophelia on earth.

He could not traverse the streets fast enough.

He noted the time, gonged across the city by Big Ben. Three a.m. If Fate still deemed to smile just a little on him, mayhap he'd find her finishing one of her after-hours sessions. No doubt she would be wandering the middle of the stage, pondering some script passage, her adorable brow furrowed. Or maybe she would be in her dressing room, nodding off in the middle of making a journal entry, curl in her chair in the same way he had first approached her...so damnably beautiful. She would be more so tonight. Her eyes would carry the alloy of self-confidence, her head high as she gazed toward the gleaming horizon of her life. Everything waited for her now. Promise and passions, triumphs and travels, daylight and dreams.

A life she would never have known with him.

He would wish her a swift Godspeed into that life, then return to the abyss of his.

He entered Drury by way of the private street entrance to his box. He was careful about it, though he had not felt the seeking tendrils of Gabriela's thoughts or emotions for well past a fortnight now. Still, he did not dare the slightest slip on his control. A stray thought could lead her straight to him.

His heart throbbed like thunder as he inched into his box and looked toward the stage.

No sable-haired angel paced the dim floorboards there.

He smiled for the first time in three weeks. Huzzah, she *was* in her dressing room.

He hastened along the stage right catwalk, nearly breaking into a run down the passage toward the green room—

Where he jerked to a stunned stop.

The place was illuminated so fully, it almost seemed a blast of sunlight. As soon as he determined 'twas not, he had a chance to discern the second startling element of the scene.

He had never seen the green room so crowded.

Every current Drury Lane cast and crew member, as well as a few who'd moved on to other theatres, stood or sat in the meager room. Even Louis joined the throng, one beefy leg propped atop a section of "wall" from the "Castle of Denmark." Alfonso Renard, face as taut and white as the bandage around his hand, stood next to him.

Everyone held either a lamp or a candle.

And all of them stared at those straining walls and doors as if someone had died.

All except Gabriela...who was nowhere to be seen.

"Are you certain that's what the doctors said, Mister Harris?" rasped a dark-haired waif from the ballet. "They said 'no hope?' That's what they really said?"

Marcus snapped an amazed look the same direction as the waif. Bloody hell, it was true. He had not noticed Augustus before, with his face buried so deeply into his overcoat. Now, as his partner looked up to the group with hollow eyes, dread began to claw Marcus's chest. The feeling cut the breath from his throat and the blood from his veins.

"I came directly from St. Anthony's," Augustus said. His tone was actually underscored with tenderness. "I spoke to the physicians for an hour. They told me exactly what I have told you all. Gabriela was found a fortnight ago by a city plumber, wandering in a drainage corridor beneath St. Martin's Lane. She was damn near dead *then*."

"Bollocks," somebody muttered.

"Damn me," somebody else added.

"As most of you know, it hasn't gotten better since," Augustus went on. "The fluid in her lungs will not drain. She has no strength to cough it up anymore. But that's because the little fool refuses to eat. That, of course, is no help to the fever, or the unexplainable spasms..."

Augustus stopped himself there. An oath escaped him,

filthier than the ones already uttered. He finally continued on a bare croak, "She has lost the will to live. Nobody can justify or explain it. I am sorry, everyone. She simply...does not want to live."

The group released a collective sigh.

Which muffled the thud of Marcus's collapse.

Into the ensuing silence, someone whispered, "Why?"

"She had so much to do," whispered one of the ballet girls.

"So much she'd dreamed," said another.

Augustus turned from them, casting his stare away.

Away and up. His red-rimmed eyes searched the ceiling, but not with the same confusion blanketing the others' faces.

A *definite* kind of dread pounded at Marcus.

Augustus knew precisely what he looked for in these rafters. And precisely who.

With his gaze still lifted, Augustus answered the group's question in a fatally calm tone.

"We know nothing save that any time G*abriela* has roused, she has only said one word. A name."

The crowd snapped stares to Renard.

The dandy dick rendered no reaction—except a seething flush that crept higher up his neck in anticipation of the information about to spill from Augustus's taut lips.

"Marcus."

CHAPTER NINETEEN

He doubled over and let out a moan so violent and tortured, the mortal ears below never heard a note of its unearthly anguish. The pain burned a path *through* every cell in Marcus's body. And hers. Jesu and Mary, aye; in her body, too. The awareness flogged him with full, furious force now that he ripped away the walls on his mind and flew to her on psychic wings.

He should have known she would do this. He could have known, had he not been so senseless, so eager to confirm *his pathetic nobil*ity and prove his nonexistent honor. What the hell was he thinking in that warped little Camelot? That self-sacrifice equaled tragic perfection? That heaven was maybe listening—and had an extra redemption sitting around to squander on him?

Bloody fucking hell.

How far off the mark he had landed! And how damnabl*y, despicably right Raquelle had been. Heaven did not give monsters a* sanction for self-sacrifice. His pitiful grasps at morality only became, as the bitch had so perfectly summarized, a rendition of martyrdom fit for nothing but a two-shilling minstrel hall.

Gabriela, I am so sorry. I am so wrong. Please hear me. Hear me now!

But only fog swirled in and answered his heart's plea. Only a she*ll of half-consciousness loomed where he had once been* *able to feel her heart beating, her desires burning, her thoughts and dreams growing.*

Agony ate at him like a three-pound parasite. As teeth, the creature used blades of memory from the far and near past.

"I love you, Marcus. Don't you know I'll always love you?"

"Blazes, guv. Sounds like ya truly love this chit."

"Don't ever leave me, Marcus...please don't ever leave me."

"They said there's no hope. Her condition has only worsened."

"I shall surrender the breath in my body before I stop loving you."

The breath in my body...

His throat convulsed. Every cell of his body shivered. Her words echoed along the stones of his soul, the acoustics there more harrowing and haunting than the longest arteries of the London underground.

The breath in my body...

His soul instantly answered that.

The hell you will, Gabriela.

And I am going to make assured of it.

He lifted his head. The movement came slowly and steadily, as a very new sensation took the place of the usual silvered fire behind his eyes. Tonight, it was silver ice, comprised of every tear he never shed and every dream he never lived, congealed into a block of resolved conviction.

The only choice he had left to make.

The one dream he could still make right.

With that realization, the ice deluged the rest of his body.

Yet as he rose and made his way back outside again, he did not resist the invasion. The cold conqueror became an increasingly best friend, his body's *aide-de-camp* as he turned south down Bow Street without a break in stride. The ice lent fortitude to muscles already turning sluggish, dripped cool drops into a bloodstream beginning to simmer as Big Ben sent four gongs across the city's rooftops. The tolls resounded into a sky full of dwindling stars and awakening morning birds...

So odd, he pondered then. When had the sun ever risen on this city in such a sky, without a wisp of fog or a tendril of coal smoke?

He instantly grunted at the musing. As if he were qualified to know how London sunrises behaved!

Still, it all seemed *odd.*

The fresh-doughy warmth of a baker's shop he passed...

Surreal.

The morning dew which clung to the daisies he purchased from a flower girl...

Unreal.

The whistle of the early Brighton train, and not the midnight constable...

Unnatural.

And suddenly, at that conclusion, it seemed a fitting dawn, indeed.

A fitting end.

★ ★ ★ ★

They had her in a room at the end of a dim hall on the fourth floor of the hospital, which still smelled of age and death despite the nurses' delusions that bleach and turpentine wielded the same might as claymore and crossbow. Or maybe wooden stake and silver bullet.

Following the instinct behind that thought, Marcus

avoided the temptation to simply race the near-empty hallways to Gabriela's room. Instead, he went around to the back of the building. Reluctantly diverting a piece of his psyche from Gabriela, he hypnotized the two orderlies slouched there before swinging up to the bricks over the door frame. One careful, suctioning hand grip at a time, he pulled himself up the wall, across a window ledge and into the corridor at the dark end of Floor Four.

The feat did not come without its price. His strength was draining from him rapidly enough without the climb. Marcus managed no more than two steps down the hall before grappling for the wall, sliding down the rough surface, and dropping his head between his knees to wait out a surge of vertigo, nausea—and *terror.*

Almost there.

Only now he saw that his biggest obstacle had yet to be assailed.

He looked past the dust, scuffs and nicks on his boots—to a set of feet squared against them in freshly-shined, patent leather oxfords. He remembered those oxfords well—from when he had snapped his wolf's jaws at them.

With purposeful leisure, Marcus raised his gaze up the length of tailored black trousers, over a tailored gray waistcoat, around a tailored black jacket, and finally to the bastard's vacuous face.

"Alfonso Renard." He dragged out the words, making sure his mocking intent was clear. "Good morrow to you, sir."

The rake's nostrils flared. Marcus wondered whether Renard had patterned the look after Kean's Richard III or Beerbohm-Tree's Macbeth. Either way, the killcow had pitifully miscast himself.

"How do you know who I am?" As the bastard intoned it, he took the bearing of yet another role he so erroneously fancied himself: Grand Spanish Inquisitor.

"I trow we both know the answer to that," Marcus replied softly.

The man's lips contorted. His aquiline brows fell, almost menacing, as he loomed an inch closer. In his stare, Marcus watched a battle of fury and fear. "Who—what—the hell are you?"

"I trow you know the answer to that, as well." He rose in a single, fluid movement. "Just as I trow you shall not try to stop me."

But the bastard's reckless rage blinded him. "Well, you trow wrong." He lunged forward, both fists raised. Marcus anticipated the move a dozen seconds earlier. A countering growl exploded from him; his grip awaited Renard's wrist— and started to crush. But as much as he longed to do so, he did not turn the man's bones to dust. Instead, he used the hold as ballast to slam Renard into a heap against the footboards.

Holding himself back from doing more was sheer hell. Wildfire blasted away the glaciers in his bloodstream; his lungs pumped like blistering bellows. As he battled for calming breaths, he hung over Renard's tremoring form. An unworldly silver glow reflected off the bastard's waxen complexion.

"*Do not think* of getting up, you blackhearted son of a whore," he snarled. "Just as you will not think of stopping me from seeing her. Just as *you* will not think of seeing her, even after this night; even after she leaves here—for she *will* leave here."

He lowered his head two inches, forcing Renard's down until it almost hit the floor. "Aye," he continued, "you had best agree, for this contract is not up for haggle. And if you ever deem it to be, I swear by all of heaven and hell that I shall find you, no matter where I am. I shall find you—and I shall make you pay for hurting her with more than a few fingers."

Not waiting for the whoreson to answer, Marcus advanced to Gabriela's door, and swiftly slid inside.

He closed the portal with his back then stood there for an eternity of moments. Then an eternity more. He quaked with the presence of her, rejoiced in the nearness of her.

Hated himself for the sight of her.

Much felicitations, Stafford. You have completed the circle; become a perfect monster. Behold the proof, laying in that bed. Behold her there, with her black eye sockets and her white lips. And that skin, such a flawless gray match for her tombstone already. 'Tis a befitting way for a demon to leave the world, aye? By taking an angel with him?

His spirit roared in grief.

The dark, dead agony crawled from the depths of his dark, dead soul, an outcry so despairing, he fell to the floor next to her bed from it. He stared down at his hands, watching with rapt fascination as the skin began its slow, retracting burn across his bones.

No time to waste now.

He flung the claws up and groped for the bed. Once there, he pulled his shaking, afflicted body closer to the motionless seraph in the sheets.

Closer.

Oh, the sweet, soft heaven of her...

He fell to the mattress next to her, every inch of him thrumming and heaving from the sweet nearness of her. He reached to brush a dark hair from her ashen cheek but yanked back at the last moment. What if he infected her face with his new deformity just as he'd ruined her heart with his soul's distortion?

He simply didn't move. He was an impotent fiend, a dying demon...but he was happy. His only remaining misery? The words unsaid. There were so many of them...and yet he could speak none.

"I want to tell you so much, my angel." He rasped it beneath his breath. "To give you so much."

There was so little time now.

So little time.

The thought struck at the same moment a peach glow warmed the rooftops beyond the window. Sharply, Marcus breathed in. Desperately, he grabbed for Gabriela's hand. Damning himself for betraying his own mandate, he pulled her small fingers hard against his chest.

"Gabriela." He leaned and whispered it against her cold, thin fingers. "Sweeting...I am so sorry."

He worshiped her, kissing each of her fingers, even every dry wafer of a fingernail. "And oh, Gabriela Angelica Rozina," he breathed, "I am so in love with you."

He looked back to her face, so unmoving and still. He delved into her mind, so silent, so sepulchral. "Do you hear me?" he grated. "Somewhere in that darkness of yours, I need you to hear me, angel. I love you, Gabriela. I love the life you forced on me, the world you opened for me, the light you gave to me. And from the ashes of my body, from the damnation of my spirit, from wherever I am going, I shall still love you with all my being. I shall love you with all my wretched, irredeemable soul."

He slowly turned her hand over in order to press his lips

to the faint pulse inside her wrist. "Throughout time," he told her between aching, broken gulps. "Throughout eternity."

No more time.

Except to wait.

The sky turned from peach to amber.

She did not move.

Marcus roared again.

He poured the sound into her now, burying his face below her breasts as he clutched her like a last piece of driftwood to a drowning seaman. "Damn you!" The curse ripped through him along with the memory of the first time he had pounded her with it, in the hall outside her dressing room. She had been so persistent, so alive—ah God, so *alive*—

"Damn you, Gabriela! You *shall* live!"

The command streamed from him a litany of desperation, over and over. He held her tighter with every passing minute, clutching as morning twilight approached full dawn, trading the heartbeats of his existence for the sole quest of renewing hers. Every thought of his mind, power of his spirit, and passion of his soul united in the siege, each effort squeezing the last drops from the night...the last seconds from his life.

"You shall live. You shall live!"

He roared it. He raged it. He cried it—as sunlight streamed into the room, brilliant and blazing.

And lightning struck his world.

The heat blasted first through his mind. That struck him as odd, since he still felt the rest of his body going up in flames, a conflagration that rendered him aware of everything and nothing at once. Every blood cell and muscle ligament, all the marrow in every bone and all the follicles of every hair; Marcus knew them, felt them, heard them. He was ignited in a fiery orchestra of nerves and instincts and feelings...*oh, so many feelings.* And yet—

No feelings at all.

Nay, he amended to that a moment later. 'Twas not an utter absence of feeling, but a diminished realm of the stuff. Like a pot of kitchen grease had been thrown onto his senses.

He felt his head raising. His eyes opening.

Opening to look at his trembling, upraised hands.

His hands. Both still whole. And both very wet...but with what? That could nay be the shine of his...tears? His body had not shed a real tear since—

And why were his fingers so dark? His skin looked like he had been out hunting all day. He nay remembered the tone of it being so dark since that fateful day he had gone to the forest to meet Raquelle—

"Sweet Jesu," he heard himself blurt. "Sweet, merciful, incredible Jesu."

★ ★ ★ ★

Through the haze of Gabriela's awareness, his voice came. Strong as an Italian concerto. Melodic as a French love ballad. Tormenting her. Calling her again; coaxing her from her black cocoon. Even *ordering* her out—the maddening bastard—but getting out of *that* by crying to her...

A dream. It couldn't be him. She'd looked for him. Called for him. He was gone.

Gabriela. Sweeting, wake up.

No. So impossible. So beautiful. She had to forget him. She had to *forget.*

She had to return to the blackness. The wonderful, numbing blackness.

"Gabriela."

She answered with a moan. The effort of it hurt, grating up her throat like wind across a desert.

"Gabriela. My love. Gabriela."

"Mmmmphh. No."

Damn him, even in the realm of her imagination, he was relentless. The man had the same tenacity of the queen who'd originally taught him the trait.

First, he leveled the attack of his touch. He slid his smooth fingers over her brow, along her nose, over the crook of her neck, between her breasts. He waged his next campaign with his voice, softly singing that ballad from the night they'd walked in the wonder of a London midnight. The memories of that journey formed the arrows of the third assault: her mind seeing him as if he walked next to her again, gazing at her, smiling at her, so proud of her, so in love with her.

She could endure the barrage no longer.

With an anguished cry, Gaby opened her eyes.

At least she thought she opened them. But several bewildered blinks later, she wondered why Marcus wouldn't fade away. She still must be very ill. She was definitely still in hospital—the dingy walls, trays, sheets, and even window were still in focus. Especially the window. Through it shined the rare, clear light of an early spring day.

It was just that Marcus wouldn't disappear from the scene.

She didn't doubt why her imagination refused to give him up. He sat there so breathtaking, so incredibly handsome. A streak of sunshine fell over his swarthy features. His darker skin was a magnificent contrast to the dancing blue-silver lights in his eyes, and the perfection of his ear-to-ear grin.

He made her heart swell.

He made her heart break.

"Marcus," she whispered. She longed to reach to him, to touch him, to feel him just once more. But the fear was more powerful than that. Fear of shattering this mirage of a moment.

"Marcus." Her voice wavered with her grief. "Marcus, why can't I let you go?"

"Because I will never let you."

That settled it. She still raged with fever. Healthy people didn't let fantasies send quicksilver down to their toes. But bloody blazes; if this was insanity, then she'd be infirm for the rest—

Her piercing gasp echoed off the walls.

With her rebellious thoughts, she'd decided to reach for him.

But then she'd touched.

Dear God.

She'd touched.

She sobbed. And she grabbed. She couldn't hold tight enough; fingers digging into his flesh, hands wrapping around his muscles, so hard and warm—

And real.

"Marcus? *Marcus!*"

He laughed as she ran furtive fingers over his eyes, his nose, his lips and jaw. He returned her ministrations, finishing by tunneling a hand into her hair, pulling her close against him, and kissing her as he never had before. A searing, possessing, aching kiss.

A mortal kiss.

She reveled in his assault until tearing away, unable to silence her questions any longer. "How?" Her lips wouldn't work fast enough. "Why? Where? Who? What happened?"

"Ssshh." He ravished her mouth with more tender intent this time. "You need to get your rest." He laid her back against the pillows but extended his magnificent body alongside hers. "There will be time for your answers later. There will be time for everything. A lifetime's worth of everything. I promise."

Gabriela, as usual, couldn't obey him at the expense of her love. Through secretly-parted lashes, she peeked at him once more. She hardly dared to believe he was here beside her, never to leave again.

But then a morning breeze wafted aside the room's curtains, sprinkling petals of sunlight across the room, across the commanding face and broad form of her dark angel.

And she dared to believe—just as she knew Marcus had dared, at the risk of everything he was or ever would be.

Dared to believe in the power of love...*and its magical redemption.*

EPILOGUE

"'Tis the most beautiful yet."

Marcus's murmur mingled with the sea wind in Gabriela's ear. "You say that about every sunrise." She laughed and snuggled tighter into his embrace, "But today, I may have to agree with you."

And she did. The entire world seemed to have come to life, even the ancient Cornwall cliff they stood upon, and the newer—but not by much—watchman's house they'd just left. Inside, they'd shared a predawn breakfast of raspberry tarts, hot coffee—one Marcus's new mortal passions—and...other blazing pursuits.

The cliff overlooked an expanse of restless waters, the foamy crests reflecting the changing hues of the sky. Aqua and orange played hide-and-seek with the silvers and sapphires of an approaching October storm.

She felt deliciously, delightedly alive. Deliciously, delightedly mortal. Life was good.

Marcus's lips again nudged at her. "Aye. I agree."

She smiled. He chuckled. But the next moment, she gave in to a perplexed scowl. "Marcus, I don't understand something."

"What?"

"How can you still do that? How can you still see into my mind, even after you've become....well..."

"Normal?" he supplied, grinning.

"Yes. How can you do that, even though you're normal again? All your other supernatural abilities and powers have disappeared, but you still read me like a Palladium showbill."

He laughed softly again. "But I was not supposed to understand you so clearly to begin with, remember?" He pressed a kiss to each corner of her mouth. "Which actually eliminates all but one answer," he continued—so breezily succinct, he'd apparently shared the answer with all the world but her.

Gabriela curled exasperated fists into his shirt. "What?"

"Magic." He revealed lingered over his kiss a little longer this time. "The simple magic of me and thee, my sweet."

"Mmmm," she purred. "Now I'll agree with you..."

She was the instigator of their next embrace, and she paced it with languorous seduction. She loved making him shake with mortal desire, even at her tiniest touches. But she loved discovering parts of the ageless Marcus that were still intact, such as the shudder she gave him by simply dipping her mouth to his collarbone.

"Magic," she repeated when they finally, reluctantly pulled apart. But she waited before issuing her next words. "So is that what happened in my hospital room last month?"

A thick pewter cloud skudded across the sun—as if the man in her arms had retained specific superhuman powers, and summoned the haze with his thoughts. But she couldn't determine that for certain. Marcus had suddenly found the moss on the rocks to be terribly stare-worthy.

Audacious man. As if he thought she'd concede to such paltry evasive maneuvers.

"Marcus," she persisted, "you...were not expecting to survive that sunrise, were you?"

He shook his head. Sort of. The motion was enough to confirm her assertion.

"But you came to the hospital to see me, anyway."

With the same taut difficulty, he nodded.

"Why?"

He lifted his head. As always, the silver sheen in his gaze there drove to the center of her soul—especially this moment, as he discernibly held his breath. When he released it, coarse words erupted, too.

"Because I love you more than I do my own life."

The desire to kiss the man surpassed any such urge Gabriela had known so far. "Marcus," she whispered after she did.

He emitted a soft chuckle when they pulled apart. "To think the answer was as simple as that," he murmured, "yet I never saw it." He shook his head again. "Nay," he amended, "I was not *meant* to see it. Not until now. Not until you."

Gaby took no pain to disguise the extent of her confusion *now*. "What are you talking about?" Invoking a favorite private quip they'd adopted during the last few weeks of intensive rehearsals, "Excuse me, Mr. Webber, I think I missed a line." She appended in a grumble, "Perhaps a whole scene."

Marcus scooped up her hand and squeezed it. "Prompter's fault." He took a deep breath before adding, "And Mr. Danewell's turn to explain." He tugged her toward the cliff's winding footpath. "Walk with me. There is a story I must share with you."

When they reached the trail, Gabriela took a chance on slanting him a knowing glance. "Does this story, by any chance, begin with, 'once upon a time, Raquelle turned Marcus into a vampire'?"

His left eyebrow plummeted. Confirmation rendered. But following the same instinct which inspired her assumption, Gabriela didn't indulge a victory grin. She waited for him to clasp her hand tighter, then lead her down that path between the ocean and sky.

"There's much more to that story than I have told you," he finally said.

"I know." She felt his startled stare upon her but didn't return the look. Something told her to garner all the fortitude she still had, for his following words would be much more than just a story.

They were.

Marcus held true to his premise and began the tale from the moment Raquelle forced him into immortality. But from there, the narrative took on so many new details, she discarded the hope of matching any parallels to the account he'd first shared back in their Drury apartment.

This time, she heard of the horror—the tormenting extent of it. He told her of the sickness—the actual chemical shock of suddenly finding one's body prey to a hunger so vile, it churned the stomach; yet so consuming, dream landscapes turned one color: blood red.

But she also heard of the hope.

Oh, yes. The hope. That fleeting, flippant comment from Raquelle on that first harrowing night, tossed like a rotted bone to a begging mongrel, but which, in Marcus's desperation, became a nugget more precious than gold. For the first century of his vampiric existence, it had given him a purpose higher than a priestly calling.

"And what did you find out?" Urgency finally made it impossible not to ask. "The woman said there was a cure but told you nothing more? Not a hint of where to start? An idea of what to do?"

The path ended at a wide boulder overlooking the Channel. Marcus guided her to the ledge and waited until they both sat to answer. "Nay," he stated. "She gave me nothing more than that. *But,*" he swiftly justified to Gabriela's glower, "I should not have expected such. Vampirism *was* Raquelle's cure. She sought no other remedy for her unhappiness, nor did she care to. So how could I have expected her to be my expert tome on the subject of a solution?"

He concluded with a shrug, again the all-believing, ever-understanding Elizabethan lad. And again, swelling Gabriela's heart a little more for him.

"So what happened when you went looking for the answer?"

As she'd expected, another shadow befell his features. "Very obviously, nothing. Oh, I had a grand tour of the earth without having to hurry about it. But after a hundred years, I stood atop a mountain in the Himalayas and decided I had cursed heaven for the last time. I returned to England the next week, settled into the catacombs under Drury and prepared myself to be perfectly but peacefully miserable for the rest of eternity. Until"—he slanted a potent look at her—"I accidentally stumbled over the green room while you rehearsed one eve."

"Oh." She pitched the word with a flirtatious edge. "So *that's* how it all happened."

"Little minx," he growled back good-naturedly. "In the space of a heartbeat, you muddled my plans to hell."

She couldn't resist tossing him a saucy slant of eyebrows and a short but sensual kiss. She also used the gesture to press a hand to his cheek, directing his gaze into hers as she queried,

"Why didn't you tell me all this before? Why didn't you share it when you first told me this story?"

Beneath her palm, a pulse jumped in his jaw. "Because I had ceased believing in a cure myself," he confessed. "I had finally discarded the concept as the capping triumph of Raquelle's little 'prank' on me." His eyes slid shut. "Even after the night I first told you the whole story...even after all the magic we shared after...I never fathomed the impossible 'cure' lay right next to me."

Gabriela frowned. "What do you mean?"

"What I mean"—he pulled her closer and pressed a quick kiss to the furrow of her brow—"is love. *You* were my cure, sweeting. I had to love another so much that I would face a sunrise for them...hand over my life to them." His chin, resting against the top of her head, turned back toward the sun. "My God," he uttered. "It sounds so unfathomable."

Gabriela smiled against his chest. "No, it doesn't."

Another husky chuckle. "Aye, my heart. After all that has transpired, I suppose it does not." He curled a finger under her chin, lifting her lips for another lingering kiss. "And," he whispered, continuing to taunt her mouth in tiny circles, "I think I shall start thanking you for that right now..."

He began a trail of nibbles over her jaw, down her throat... down the bodice of her walking gown. "Ah...we have a ship to catch, Mr. Danewell," she managed, only to cut herself short with a gasping giggle as his tongue slid beneath fabric and across her expectant flesh. "R-Remember?" she prompted. "The tour begins in one week...Paris..."

"God's bloody bodkin," Marcus grumbled, dragging himself back, "I remember."

She laughed softly, indulging another gaze full of him.

The noble angles of his face were dark and swarthy, and dusted with an arousing beard stubble that she longed to caress.

"You have the rest of your life to thank me," she reminded him. "And the rest of *our* life to love me."

At that, he gave her his wide, blinding smile...and a deep, consuming kiss. "Oh, my Gabriela...now I wish I *did* have eternity at my disposal."

Continue the Lords of Sin Series with Book Four

A Fire in Heaven

Keep reading for an excerpt!

EXCERPT FROM *A FIRE IN HEAVEN*
BOOK FOUR IN THE LORDS OF SIN SERIES

CHAPTER ONE

Run! No one would blame you. No one would care. *You don't belong here...you don't belong here. Run!*

The thought clung invitingly to Kira Sergenkov's mind, warming her more than the cold muck attaching itself around the rest of her body. "Fog" was what all these Englishmen kept calling the sludge, yet the stuff wasn't like anything *she'd* seen before. The disparity, however, didn't surprise her in the least. Nothing had been familiar in her life for the last four weeks.

The mighty mausoleum of a house towering before her didn't help matters, either.

The only building she'd ever seen which dared to rival this place was the White House, home of President Tyler himself. But beyond the polished brick driveway and column-framed entrance of *this* mansion, she reminded herself, no president dwelled. No influential man made world-changing decisions. A man had instead used this palace as a hiding place.

A man who had forsaken the fact he ever had a daughter named Kira.

Trepidation clogged her throat again. She was suddenly

conscious of her faded walking boots, the missing tassels on her shawl, the worry-wrinkled ribbons dangling from her bonnet. She swore the holes in her thin gloves grew as she reached a trembling hand to an unsmiling footman.

Saints, she was really here. Really about to meet *him.* Had she imagined this day, even in her most far-fetched visions, but four weeks ago?

Four weeks...twenty-eight days that now represented the expanse between two lifetimes. But she shouldn't find *that* fact so hard to believe. It had only taken an hour for the only life she'd known to burn to the ground. Another two days had successfully scattered the fire's other survivors—the last of the rag-tag troupe she'd called family for eighteen years—to the four directions of the wind and then some.

And then, the most bizarre shock of all had come: the father she'd thought long dead was suddenly very much alive, very much an English lord, and very much "requesting" her presence by his side.

Kira wondered just what a child-abandoning coward would look like.

She would have to wait for an answer. Appearing at the mansion's door wasn't the looming London lord she expected, but an imposing figure nonetheless. Even with its distinctly feminine outlines of graceful posture, ruffle-edged sleeves, and multiple-layered skirts, the silhouette momentarily snatched Kira's breath away with its regal presence and commanding height.

"My Lady Kira, I presume," the shadow issued in a tone that could have been pulled from the foreboding mists themselves.

Kira averted her gaze momentarily, feeling certain she'd

be more comfortable center stage at the Paris Opera. Finally, she attempted an unsteady bow. "H-How do you do," she stammered. When only a prolonged pause answered from the doorway, she grew even more painfully aware of how like a fish on land she appeared.

Of how like an outsider she felt.

She forced a breath past a chest suddenly full of a hundred knives, the blades all sharpened on memory's ruthless whetstone. But she hadn't learned to throw knives—literally *and* figuratively—at the age of five for nothing. Fury welled within her, summoning daggers of defiance. Kira jerked her spine straight and affixed her gaze back to the figure atop the entrance stairs.

Easy as pie, she inwardly congratulated herself. Oh, yes; she'd faced more intimidating strangers than this haughty housemaid before celebrating her tenth birthday—and she was more than passing proud of that claim, as well. Growing up on the front seat of a circus performer's wagon showed a person many of life's more "unique" aspects, including the inclination of folks to turn a hateful eye at anything or anyone different from themselves.

And Kira, nervously fingering one of her unruly auburn curls, certainly knew what it was like to be different.

"Well, inside with you now," the figure at last bade, punctuating with a pinched sniff. "Before those threads give you pneumonia, or worse."

The remark again rendered Kira irksomely conscious of her attire, which set off yet another flash of pride-filled indignance. She wasn't allowed half a moment to indulge the fury, however. It was barreled out of the way, flattened in the path of an enthusiastic ball of sopping fur, hurdling into her legs. Equally sodden limbs gripped her knees, her waist then her neck as the creature climbed her like a miniature palm tree. But she couldn't be angry at the invasion if she tried, especially as a five-fingered paw thumped the top of her head, and blissful primate grunts resounded in her ear.

"Well, hello to you, too." She laughed, hugging the fur ball closer, shutting her eyes and for the briefest of moments believing the two of them were wrapped in Boston fog, instead...or perhaps an evening mist off a lake in the Carolinas, where Chico had deemed it best for the wagons to stop for the night...

"Dear God!"

Boston became London again before Kira reopened her eyes and beheld the face of the maid for the first time. Obviously, flying fur balls were deemed cause enough to descend a few steps, even in England's gray and goopy capital. From where the woman now stood, her features were clearly discernible.

Beholding her, Kira kicked up both brows in shock. The woman's height had deceived her into expecting a mannish matron, but now she gazed at the epitome of the opposite. In a simple but stylish dark-blue gown, topped by impeccably chiseled features and intricately coifed hair, the woman was dipped from head to toe in proprietous English femininity—and, at the moment, in proprietous English horror, as well.

"What—is—*that*?" A manicured hand extended in shaking shock, to which Kira replied with an amused grin.

"His name is Fred. I've had him since he was a baby. His own mama was accidentally killed." She pursed a momentary frown. "She was playing around on the trapeze, just as we'd told her *not* to."

"He…it's…a *monkey*."

"Chimpanzee." Kira had no trouble slanting her expression with ire instead of grief. "Fred is a chimpanzee, not a monkey." She added in a tight undertone, "I'll thank you to inform everyone of that."

But instead of compliance, Kira was struck with a stare of contempt. "I'll thank *you* to take that…*animal* to the barn. They can bathe it…then perhaps trim it, or something."

"They won't touch him." Despite the menace of her glare, Kira railed at herself for allowing her vulnerability to show through about this. As if the threat of *her* fury would force someone to give Fred even the respect they'd afford their dog.

But Fred was different, too. *He'd* come to accept it a long time ago. Tarnation, the imp even flaunted it.

Kira supposed that was why she'd threatened a bullet through the gut of anyone who'd tried to sell him off after the fire.

She supposed that was why she pulled him closer to her right now, and continued leveling her determined stare along with her next words.

"Fred will be staying with me," she stated calmly, but firmly. She wasn't surprised at the reacting gasp from the steps.

"I think not!" Each word was its own production of horror-filled breath.

"I think so." Kira lauded herself for the peaceful smile she managed off the side of her mouth. "He's my pet, and he goes everywhere with me."

"A *pet*, my lady, is a poodle, or—or a cat—"

"And I'm certain they're very nice pets, too."

"But—but a chimp—"

"Is infinitely more agreeable than a poodle, and more

affectionate than a cat. May we come in now?"

At first, only a pair of sighs answered the continuing serenity of her smile. When no other response came except the maid's militant pivot and subsequent retreat, Kira interpreted both actions as a well-earned victory. After a quick kiss to the top of Fred's head, she ascended the stairs with a dash more confidence than she'd had ten minutes ago.

The feeling was very short-lived.

Clean. As soon as she recovered enough from a blindingly up-close view of the chandelier, that word resonated as her first impression of the mansion. The butler who stepped forward to take her shawl was impeccably clean, his face betraying no surprise at the drab garment draped over his arm—though it showed in the glint of his eyes. The marble floor beneath her feet was gleamingly clean, actually mirroring each of her steps. And the pervading scents in the air were so clean, they hurt to breathe: lye, lemon, and bleach.

There was no enticing aroma of simmering soup in the kitchen, or freshly-arranged flowers from the garden, or even the rain that seemed certain to form from the muck outside. Everything was clean and cold...and daunting.

Kira clutched Fred closer and wondered if her father might be Prince Edward himself.

She followed the maid past a winding stairway of well-oiled mahogany and into a perfectly-arranged sitting room. As they entered, the woman addressed a petite maid who was finishing her duties before a fireplace at least five feet wide, bordered by the same marble they'd just crossed in the foyer.

"Emma," the woman directed, "we shall take tea and cider in here now, and be seated for dinner in one hour."

Kira pondered if that was when she'd at last meet her

father. She also admitted she didn't anticipate that encounter as eagerly as she had an hour ago.

Just as her heart formed that thought, another voice surged through her senses, swirling into her mind through the mists of memory. *Be strong...oh, please be strong, my* lipistok... *my little rose petal. Be strong for me now.*

"Mama!" Kira rasped into Fred's fur as the two maids discussed some last dinner details. "Oh, Mama, I don't know if I *can* be strong!"

But the words came again, echoing through her soul now as well, just as Mama had rasped them past smoke-filled lungs and a body crushed by the scenery flats she'd been trapped under. The backdrops, Kira recalled with a wince, which had depicted London Town—in laughably bright colors.

There is so much ahead for you, my Kira...so much...the spirits and the saints have blessed me with this knowledge, even long before tonight. You must believe this, lipistok; *you must believe in the destiny of all this. You must believe in your destiny...*

This story continues in A Fire in Heaven
Lords of Sin Book Four!

ALSO BY ANGEL PAYNE

Lords of Sin:
Trade Winds
Promised Touch
Redemption
A Fire in Heaven
Surrender to the Dawn

The Bolt Saga:
Bolt
Ignite
Pulse
Fuse
Surge
Light

Suited for Sin:
Sing
Sigh
Submit

Honor Bound:
Saved
Cuffed
Seduced
Wild
Wet
Hot
Masked
Mastered
Conquered
Ruled

Secrets of Stone Series:
(with Victoria Blue)
No Prince Charming
No More Masquerade
No Perfect Princess
No Magic Moment
No Lucky Number
No Simple Sacrifice
No Broken Bond
No White Knight
No Longer Lost
No Curtain Call

Temptation Court:
Naughty Little Gift
Pretty Perfect Toy
Bold Beautiful Love

Cimarron Series:
Into His Dark
Into His Command
Into Her Fantasies

For a full list of Angel's other titles,
visit her at AngelPayne.com

ABOUT ANGEL PAYNE

USA Today bestselling romance author Angel Payne loves to focus on high-heat romance starring memorable alpha men and the women who love them. She has numerous book series to her credit, including the action-packed Bolt Saga and Honor Bound series, Secrets of Stone series (with Victoria Blue), the intertwined Cimarron and Temptation Court series, the Suited for Sin series, and the Lords of Sin historicals, as well as several standalone titles.

Angel is a native Southern Californian, leading to her love of being in the outdoors, where she often reads and writes. She still lives in Southern California with her soul-mate husband and beautiful daughter, to whom she is a proud cosplay/culture con mom. Her passions also include whisky tasting, shoe shopping, and travel.

Visit her at AngelPayne.com